Jagua Nana

Cyprian Ekwensi was born in   of a famed storyteller and elephant hunter.   orked as a forestry officer in Nigeria and as a pharmac   d, Essex. On returning home, he wrote his first novel, *People   City* (1954), which was one of the first Nigerian novels to be published internationally. *Jagua Nana*, his most famous book, appeared in 1961 and won the Dag Hammarskjöld prize in literature, though it was banned in schools and attacked by the church. In later life Ekwensi worked in broadcasting, politics and as a pharmacist, while writing over forty books and scripts. He died in 2007, survived by his wife and nine children.

CYPRIAN EKWENSI

Jagua Nana

PENGUIN BOOKS

PENGUIN CLASSICS

UK | USA | Canada | Ireland | Australia
India | New Zealand | South Africa

Penguin Books is part of the Penguin Random House group of companies
whose addresses can be found at global.penguinrandomhouse.com.

First published in 1961
Published in Penguin Classics 2018
001

Set in 10.5/13 pt Dante MT Std
Typeset by Jouve (UK), Milton Keynes
Printed in Great Britain by Clays Ltd, St Ives plc

A CIP catalogue record for this book is available from the British Library

ISBN: 978–0–241–33499–7

www.greenpenguin.co.uk

MIX
Paper from
responsible sources
FSC
www.fsc.org   FSC® C018179

Penguin Random House is committed to a
sustainable future for our business, our readers
and our planet. This book is made from Forest
Stewardship Council® certified paper.

Jagua Nana

Jagua had just had a cold bath, and, in the manner of African women, she sat on a low stool with a mirror propped between her bare knees, gazing at her wet hair. Only one cloth – a flowered cotton print – concealed her nakedness, and she had wound it over her breasts and under her armpits. Her arms and shoulders were bare, and she sat with the cloth bunched between her thighs so that the mirror bit into the skin between her knees.

She raised her arm and ran the comb through the wiry kinks, and her breasts swelled into a sensuous arc and her eyes tensed with the pain as the kinks straightened. From the skin on her long arms and beautiful shoulders the drops of speckled water slid down chasing one another.

She saw Freddie pass by her door just then, saw him hesitate when he caught a glimpse of the dark naked hair under her armpits. Then he hurried past into his own room on the floor below, calling as he went:

'Jagwa! . . . Jagwa Nana! . . .'

She knew he was teasing. They called her Jagua because of her good looks and stunning fashions. They said she was Ja-gwa, after the famous British prestige car.

'I'm comin' – jus' now! . . . Call me when you ready!'

She could sense the irritation in his voice. As always when she did not like where they were going she delayed her toilet, and Freddie must know by now that she disliked intellectual groups, especially the British Council groups which she thought false and stiff. On the other hand, Freddie could never do without them. He said they were a link with Britain from which stemmed so much tradition.

Like Freddie she was an Ibo from Eastern Nigeria, but when she spoke to him she always used pidgin English, because living in Lagos City they did not want too many embarrassing reminders of clan or custom. They and many others were practically strangers in a town where all came to make fast money by faster means, and greedily to seek positions that yielded even more money.

She heard the clatter of Freddie's shoes as he hurried down the steps to his own room on the floor below. She waited for him to come up, and when he would not come she went on combing her hair. By an odd tilt of the mirror she saw, suddenly revealed, the crow's-feet at the corners of her eyes and the tired dark rings beneath.

'I done old,' she sighed. 'Sometimes I tink say Freddie he run from me because I done old. God 'ave mercy!' she sighed again.

The sigh was a prayer to God to stay back the years and a challenge to herself to employ all the coquettish arts to help Him. She did not often remember that if her son had lived he would today be roughly as old as her lover. Freddie was hardly more than a boy, with his whole ambitious life before him. He was a teacher at the Nigerian National College who badly wanted to travel overseas to complete his law studies. He had applied for a Government Scholarship, but did not pin his faith on being selected. She knew Freddie deserved a good girl to marry him, raise his children and 'shadow' him in all his ambitions. But Jagua was too much in love with him to make a reasonable exit. And she wanted Freddie as her husband because only a young man would still be strong enough to work and earn when she would be on the decline. Men would not be wanting her in six years' time, when – even now – girls of eighteen could be had. At forty-five, she had her figure and her tact to guide her.

She knew that, seen under the dim lights of her favourite night-spot, the *Tropicana* – and from a distance – her face looked beautiful. In any light she was proud of her body, which could model for any painter or sculptor. When she walked down a street, male eyes followed the wiggle of her hips which came with studied uncon-sciousness. Sometimes she was ashamed of her too passionate love-making, but Freddie did not seem so embarrassed now as he used to be at first. When she painted her face and lifted her breasts and exposed what must be concealed and concealed what must be exposed, she could outclass any girl who did not know what to do with her God-given female talent.

Freddie came into the room when she was dressed. He stood at the door and looked at her exposed shoulders and neck (they were magnificent, Jagua knew), at the transparent material of the blouse through which her pink brassiere could be seen – provocatively – and much more besides.

'You no like my dress?' she teased, knowing his prejudices against 'going out naked' as he called it. 'You vex wit' me?' She had already noticed the redness in his eyes.

'Jagwa, how many times I will tell you not to shame me? You never will satisfy till you go naked in de street!'

She smiled. 'I know das wat you goin' to say. But speak true, dis be naked?' she pouted, holding the flimsy edge of her skirt and twirling round and round. 'Dis be naked?' She reached for a powder puff and began to powder her face. 'You don' know de fashion, Freddie.'

'You know de fashion, das why dem call you Jag-wa!' He was talking sarcastically. 'But we goin' to a lecture, not dance. We goin' to a lecture in de British Council.' Freddie shut his eyes tight the way he always did when irritated.

'Ah know wha's wrong wit' you, Freddie, man. You too jealous! You never like de men to look at you woman body. Don' worry! All dose men in de British Council, dem got no bodies, dem only got brain and soul. Dem will not want to sleep your woman!' The tears had welled up now and she sat down and began wiping them and sobbing aloud. She sat like a log, obstinate, this live bright thing that had been aglow only one moment ago.

Freddie came and held her hands and wiped away her tears and she felt soothed.

'Make you trust me, Freddie. I not goin' to run away with any man. Look roun' and see. All de girls dress like dis nowadays. Is de fashion. We live in Africa where de sun dey shine every time; even sun use to shine when de rain fall. So we mus' show our skin and let de sun-shine kiss our body. Is nothin' bad in de sun kissin' you woman body, Freddie. When you go to col' country, like England . . .'

5

She saw that Freddie was not listening. He was looking through a window at the setting sun beyond the big banana leaves and palm fronds. The yellowness lit in silhouette the tall trees and corrugated roofs. 'When ah go to Englan', eh?' he sneered. 'You jus' wan' to laugh me. Poor teacher like me? Where I will fin' de money? Unless Government give me scholarship—'

'Nothin' is impossible, Freddie! You mus' have hope. I know how you wan' to go study in England. By de help of God, you mus' go. You better pass many who done go and come. You be clever boy, and your brain open. You young, too. You know what you doin'. You serious with you work. Yes! Government kin give you scholarship. If dem don' give you, den we mus' try pull togedder to sen' you.'

'I jus' tryin' by myself, das all. If God help me—'

'God mus' surely help you.' She gave him a knowing look. 'As long as I love you, Freddie,' she whispered.

She wanted Freddie because of his youth. He was good-looking and she knew the girls loved him but that did not prevent him being ambitious. Suppose he went to England, returned a lawyer, drove a big car, and then shunned her? No! He was too genuine a man to do that. He was not like the others, the 'Lagos' boys, the 'fast' ones.

'When you go, Freddie, promise me one ting. You no go stay dere too long; or you forget we here! Person like me won't be small gal every day. I growin' old, I want me own-man . . .'

'Don' worry, Jagua. Let me go firs'. Den when I return you kin see for youssef. Ah never gone yet. Why you begin worry how I goin' to return?'

'Is true,' Jagua sighed. 'But sometimes I use to fear. You men! Woman will put all her trust in you. Den you go and disappoint her.' She began powdering away the tear-stains. 'But ah jus' tellin' you in case . . .' She looked appealingly at him, a twinkle in her eyes. When she looked away, she was talking half to herself. 'When you come back now with you title, den you will begin to chase de small gals with standin' breast. You won' see me den, only now when you strugglin'. Dat time, Jagua go be too ol' for you.'

'Too ol'? Nonsense!' Freddie said easily. 'Jagwa no go be too ol'.'

She was glad. She finished in silence, her painting and

powdering, and when she was finally ready they stepped out into the sun, their heads raised proudly.

As soon as they entered the public lecture room a mild sensation swept through the audience. The speaker had already begun his lecture, but it seemed to Jagua that all eyes turned in their direction, and this was what she always liked. She knew Freddie did not care for this tribute to her beauty and fashion sense. One day he would know how much she was 'raising' him by being so dashing. With satisfaction she saw the whispering lips, shielded, the heads lowered behind the programmes.

A guide darted forward to take them to their seats. Even before they found places, Freddie pinched her and whispered: 'Dis man – he kin lecture wonderful.'

'So you say about everythin' in de British Council,' she whispered back. 'Wonderful!'

She looked at the lecture platform, noting the tarnished hairs piled up above each ear and around the high bald skull.

The lecturer's suit was rumpled, saggy at elbows and knees, yet had a kind of careless elegance. Perhaps this one would be different from the others, but to Jagua all lecturers were the same: boring.

She took her seat and peered hard at the programme Freddie was offering her.

2

Once when she caught the lecturer's eyes Jagua was surprised to find that they watered and gleamed against the light. She could not understand why. The old man kept wiping his face with a handkerchief though the evening was quite cool. His black face, a trifle oily at the cheeks, was unlined and quite young looking. The voice was authoritative but hoarse, probably from drinking too much whisky-soda Jagua thought, in the too humid heat of the Lagos Lagoon.

The breeze blowing offshore from the lecture hall made her feel drowsy and the hum of the ceiling fans deadened her sensitiveness. Freddie sat near the window looking out towards the jumble of cargo vessels and fast mailboats from Europe and America that cluttered up the lagoon. Local yachts, motorboats and canoes occasionally sped by, chugging up the water.

The lecture was entitled *Some Personal Recollections on the Passing of White Imperialism in Nigeria*. It seemed to be progressing satisfactorily. It was obvious to Jagua on glancing round that these were the intellectuals of Lagos City. The same group always met at cocktail parties: the American and Swiss Consuls, the oil prospectors and the public relations men, the managing directors in the merchant houses. They always wore the same suits, and the Nigerian intellectuals wore fez caps or turbans and cotton or damask robes in technicolour.

Jagua closed her eyes, striving hard not to offend so *élite* a gathering by simply shouting at them to stop all the fuss. In the distance the voice came:

'Times have indeed changed . . . Yesterday, the Legislative Council was composed entirely of white men. They made all the laws and the Governor looked on . . .

Talking of Governors reminds me of that first Governor Sir Dalton Thomas. He was a man who loved ceremonials. He would issue circulars: "His Excellency the Governor will attend Divine Service at Holy Cross Cathedral on Sunday the 15th of March . . . His Excellency will officiate at the opening ceremony of the new Railway Terminal . . .

Now, Sir Dalton Thomas (bless his memory) fostered in our Colonial minds the idea that a Governor must ALWAYS be seen in uniform. So when he retired, we expected the new Governor to behave in the same way. But no! What happened?

The new Governor, Sir David Arlington, HATED uniforms. Absolutely. He was a Cambridge man, an easy-going sort of chap and he was scheduled to visit the great Moslem town of Kano for some opening ceremony or other, you see . . .

The town had a holiday, the streets were hung with flags; a durbar was arranged, and everyone turned up at the railway station.

The train came in late. There was a guard of honour mounted at the station in full colours. Everyone looked round for the new Governor. Out of the special railway car came a young white man, wearing a battered old felt hat, flannel trousers, and – oh dear me! – a college blazer!

As he walked down the ranks, the Emir of Kano shouted: Governor *Banza*! which means, Governor of no value. Tell the King of England to send him back! He has no uniform. Nigeria demands a real Governor, not an APPRENTICE, one unfit to wear uniform . . .'

Laughter burst from every throat. Jagua did not catch the joke. She glanced at Freddie, noting his taut brow, the intent admiration in his eyes. The lecturer went on, now humorous, now serious, now satirical . . . Jagua studied his fine head, felt the mobility of brow and eyes, followed the gestures . . . the old man appeared to her to be reliving his younger days when there were few roads or railways and the white man lived on quinine or died in fevered swamps.

Freddie appeared restive. He raised his hand, interrupting the old lecturer who immediately nodded at him. Freddie jumped to his feet and asked a question. For a moment there was silence. It seemed to Jagua that Freddie had asked either a clever question or a dangerous one. She saw the lecturer raise his handkerchief to his face and mop the sudden outbreak of sweat. His brow furrowed and he shot back a reply, raising his right arm the way Jagua had often seen preachers do. Laughter broke from the audience. While they were laughing, Jagua decided that she no longer belonged to the group. She felt ostracized by the chorus of inhibited enjoyment and that herd instinct she always sensed among intellectuals. She rose and began walking away, while Freddie was still on his feet.

She clicked her high-heeled shoes, but the listeners were still convulsed with laughter and few male eyes followed her wiggle. She cared little for the mixture of anger and embarrassment which she knew must be gnawing at Freddie's guts.

3

Jagua stood outside the Lecture Hall, searching the street for a taxi. She saw Freddie emerge and come straight to her, shouting at her all the while. She ignored the scowl on his face and the ceaseless flow of harsh words he was hurling at her. She had learnt that men had best be left uncontradicted when they lost their tempers. She saw the taxi and stopped it.

'Tropicana Club.'

'We use meter, or we don' use meter?' grinned the taxi driver.

Jagua distrusted the new meters on the taxis. They always seemed to cheat her. 'No use meter.'

In the taxi Freddie sat at one end of the seat and Jagua sat at the other extreme end. No talking to each other. The taxi driver, with an eye to the entertainment of his passengers, talked about the political leaders and their latest disagreements, about the last football match between Nigeria and Libya. His conversation fell flat.

Jagua was not listening. Looking up for a moment she saw in the rear-view mirror the angry eyes of Freddie. She knew he must be angrier than ever because he had failed again to drag her up into the society of the snobs. Instead she had won. She was pulling him down to the *Tropicana*, trying to teach him to relax. You die, you're dead, Jagua thought. It's over. You've left nothing, not a mark. Freddie always resisted her own philosophy but she would go on trying.

When the taxi passed over the bridge she barely glimpsed the half-naked fishermen in the canoes on the flat lagoon. They had their sails out, so she guessed they must be fishing. Now, these fishermen did not worry about lectures, Jagua thought; and they were happy. She loved this hour when the lights were coming up in the causeway: white and blue and orange lights and the hotels and coloured adverts ablaze but not yet effective in the pale twilight.

The taxi rattled over a level crossing and pulled into the side of a road. She heard the trumpet shrieks from the *Tropicana* and felt genuinely elated. Jagua got out on the side of the road near the woman selling cooked yams. She stopped for a moment to straighten her dress, and the woman stopped blowing the fire and started looking at Jagua's sheath dress, painted lips and glossy hair.

'Heh! . . .' the yam seller burst out. 'One day ah will ride motor car and wear fine fine cloth . . .'

She said it aloud to Jagua's hearing and Jagua felt her ego pumping up. She pulled Freddie across the road to the little hatch of a door and they went inside. The *Tropicana* to her was a daily drug, a potent, habit-forming brew. Like all the other women who came here, alone or with some man, Jagua was looking for the ray of hope. Something will happen tonight, this night, she always told herself.

The music was tremendously rhythmic, coming from the bongo drums, and the bandleader, pointing his trumpet skywards blew till the blisters on his lips widened and he wiped his lips, and the sax snatched away the solo, distorting it. This was it, Jagua felt.

All the women wore dresses which were definitely undersize, so that buttocks and breasts jutted grotesquely above the general contours of the bodies. At the same time the midriffs shrunk to suffocation. A dress succeeded if it made men's eyes ogle hungrily in this modern super sex-market. The dancers occupied a tiny floor, unlighted, so that they became silhouetted bodies without faces and the most unathletic man could be drawn out to attempt the improvisation which went by the name *High-life*.

Jagua saw them now as with white collars off they struck a different mood from the British Council: the 'expatriate' bank managers, the oil men and shipping agents, the brewers of beer and pumpers out of swamp water, the builders of Maternity Block, the healers of the flesh. German, English, Dutch, American, Nigerian, Ghanaian, they were all here, bound together in the common quest for diversion. Bouncing off the roofs, Jagua heard the trumpet choruses from the adjacent club, reaching out to the *Tropicana* with a kind of challenging virility.

She glanced round but could not get herself a seat among the dozens of empty chairs. She wanted most to dance. 'Take me Freddie. Take me and dance me, quick!' She put down her handbag on a chair and offered him her arms. He still moped.

The band was playing a new hit tune from Ghana, good enough to melt away all anger, something weepy but rocking, the kind she knew Freddie liked. She rubbed his hand caressingly. 'You still vex wit' me?' she cooed at him. 'You still wan' to go back and lissen to de ol' man lecture? Come on, man! Forget de lecture. You young man, enjoy youssef!'

Jimo Ladi and his Leopards always played well, though rather loudly, but dance *High-life* must be loud to fire the blood. White men and black men, they all rose, and crowded the floor. The black men chose the fat women with big hips: the white men clung to the slim girls with plenty of collar bone and little or no waists. There were girls here, and women, to suit all men's tastes. Pure ebony, half-caste, Asiatic, even white. Each girl had the national character-istic that appealed to some male, and each man saw in his type of woman a quality which inspired his gallantry. So the women enticed their victims and the *Tropicana* profited.

Jagua clung to Freddie and they rubbed shoulders and bumped hips against softer hips and knocked down cigarette-ends in the compression chamber they called a dance floor.

After the dance, Freddie went over to the bar, leaving Jagua for barely a moment. A Syrian gentleman came to Jagua's table at once and covered it with lavish drinks. He was not a young man and he had the unsober looks of one who came to the *Tropicana* every night. Jagua had often seen him in the company of Mama Nancy. But tonight Mama Nancy was not in the *Tropicana* and she wondered what the Syrian was planning. He was said to have a lot of money and to be quite lavish with it, and she would not mind taking him home. On his invitation she helped herself freely to his cigarettes. She felt flattered by his admiring smile.

Freddie came back and threw her an angry glance. 'Get up, Jagua, an' let's go!' he scowled. He was all tensed up.

'Why now, Freddie? Siddown and greet de gentleman,' she said lazily. 'We only jus' come and he dyin' to meet you.'

'Le's go home, I said.' He glared at the Syrian who calmly offered Jagua another cigarette. Jagua took it. This was her bread and but-ter, she told herself. The Syrian's money would buy her that new dress from Kingsway. She had already pictured herself in it. She loved Freddie well, but his whole salary could not buy that dress. He must understand that taking money from the Syrian did not mean she loved him less.

With the match-light catching the points of his chin and etching out the bushy eyebrows, the Syrian squinted and puffed his cigarette alight, offering Jagua the flame. Jagua smiled at Freddie. The Syrian smiled too.

'I waitin' for you, Jagua.'

'But you never dance me enough, Freddie.'

'We done dance finish. Le's go home.'

Jagua turned a smiling face at the Syrian. Out of the corner of her eye she saw Freddie's fist tighten. Then, raving mad, he turned and walked out of the *Tropicana*. At that instant Jagua forced back a small spark of pity for her loved one. He should know by now that in the *Tropicana*, money always claimed the first loyalty.

4

Freddie stood at the door of the *Tropicana*, shaking his shoulders to the bright *High-Life* which Jimo Ladi and his Leopards were weaving within. He toyed with the idea of returning but resisted it. Jagua's behaviour within the *Tropicana* was one reason why he never liked bringing her here. Once inside, the lights, the influential people, the drinks, the flattery, the voluptuous stimulations, the music, all combined together to change her into something beyond his reach.

He became aware of a girl's young body brushing against him, squeezing tight against the passage. Her voice excited him too. 'Freddie, you seen me mother inside?'

He looked at her. 'Nancy, what you doin' here?'

'Lookin' for me mother,' said Nancy sweetly.

'I don' see her inside. Wait! Don' go yet! I wan' somebody I kin talk to.' He seized her wrist.

Nancy looked at him in surprise. Freddie knew why, but now he had no time to worry about that. He had always treated girls with indifference, and someone like Nancy must believe he was not interested in her.

She twisted free. 'You done gone mad, Freddie? Look you eye like you wan' to eat me.'

'Yes, sometime I kin eat you.'

In that tight little passage leading into the *Tropicana* Freddie was confronted with this mere slip of a girl: slim and bright in the manner of the young Nigerian girls of the day. Hair matted and boyish and glistening wet with too much pomade; a sky-blue blouse that exposed a bare graceful neck; slender arms and shoulders; hard breasts, upright.

Her complexion glowed livelier than the twinkling lights of the *Tropicana*, her ever-smiling teeth, the ripeness of her lips, charged Freddie with a boundless thirst for her. This to him was a discovery. It was the tearing away of a veil from his eyes. She walked out with him, smelling faintly of *Miraba*, squeezing her way deftly through the taxis which were now piling on both banks of the road while white men, coatless, were paying-off their taxi drivers and hurrying to the *Tropicana*.

Soon the noise became a murmur.

Nancy said, 'Freddie, I sure my mother's in there!'

'No, Nancy; I should've seen 'er.' He took her arm, and now that it was not so bright she let it be. He felt a sweet thrill run through his veins and he quickly began to tell her sweet words, any words that would keep her from wondering where they were heading for and why.

He himself was driven partly by impulse and partly by instinct. He only felt that he must be with Nancy, must confide in her. It was all rather vague to him and he knew she must be thinking now about the friendship between her mother and Jagua. Sometimes when her mother Mama Nancy came to see Jagua, Nancy came along too and they often found Freddie in Jagua's rooms. They had all come to accept Freddie as Jagua's young man, one who had no interest in girls like her. Often they teased him, telling him what a pity it was that he Freddie – young, studious and ambitious, should be the lover of the ageing and experienced woman of the city, Jagua; and though Freddie always spoke up loyally for his mistress he knew that they were genuinely concerned that he had 'fallen into her clutches' and were afraid that he could never get out of her control.

'Freddie, where you takin' me?' Nancy asked, as they cut away from the motor road.

Her voice, the female cry of distress, fired his blood. He felt a hot surge towards his eyes. Her hand was slipping back from his and he gripped it firmly: silky and smooth, it warmed the inside of his palm. Her body smelt so different from Jagua's. Why, Freddie told himself, she was just turned twenty, and Jagua must be well over forty.

'Siddown, Nancy. I beg you. Sit on de tree. Ah goin' to tell you everythin'.'

She glanced at the fallen tree over which the ferns grew, matty and damp. 'What you goin' to tell me? I can't sit here, Freddie. I fear for snake.'

'Snake?' Though he tried to sound casual and reassuring Freddie remembered going on a car drive with a friend and seeing a mamba lying in the middle of the tarmac, warming its belly. They were standing now in the woods, well away from the motor road. Occasionally distant headlights etched out the trees and lit up her face, but Freddie was sure the shadows concealed them both from passers-by on the main road.

Impulsively he reached out and circled Nancy's waist and drew her to him. 'Freddie!' she whispered. Her sweet breath beat warmly against his lips. The hard slim bust strained closer to his shirt. In that brief contact when her body rubbed against his and she struggled to get free, Freddie experienced a rare elation. Was sex not a monopoly of sophisticates like Jagua? Jagua with her arty make-up, seductive bosom and hips? He felt his heart aglow with the new pleasure. Sweat sprang to his pores and soaked his clothes.

'Freddie, what you tryin' to do?' she breathed. Her secretive voice excited him.

'Now lissen to me, Nancy.'

'No, Freddie, is dangerous.' She drew back.

'Wha's dangerous? I done anything to you?' His hand slid beneath the blouse and grasped the nipple of her breast. It was a hard little breast, fitting into the cup of his hand and bouncing restively within the cup.

'What you tryin' to do, Freddie? Is not right.'

'Nancy, I can't let you go. I wan' to tell you somethin'. Stay a little.'

'No! Le's go. You kin tell me in de house.' Her voice was weak and she leaned against him. 'I afraid, Freddie. I don' know why. I just fear in my mind.'

'I feel all hot inside me, Nancy. You know what you doin' to me?'

'Go 'way!' But she was leaning on his arm and holding it dearly. 'Am a decent gal, Freddie,' she whispered.

'But ah love you, Nancy. True!'

'So you say to every gal. What about Jagua? If she know, she will kill me.'

'Know what? We done nothin',' Freddie cried. 'What we done?'

'You soun' like you vex with me. Because I don' give you myself quick-quick, like Jagua. Not so? You disappointed wit' me?' He detected the note of pleading in her voice. 'Er? Because we done nothin'?'

'Lissen, Nancy! Me an' Jagua, is different from this!'

'Different?'

'Yes.' How could he explain it to her? He had suddenly discovered that she was young but mature. She was clean, sweet, desirable. Jagua was not young. She was beyond awakening his finer feelings, no matter what she might do. 'She too ol' for me, you understan'? I can't marry her.'

She looked at him with interest, but still the distrust was visible in her eyes. He said to her, 'Nancy, I want young gal like you who understan' love, not money. If a person have somebody he *love*, I mean – really love – everythin' mus' come right in de worl'.'

She said, 'Somebody like me?'

'Sometime! Nancy I not tryin' to deceive you or do you anythin' bad. You young and I young. Is right for me to love you and plan for tomorrow. And—'

'At firs' I fear, Freddie. All de young men in Lagos dem talk sweet sweet – like you doin' now, Freddie. But when dem get a gal on de bed, you never see dem again. And if dem give de gal belly, she mus' carry de belly alone, and dem will run and lef' her. Is very bad of de young men. So I use to fear.'

He smiled. 'No! I not tryin' to give you belly to carry, Nancy. Tha's what I tryin' to tell you.' Could she sense the voice of truth in him, he wondered.

She sighed. 'If Jagua know—'

'Don' worry 'bout Jagua. You got you own life, Nancy.' He knew that in her own way Jagua loved him and he owed her a world of gratitude for her sweetness, the physical satisfaction she gave him; but was there not something else besides physical satisfaction? Nancy, he felt, could supply both the physical satisfaction and the 'something else' he needed. She was young and still not yet set in her ways. 'Look, Nancy! Is only I can't help myself. I don' want to hurt Jagua. She fine and she have some money an' she know how to dress smart and hook all de men in Lagos. Das why we call her Jag-wa. But she's not for me. She too high up in de sky. You know, de woman take a fancy to me because she say I young and handsome. But she take money from de other men, and sleep wit' dem. And she tryin' to keep me for marriage when she get older, like I'm somethin' from de museum. 'I too young to sell my life like dat.'

'Freddie, you very handsome.' She tucked herself close to him and he kissed her. 'Freddie!'

'Nancy!'

'Kiss me, Freddie! Why you so blin' all de time?'

He kissed her and her mouth tasted young and her body was all afire with an electric fire he had never felt before, sending voltages of passion through his veins.

'You very beautiful, Nancy; and sweet!'

'No!' she breathed, as his fingertips slid beneath her skirt and down her belly. 'Not today, Freddie. Another day, I promise you, Freddie. Is too sudden.'

She disengaged herself and started walking quickly to the motor road, straightening her dress. He called out to her: 'Nancy, come now!' But she did not turn her head. He stood there waiting, and when he could not get her obedience, he left the woods and came and joined her.

They walked in silence, for this new discovery was too all-consuming; something deeper than a promise had been born this night. If it would last, this new feeling would weld them together. He could feel that; and he could feel too, that this meeting was going to be their special secret. Jagua would never know, and therein lay its savour.

They came to the roundabout that blazed with lights. Indian Almond trees threw shadows which concealed the lovers nestling on the benches. All roads from the city and into the city met at this point, a good hunting ground for the *Tropicana* girls who liked street work. Freddie saw some of them now, moving so that the beam thrown by approaching car lamps would pick them out. They walked self-consciously, wiggling their hips extravagantly like stunt women.

Near the bus stop Freddie paused and looked at Nancy's youthful profile. 'Don' pay any attention to Jagua, Nancy. You hear me?' He had never before felt the real difference between pure love such as was exalting him now, and the casual encounters with the *Tropicana* girls.

The bus, a long affair in red and cream, swung to the stop with the conductor hanging out in his khaki shirt and shorts and yelling, 'Are you goin'?'

'Goodnight, lovely one,' said Freddie. 'You will dream of me?'

'Yes, Freddie. I don' know how I kin sleep dis night.'

The bus was already swinging away, and he watched the lights, and the well-groomed head of the girl whose world must be nearer his.

As he stood waiting for his bus he remembered the carefree days. Mama Nancy would come up to Jagua in her room with Freddie lounging in a chair.

'You got chance to do me hair, Jagua?' she would ask. 'Or you boy frien' need you?'

Jagua would not look at Freddie's face, but would say: 'Siddown, Ma Nancy. Me house be you house. Sure, I goin' to do your hair – in de latest style, too. I sure Freddie won' mind.'

Nancy would sit through it all, the Junior Miss, miles removed from their adult world. In those days it never occurred to Freddie that here was a girl, full of feeling. She was simply Ma Nancy's daughter. To him she was just a monument. He did not even associate a bed with her.

He would sit by, reading his correspondence course on law,

or – more often – he would leave the women and go downstairs to his room. Mama Nancy and Nancy had never been to his room. They only met him in Jagua's. Often they came to Jagua's room and played discs and danced to her collection of jazz, *High-life* and rhumba music.

They had been good friends but now, with this new taste of Nancy on his lips, Freddie felt fortified to face Jagua's possessive love for him.

5

The bus put him down at Skylark Avenue where he bought a loaf of bread and lingered for a while. At this time of night Skylark Avenue exploded into life in a manner to attract even those who lived on it. Above the noise he could identify the *High-life* rhythm gushing from a record-dealer's loudspeaker. On the opposite side of the street cars were gliding into the petrol-filling station where the girls in their spaceman cloaks lunged about like red dervishes charging one car after the other with power.

A hundred yards from his room he recognized Mike – Jagua's houseboy – standing on the steps, wringing his hands.

'Sir! Tenk God you return! Madam, she say make you come quick.'

'Madam? But ah lef' her in de *Tropicana*.'

'No, sah. She sen' message from police station, sir. She say make you come bail am.'

'Bail – what? Police station?'

'Dem fight in de *Tropicana*. She and Mama Nancy, dem broke all de table, them wound themself with bottle.'

'Hold on! What you talkin'? Jagua fighting Mama Nancy?'

'Yes, sah! She say make you come and bail am. Dem arres' de two and lock dem up in de guardroom.'

Freddie knitted his brows. No self-respecting teacher would like to be mixed up with Charge Offices, certainly not he. When he had changed he had a quick bath, and like a man running away from his own shadow, Freddie got into bed and switched off the light.

In the darkness he could see nothing at first, and then the accusing face of Jagua began staring at him. 'So you treat me, Freddie?' There was a twisted smile on her face, cold, unforgiving. 'When trouble meet you woman, you turn into de bed and sleep. You lef' her to suffer?' The face was so real that he could not stand the terrifying judgement contained in the eyes. He found himself getting quickly out of bed and switching on the light. He took a law book from the locker, put it under his arm and set out for the Charge Office.

At the counter he saw a sergeant making entries in a fat book.

'I wan' to see Jagua, Sergeant.'

'You tink I playin'?' the sergeant said. He looked up and waved his pen at the others on the counter, 'All of you, see dis man, who tink I come here for play. Man, go siddown till is you turn. Ha, ha! Dis be Charge Office, not school!'

A young woman in the corner of the smelly room seemed to be making a statement which Freddie had interrupted. She stood away from the counter which ran across the room and began bawling swear words at the young police constable, who ignored her and kept on writing steadily. Freddie observed at once that other constables were deriving some lecherous satisfaction from the young woman's behaviour. She had a defiant twinkle in her eye, her breath smelled of alcohol and her blouse – one arm of which had been torn in some scuffle – slouched over a naked young breast with a dare-devil abandon that could not but be comical. She seemed by her manner to be conscious of the power of her femaleness over the males in the khaki uniforms.

Freddie stared at this ragged woman who confronted him with the eternal struggle to live, so tragic in the lower reaches of Lagos life. She must be a 'habitual', Freddie concluded from the brusque manner in which all the men mocked her. He was interrupted by the loud voice of the sergeant who took him to the back of the Charge Office where the cells were. The strong smell of human urine hit his nostrils in the warm air. It seemed to hang in invisible walls of mist along the corridors.

By this time it was nearly midnight and some of the 'prisoners' had already accepted their fate and were lying on the cold cement floor, no bed, no pillow and rolling in their own excrements. But Jagua was wide awake. Freddie saw her standing behind bars, and looking directly at him with an animal muteness not unlike the face he had just visualized in his own darkened room. This was his mistress, and this squalor all came along with the kind of life she had chosen. He felt a mixture of shame, grief and pity. He wished that no one would recognize or identify him. He could not say a word as the big key rattled in the lock and Jagua, subdued and silent, her head swathed in bandages, came out and walked away with him after all the papers had been signed and the undertakings given.

Freddie was downcast. Jagua would yet see him in even less reputable places. How often had they quarrelled over her madness at the *Tropicana*? Once there, she became transformed into a she-devil. What angered him now was that her face showed not even a glimmer of distress. She seemed ready for more.

'Why you fight, Jagua?' Freddie asked when they got back to her room. Jagua was taking off her clothes as if they were already contaminated. Even in his anger the sensual feeling was creeping in on Freddie. Her skin was silken and paler than her face, especially at the back of her neck and sloping down her back beneath the arms. There were no collarbones to be seen when she faced him, and when she turned her back at him, stepping out of her clothes, the voluptuousness of her big moulded hips seduced him and made his anger sharpen at his own weakness for her. 'You no wan' to answer me? Why you fight?'

She was nonchalantly lighting a cigarette now, and Freddie watched her put it to her lips and draw in a deep one. 'Why you sen' for me? I don' tell you make we lef' de *Tropicana*. Yes, I tell you make we lef' but you done see de Syrian man and you tink you kin get money from him. So you disgrace me. Instead you get money now, you goin' to pay fine or get into de white college for assault . . . you see?'

When she had had her bath and combed out her hair she came and took him to bed and whispered to him. She would not be bad any more. 'True, Freddie, ah mean it dis time.'

She cuddled him and kissed him, and mothered him, bubbling over with love as she always did whenever she knew she was in the wrong and wanted to be restored to his favour.

'I goin' to return proper to mah trade. Ah already arrange to speak wid de manager of de company. He goin' to open branch shop for me, where I kin sell Accra and velvet cloth and lace. When ah pay security, de shop will be under my control.'

Freddie made a face to show her he was not convinced. Jagua had always promised to be good, to settle down, to open a retail shop and engage in petty trading, mainly cotton-wax prints. He knew she had already made some money in the cloth trade, selling Georgettes and Damasks, and sheer brilliant Manchester prints – the kind which girls like Nancy tied skirt-wise over blouses. Jagua knew the West Coast of Africa from Gambia to Lagos, with Ghana as a kind of Parisian centre of fashion. Before Freddie met her she used to travel regularly to Ghana and beyond, buying there and selling in Lagos. It was partly one reason why they called her Jagua. She had style. Whenever she put on anything it became the fashion in Lagos, and the girls and women came flocking to her and wanting to know where the article had come from. Then she would go into the room and produce the material and more women would hear about it and come too. During that time Jagua was well known to all the Customs men and the Border Police. What had happened to her Freddie could not say. Sometimes she talked of going to Onitsha by the Niger. There she hoped to become one of the Merchant Princesses who controlled tens of thousands of pounds. Freddie had an idea that she was capable of doing it, but she would not leave Lagos. Or while in Lagos she would not exert herself. It was three years now since she had been to Ghana. The *Tropicana* had sapped all her energy. She seemed to be one of those women who are always trying to prove to men that they are still young. And to do so, she must always remain focused in their sights. Going away from the social centre might make them forget her.

Freddie soon learnt what had happened in the *Tropicana* after he had left. Jagua told him that Mama Nancy had come in and had lured away the Syrian gentleman from her. He rightly belonged to her, but why should Mama Nancy come and claim him when – that night – he had decided to change over to Jagua. Freddie was so irritated with her story that he cut her short halfway through.

'You know sometin'?' Jagua confided now. 'Freddie I sorry for wat happen. I shame too much. If I tell you I no shame, I tellin' you lie. So I begin tink, as I lay down in de cell. If to say ah get me own man!'

Freddie grunted. He was used to these fits of repentance.

'If to say ah get me own man like you, Freddie. I mean – not jus' lover, but man forever! Den people will point and say, "Das Freddie Namme, husband of Jagwa." Oh, my heart will full up with proud. I no go care anythin'.'

'Why den, Jagwa? You keep findin' trouble. I already tol' you, le's leave de *Tropicana*. I tol' you I been tryin' to read de law, so I kin pass all de exam and become a man. You won' let me learn. Always findin' trouble for me. How I kin get peace of min'?'

'No worry, Freddie. I goin' to sen' you to England. If you don' find peace of min' dere, den. God don't say make you become lawyer. I goin' to send you to England so you kin read proper law in de inns of court!'

Freddie's smile was tolerant. 'Nonsense! You jus' jokin', Jagwa. You not goin' to sen' me to England with you own money. You got odder thing to do wid de money.'

'Ah got odder thing to do, but sendin' you is de best of all. I goin' to send you to Englan'; and you goin' to return and marry your Jagwa. Yes, Freddie. I wan' me own man now. Dem insult me too much. But as you is only a poor teacher you no reach yet for marry Jagwa woman. You mus' go train youssef to be proper man . . . Den I kin born chil' for you. An' you kin look after me, in me old age.'

'So you sendin' me to Englan' to return an' marry you?'

'Ah got anodder reason. I hear say Mama Nancy, she want to bluff me. She say she sendin' her own young man to Englan', so he too kin return an' marry her.'

'Oh! . . .' Freddie turned in the bed and faced the wall. He really had no wish to marry Jagua. As a mistress she was brilliant, but he

23

could not imagine her as a wife, when young ones like Nancy were available.

Jagua pressed her lips against his ears, and her arms enfolded him in a soft embrace. 'I goin' to sen' you to England, so you kin come back and marry me.'

Freddie did not share the delight she felt in the underlying condition.

6

As the weeks slipped by, Freddie began to see signs that Jagua meant every word. How she surmounted most of the hurdles the Government placed in the way of the private, ill-equipped but ambitious student he never could tell. The Nigerian Government regarded the student 'adventuring to England' with the same dark frown that the French Government viewed the globe-trotting fool attempting to cross the Sahara on a pedal-bicycle.

Jagua revealed that she had some money saved up from her cloth trade in Ghana and this money she now drew liberally. She paid for Freddie's dinners at the Inns, transferred enough money to pay Freddie's rent for one year and clothe him and buy him books.

Life began to acquire a new meaning for Freddie when, after months and months of waiting for letters from the immigration and the shipping authorities, they told him he would be travelling on a Norwegian cargo boat. The journey would be slow and long, but the food would be a compensation, he was assured. The sailing date was not definite – they still had a lot of cargo to take on board; and for this reason, Freddie could not tear himself away from Lagos and journey to his native Bagana in the East to say goodbye to his friends and relatives. He particularly wanted to see his mother, and if Jagua also wanted to be introduced to his parents, what harm could that do?

But Jagua herself could not readily leave Lagos now. She was still on bail, and when eventually her case came up Freddie saw her fined thirty shillings and warned to keep the peace. After that, not enough time was left for journeying to Bagana, and besides they had not been able to include the visit in their plans.

About a week to sailing time, the news leaked out among Freddie's friends, who pinned him down to a nightmare of farewell parties. He had even less time for anything else. Many were the nights when he put on his baggy velvet trousers and fez and in the warm humid air sat down and listened to speeches by his friends. He was, they said, a good example to Africa in thus 'seeking the Golden Fleece of Knowledge and Leadership'. Nigeria's future salvation depended on such trained people, they claimed. Looking at the speaker's eyes, Freddie knew he was speaking what he believed. In a way he knew that all his friends identified him with their own secret ambitions to study abroad. He did not like being fêted, but he bore it all with fortitude safe in the knowledge that he would soon be out of their reach.

What troubled him more at this time was that Jagua had become unbearably touchy and morose. Freddie noted how unfriendly she had become. She walked about with a long face and for the most trivial reasons she started yelling abuses at him. Could it be that she no longer wanted him away from her? At such times when he tried to reason with her and failed his spirits would sink and he would wish he could be with Nancy to soothe away the rough edges of his nerves.

One afternoon he ran across her in the Square. He was transported with delight. The smell of that warm night under the woods immediately filled his nostrils. In the midst of the confusion of pressing bodies and arms reaching out to grip the bus railings, he felt the silky-sweet touch of her hand. He noticed her because of the way she moved – hips fanned out by the georgette check in bold yellow and brown, the unconscious wiggle which drew him out to 'follow me'. She wore her hair short, and perhaps because she had been shopping in the sun it stood straight, without kinks, with beads of oil glistening in it. Her upper lip had gathered the crystal drops of perspiration, but she gave him a sweet smile and her eyes were keen. The greenish nylon blouse blended with the yellow georgette, and he could see the shadow of her pointed breasts with the dark nipples and soft pale sides that trembled.

They climbed into the bus with Freddie close behind her, his hand on her smooth cool arm. They sat down, intimately crushed in the seat. She mopped her brow with a soft cloth and soaked away the crystals of her lip.

'Freddie, I hear you almos' leavin' for England; and you don' care to come and see me. Is it good? And you say you love me?'

'Not so, Nancy. I try to come, but—'

She gave him an accusing look. 'When ah come to Englan', we will meet dere.'

'You jokin'?'

'I mean it, Freddie.'

He searched her face and could make nothing of her eagerly gleaming eyes. She took out two oranges from her shopping and offered him one. 'My Mama tryin' to sen' her young man; but he grown conceited, so she askin' me whedder I want to go and qualify as secretary typist. De Syrian man will pay all de fee.'

'You mean it? You really mean it?' He tried to keep back his delight.

'I coming to England and we will marry there.' She waved the orange joyfully, and pressed it to her lips.

They were nearing their destination now and Nancy looked at him suddenly and whispered. 'I goin' to be your Englan' lady, Freddie. You no glad? See how God use to do him own thing.'

Freddie helped her down, and together they walked some of the way. As they entered the home street, he handed back her shopping bag and stood for a moment under the trees, well away from the other end of the street where Jagua lived. But Nancy succeeded in enticing him out of his hiding and step by step they moved up, until Freddie found himself near the end of the street.

He watched her walk away with the young upright shoulders, dainty steps and trembling bottom. When she had vanished beyond the mango tree by the foodseller he looked up, and there gazing down at him from the balcony was Jagua Nana. The smile on her face did not mask the greenish tinge of anger. She must have seen everything.

'Freddie, who dat I see with you?'

'You mean – with me?' He looked up the street. 'Oh – is only Nancy Oll. She gone back to her modder. Is only Nancy—'

'Wat you mean, is only Nancy? Nancy not woman, yet? She no reach for sleep wit' you and born pickin'?'

'I comin' up to explain, Jagua. Have patience – is nothin'. Nothin' at all. I comin' up to explain.'

7

Freddie walked quickly to his room and threw the armful of shopping on his bed. Knowing how very sensitive Jagua was about her age, he felt now he should at least have spared her the challenge and the humiliation of being compared with the teenage Nancy, daughter of her rival Mama Nancy. And this at a time when she had sacrificed so much for him too.

At her door, he hesitated and listened. Voices drifted to his ears. He heard the sound of glass on glass. He knocked and the door opened. To his shock he was greeted by a strong smell of beer and for a moment could not see round the room through the fumes of cigarette smoke recalling the atmosphere of the *Tropicana*. Then the smoke cleared a little and he saw the three men in the room; men whom he had never seen or met before. He identified their kind instantly: the influential men of Lagos. Private business men, perhaps; dabblers in party politics, almost certainly. They were in the same age-group as Jagua, men in their early fifties, and what they lost in youthful virility and attractiveness they made up by lavishing their money on women like Jagua Nana, on letting their tongues run away with them in recalling fanciful accounts of their prowess with women in distant lands. The sight of those three men drinking ice-cold beer and lounging carelessly in the chairs of Jagua Nana threw a mist of anger between him and Jagua. He pushed past her into the room. Jagua introduced them as 'three men just back from Ghana and Overseas', but Freddie had already taken in the situation with the intuition of a lover and he was not deceived. No one told him they had come for the woman Jagua. Living in Lagos had taught him that this was the way it worked. The men came to a woman like Jagua, in the daytime, socially. Then individually they sneaked back at night or in the morning when the office workers were poring over their files beneath waving overhead fans. At such times they drank beer and paid for the 'love' they bought. Freddie took this visit by the three men as a survey of Jagua's residence, and no matter what they did to disguise their intentions, he stuck to his conclusion and it made him see all their actions in an angry light.

It did not once occur to him that he had no right to be resentful, that as a poor teacher he could not even begin to think of buying Jagua half the luxuries with which these men pampered her. But that did not ease the pain. In a city where money was the idol of the women, an idol worshipped in every waking and sleeping moment, sentiment was a mere pastime. And to Jagua, Freddie classified as sentiment.

He looked at her now, the ways she was dressed to sell her body, so that these men could see for themselves and inflame their senses with what they saw: the smooth round arms, the long neck, the smooth well-moulded calves. And when she bent forward to fill a man's glass with beer, raising the glass from the little stool and tilting it so that it did not froth too much as she poured the beer from the bottle, her breasts hung down pendulously. He could see them clearly in the nylon brassiere inside the loose transparent blouse. He noticed too with a jealous twinge that she had groomed her hair, combing it straight backwards and decorating it with a gold band. She looked to him not more than thirty now.

He excused himself and shut the door behind him. Jagua wrenched it open and pulled him in, leading the way to the bedroom. She told him she did not know the men and had never seen them before they turned up that afternoon, looking for someone who had lived at this same address before she moved in. But how, Freddie asked her, could they have missed their way into this – her own particular room? And knowing they were in the room why did she have to call him up to face the humiliation of knowing his rivals?

'Sorry, Freddie,' Jagua said. 'I done nothin' with them. I tell you, I don' know them.' She opened the cloth which she had tied sarongwise, folded it back again round her hips. Freddie caught a flash of her beautiful legs. 'You think I will tell you lie?' She looked at him fully.

He knew she was lying. 'You will finish your lies when I come back.' He saw the spark of fear in her eye and knew he was master of the situation.

The conversation of the men in the other room came faintly to them. Freddie heard the phrase 'When I was in England' leap suddenly out of the general chatter. He knew then that he had assessed them right. They were trumpet-blowers out to impress Jagua. 'Been-tos' who had been in England and acquired professional skills were regarded with great favour by the women. And since Jagua did not have a man of her own, why wouldn't they show her how superior they were to other men in Lagos. That phrase awakened nothing but anger in him. He was angry because – rightly or wrongly – women like Jagua automatically became the property of men like the three in the room. He was angry because he had already known his true position with Jagua. But now these men focused it for him.

He was the glamorous young man in Jagua's life, the lover of the elderly beauty who must not press forward when those who paid for her luxuries were around. There was nothing he wanted more now than to take his proper place. To remain in the background till they were gone; and then – for his sporting spirit – he would be allowed to play as much the lover as he chose.

He made abruptly for the door. Jagua held his sleeve. 'Freddie, you goin'? Listen, when de strangers leave, I will come an' explain.'

He did not answer. He did not want her explanation. She was still talking when he strode across the sitting room, holding his breath against the pungent fumes of smoke.

His room was at the back, on the ground floor: one of ten rooms which bounded a narrow corridor. Each floor had a communal cooking place, a bathroom and a lavatory pail. There was a small yard at the back where the children played and hawkers came in with their wares and wood was split and gossip exchanged. The owner of the building was a retired Civil Servant who erected it out of his accumulated savings over a thirty-year period of service. Freddie was tired of taking complaints to him, because he did not believe in spending any more money to maintain the house. He simply sat there in his own room and parlour, gazing out of the window and into the street, waiting for the end of the month when about one hundred and twenty pounds would be paid to him.

Freddie returned to the comfort of his own room and tried to compose his thoughts in the stifling air that exuded from the hot cement walls. He put aside his shopping and took a book from the shelves. He sat down in a low chair, turning the pages casually and thinking of Jagua. The noisy rhythm of children drumming and singing in the street, the chugging of a railway engine, the harsh triumphant laughter of a man winning his game of draughts under the mango tree outside . . . he felt them all and hated them because he felt powerless to control them now that he wanted some peace. Above them all the mocking voice of Jagua kept imposing itself on these noises, and suddenly he felt the sharp pain of degradation by the Syrian from the *Tropicana* who knew he could 'get' Jagua because he had the money and therefore insulted him; the false superiority of the three men now in her room; the torture of being held in sexual bondage by a woman very much older than he was, more cunning and more ambitious and infinitely more possessive. But if he decided to break away from her, he would be losing his chance to go abroad and study. Such a time did not come twice in a lifetime to a Nigerian.

He heard a knock at his door and Jagua came in. She put a hand on his head and he quickly shook it off. 'Freddie, you vex, not so. I sure you misunderstan' de whole ting. I goin' to show dose people some place.'

He did not say a word. She went to the door, and from there said: 'I goin' to show dem some place in Lagos an' I soon come back, so I kin clear de whole misunderstandin'.'

Suddenly he seemed to notice her dress for the first time. She had changed and she had thickened the make-up on her face. The eyebrows were marked out sharply in wide sweeping arcs that extended the natural curve by an inch on either side of the cheek.

She looked like one of the masks from a collection Freddie had seen in the museum sometime. She obviously did not know how she had cheapened herself, for she gave him one of those coquettish glances with the word whore written in them.

'Jagua, how you dress so loud? Because of de three men who 'been-to' England? You sure you coming back dis night?'

'Jus' now.' She smiled. 'I only goin' to show dem some place, den I come home! What I got to waste time dere for? I got plenty to do in de house.'

Freddie began to laugh, a laughter that mocked himself too. 'Jagua, who you tryin' to deceive? I know you goin' to do business widde men.'

'Never!' She came towards him. 'Ah swear Freddie! So you don' trust me?'

'Swear proper, Jagua.'

She put a finger on her tongue and raised the finger to the sky. 'If I goin' to do business widde men, when I reach de main road, make motor kill me dead. You satisfy, now?'

'Jagua.' Freddie rose from the deep chair. 'One of my frien' tell me say you done begin stroll in de night. You doin' what dem call solicitin'. You strollin' so de white men kin pick you up in de car and take you home. You fit swear say dat one is lie, too? I hear dis long time, but I jus' keep quiet, because am only poor teacher who got no money to maintain Jagwa woman.'

'Lie, Freddie! Wicked lie! I never done no solicitin'.'

Freddie raised his hand in warning. 'Jagwa, one of dese days we goin' to prove all dis thin'. Mind you, Jagwa, I don' care de hell what you doin'. Is not today me and you been goin' steady. But what use to anger me: you tryin' to show me you be virgin. You never known anodder man in dis Lagos, or anywhere you go but young Freddie Namme. Das what use to make me vex too much.' He caught the merest flicker of doubt in her eye.

'I mus' go now. De people waitin' for me.' She twisted the door knob. 'In de name of God, I done no solicitin'. Don' lissen to dem, Freddie. In dis Lagos, people mus' poke nose. Dem never try mindin' dem own business.'

She went out and he heard the sound of the car. It was one of the long ones, driven by a chauffeur. He remembered seeing it as he came in, but had not really associated it with Jagwa. She was indeed Jagwa, he had to admit. His jealousy had accomplished nothing. She was still Jagwa. But was it natural, he asked himself, for all women to uphold their innocence – even Jagwa? What would she do if he caught her red-handed in bed with a man? He wanted to know that one. Half his mind told him she would still deny; and he had a feeling that she would convince him it was a misunderstanding.

Jagua did not come back home that evening.

Freddie was sitting at his desk the following afternoon writing, when he heard a knock at the door. It was Nancy. She looked sweet in a simple white dress with a black belt in the middle. Her complexion glowed with youthful good looks; her eyes were dark and eager. She had a parcel in her hands and she hesitated at the door.

Freddie smiled at her. 'Come in, Nancy. You always come when my mood is bad. Don' be afraid. Jagua not at home.' He placed the back of his hand over his mouth and whispered, noting the sparkling eyes. 'She done gone out with three men since yesterday afternoon and she never return. You know what she tell me? "I come back jus' now," she say. "What I goin' to waste time for? I got plenty to do in de house!" Ha, ha, Nancy? You ever beat dat one? Jagua got plenty to do in de house and she go 'way with three men in long car since yesterday an' she don' come back to dat house. Come in, Nancy, I feelin' very low . . .'

She looked at him with tenderness. 'You talk like you drunk, Freddie!' She came and took his head in her hands. 'You feelin' hurt? Dem wound your vanity. Dem show you you got no power and no control over de woman you call your own!' She sighed. 'Sometime I sure dat you really love dis Jagua woman.'

'Sometime. But also he kin be dat I got into de habit of Jagua, an' I kin not shake off de habit. She weaken me too much.'

'Das wat I suspect, Freddie. De woman done give you love medicine, an' you drink de medicine in some sweet soup.'

Freddie looked at her with fear in his eyes. 'Love medicine – but why Jagua go worry for make love medicine for me?'

Nancy put her parcel on the table and looked about the room. It was very disorderly and the only available sitting space was the bed. To Freddie's delight, she sat on it.

'Woman like Jagua, who been in dis business a long time, dem get plenty power. Dem practise witchcraft. Dem spen' all dem money with the medicine man to make dem juju so dat man kin like dem. Jagua know dat her medicine done catch you, so she don' worry at all.'

Freddie felt hopeless. There could be some truth in what Nancy was saying. If not, why could he not shake Jagua off? She was not a respectable woman, for all her attractiveness. He knew that. He knew also that she was subject to caprices and impulses. Just as she had lavished much money on his study course in England, so also could she suddenly decide on something quite unexpected and he would be left floating.

He turned his attention to Nancy. 'Sorry about de room, Nancy. Everythin' tupsy turvy. I packin'. God know de truth. As soon as I enter de boat, ah will be a happy man. No one kin trouble me. Anythin' Jagwa like, she kin do. Is when I see all dis nonsense with me own eye; das when it pain my brain too much.'

'Is all right, Freddie.' She put her hands between her knees, swinging her legs playfully. 'I soon go, Freddie. Mama sen' me come to know how you packin'.'

'To me . . . You mean dat?'

'Why you actin' surprised, Freddie? You tink she don' know about you and me? I already tell her.' She pointed at the parcel on the table. 'She say give you dat parcel.' Her eyes shone.

Freddie went over and took the parcel. It carried a London address. He looked at her with a question in his eyes.

'Is home food,' Nancy explained. 'Home food – gari, pepper, okro. Is for our cousin. He livin' in London and studyin' engineering. Say to him Mama sen' her love and Nancy joinin' him soon. You know, those boys in London, them use to feel homesick and when de news from home come like dis, it kin make dem heart strong enough to put dem head for de work.' She tensed her brow and her eyes. Her seriousness interested him.

'I mus' see dat it reach him safe, Nancy. Unless I don' go again!' He smiled. 'As you know, not me sendin' myself.' He looked at her more closely and felt a twinge of remorse. 'I never offer you nothin'. What you will drink, Nancy? Ah kin sen' Sam to buy you some cold coke.'

'For me? . . . No Freddie. I mus' go now.'

He held her hands. He saw the flush come to her face. Instinctively her eyes went to the door. He sat beside her on the bed and took her wrist and laid it in his hand, examining the long and shapely fingers. She turned her face towards him, and, though he could read the cautionary message, he kissed her and her eyelids slid down and the soft eyelashes fluttered against his cheek. The anger was melting away and the world had become sweet with Nancy Oll and her fine skin and bewitching fragrance.

He felt the gentle push and the gentler voice. 'You come again, Freddie. You always wantin' dat. Anytime you see me always you wantin' dat one. Is all you like me for, Freddie?'

He slid his fingers along her bare shoulder and into her blouse. There was nothing else he could have done. The blouse was cut to be slipped away. She did not even wear a brassiere and her breast was dancing in his hand.

'De door open, Freddie.' She was hissing now.

He squeezed her again, then went to the door and bolted it. 'Don' fear, Nancy. Nobody fit enter now.'

'But is too hot now, Freddie. Is too hot for doin' anythin'. True. Let it be anodder time.'

'Yes, dear.' He had taken her in his arms and was squeezing her close. Through the drumming in his ears, he heard the last lonely cry of Nancy the girl reaching out for help she must know would never come from the wolfing Freddie. 'Freddie, Freddie – Oh! . . . I beg you, make we keep it till anodder time. If you love me, Freddie . . . But I not goin' to run. Is for you Freddie. I not goin' to give it to anodder man, while I love you.'

The drumming had become a roar. The fingers were trembling

around the buttons, the intricate knots which showered the clothes she had on. He caught his breath. Her superbly tanned and shapely young body stood revealed. He could not help leaning back for a moment and devouring the slim shoulders, full breasts with the long nipples. He kissed them now and they reared into a gooseflesh with a sharp intake of her breath.

'Gently, Freddie, you will rumple me clothes. Me Mama will know what you done.' She wriggled out of her frock and chemise. Her waist was so slim and her belly so flat that he laid his palm on it to believe what he saw. She had small buttocks unusual for a Nigerian-bred girl, but they were silky smooth with an eel-like electricness that sent shivers of madness through him.

He took that slim waist and marvelled at it and pressed her to him and was entwined in her teenage athleticness. The heat and sweat, the odour of mating, fused them both in a reeling bout of insatiable lust. She was crying too loud for his comfort.

'Freddie, I die! Kill me, Freddie. I die! . . . Oh, God! . . .'

He bit her ear. He felt golden-sweet with this release of his pent-up tensions. The pleasure he had found in Nancy's youthfulness, her sensitivity, came as from a fable. He could not help contrasting her skin which was firm and elastic, with Jagua's flabby and soggy for all the artifice. When Nancy cried, it was because she felt pain or pleasure; not because she had rehearsed it and timed it in advance. Her eyes rolled in ecstasy, and when she sat sobbing after he had had her he was disturbed and he kissed away the tears and smoothed her cheeks. She was genuine. Did genuine mating exist? Freddie asked himself. If only Jagua knew it, this was the greatest betrayal she had ever faced.

'Freddie, tell me you love me.' She kissed him.

'I love you, Nancy,' he murmured between kisses. 'But why you cryin'? You so sweet, I wonder if I jus' dreamin'!'

The tears came up again. He saw them fill the eyes, brown eyes that looked beyond him in a flood of grief. He took a handkerchief and dabbed away the tears and tenderly told her to get up and dress before lying back for a while. She slipped out of the bed and clumsily began putting the chemise over her head. He went and held her hips.

'Where you come from, Nancy?'

'My fadder and modder come here from Freetown, in Sa Leone. Long time. My fadder workin' in de Secretariat before he die. Since den I live with my modder who sen' me to school. She doin' a bit of dressmaking and a bit of bakery – we got a nice shop where we sell cake and bread . . .'

'So you say your modder know all about we?' He handed her the blouse. She was getting into her knickers, and she held his shoulder to retain her balance.

'I tol' my modder dat I love you an' I wan' to marry you. She think I no serious. "Don' forget, Nancy . . . We comin' a long way, from Freetown. An' if you marry dis Nigerian boy, den you mus' forsake you fadderlan'." So my Mama say, but I don' lissen to her, so she jus' go on talkin'. She tell me dat if I wan' to marry you, I must kill Jagua firs' before I kin get you. I mus' kill Jagua firs'. She talk true, Freddie? Tell me, Freddie, is true dat if I want you Jagua will fight me? Answer me true – not because you and she quarrellin' or anythin'. Answer me true, because I love you, Freddie.'

He looked at the pain her eyes tried to conceal. 'No, Nancy. I not goin' to marry Jagua. At firs' I think Jagua serious with me. But is all lie, lie, lie! She got dis habit of runnin' after men with money. Now if she don' sleep with one man every day, she never feel happy. Den on top of dat, she takin' me as small chil' and she always deceive me under me own nose. If I catch her, she begin to tell long story. I got too much pride, Nancy. But jus' now, it won' be de right thing, if I let her know. Ah mus' wait till ah enter de ship firs'. Till I land in Englan'. Den I will show my hand.'

She threw herself into his arms and he folded her, soft and sweet and dainty. 'But Freddie, what you goin' to do? Jagua put a lot of money on you head. How you goin' to pay back?'

He stroked her hips. 'Easy. Jus' let me reach England and begin to study de law, firs'.'

'You know what, Freddie? I goin' visit your home town of Bagana. Before I cross over to Englan' I mus' go and know Bagana and salute you Fadder and Modder. I will tell Mama to take me wit' her, so she too kin see dat Nigerian man is good for her chil' to marry. Is true we comin' from Freetown, but is here dem born me, and here I go to school. Nigeria is me secon' home.'

Freddie kissed her again; then he heard the loud, insistent knocking on the door.

8

'Open de door! . . . Freddie, open de door! . . . You hear me? Open de door quick, or I will burs' de door!'

It was Jagua. She would bring the house down on their heads if he did not quickly calm her down. His first impulse was to dart through the window, to pull Nancy after him. But the meshes of the mosquito netting were too fine to allow that. Glancing at his bare legs he reached instead for his trousers, jumped into them, fastening the wrong flap buttons in his headlong hurry. She was banging the door now with a heavier object.

'Just a minute! Wha's de matter, Jagua?'

With one quick glance at Nancy and a finger pressed over his lips, Freddie went to the door and slid back the bolt. Jagua crashed into the room. She lunged straight at Nancy.

'What you doin' in dis room?' she panted. 'You good for nothin'. You call yourself decent gal. What you doin' with my man with de door all locked up and—'

'Is your man, then? Why you runnin' about wit' odder men, you can't sleep in you own bed.'

Nancy's nerve surprised Freddie. He immediately sensed the fight coming and stood on his toes. What a scandalous thing for his teacher reputation. 'I beg you, Jagua. Don' make trouble. Is a misunderstandin'. I goin' to explain.' His words had the reverse effect.

'Shut up, Freddie! Got no business with you – yet!' She turned to Nancy. 'Dis is de poor bastard I got to teach a lesson so dat she will know next time about taking de man of her senior. Nancy, who tell you dat I goin' with odder men?' Her eyes were aflame and Freddie seeing them, went and shut the door. 'Who tell you dat? Answer me!'

'Yourself! Who tell you dat am in de room with Freddie? Why

you hurryin' to enter de room. Somebody tell you am here, das why you running and ramming de door with stone.' Nancy was speaking with a spirit which made Freddie want to raise her by the arm and shout: 'Champion! . . .'

'I tell you, Jagwa! I love mah Freddie. He goin' to England and when he coming back he will be my England man!'

'Close you mout', you small pickin'! Who born you to talk to me like dat?'

Jagua sprang at her. 'I goin' to teach you pepper! And you kin go and call you Mama too an' I will give am fire to chop!' Freddie scarcely saw the flash of her hand but he heard the smack and saw Nancy wince and place a hand on her cheek. The two women clinched, and it was Nancy who screamed. 'Oh! . . . Freddie, she bite me! De witch-woman bite me! . . .'

'Bite her back! You got no teeth? Nancy, bite am back good and proper!'

He saw Nancy butt into her and Jagua screamed. Freddie felt a sweet glow at Jagua's humiliation and Nancy's incredible nerve. Quickly he slid between the two women and tried to tear them apart. From both sides blows buffeted his skull and ribs. Jagua landed a good right on his cheek. He seized her by the wrists but with the enraged strength of a jaguar she wrested free.

'Leave me, Freddie. You never gone England yet, and you done begin run after anodder woman! You tink am a fool?'

'I don' run after her, Jagua. What I goin' to do when her modder sen' her to me – an' you run away with other man?'

'What you goin' to do? You done what you mus'! You slept with Nancy. Yes! What kin' young man you be if you don' sleep with such fine gal? You tink Ma Nancy don' know what she doin' to sen' her alone to your room?'

Freddie sneered. 'When you and de three men ride away in de big car, where you go? What you wan' me to do? Sit down and cry? I must to console myself! Das how poor man who no get long car kin console hisself.'

'What concern you wit' Mama Nancy, dat she sendin' her only daughter to your bed?' Jagua snapped at him. 'So she sendin' Nancy to you now, so you kin marry her? By de way, Freddie, who help you get passport? Who suffer and bribe de men till dem 'gree to give you passport? Or you don' know about de Government control, how is hard for obtain passport? Why Mama Nancy don' try for you? And who pay for your study and your room in de U.K.? Not me? Where Nancy and her modder hide when I doin' all dis?' She stood arms akimbo, half her blouse torn open, glaring at Freddie and Nancy so young and sweet.

Freddie saw her make straight for one of his suitcases. 'What you want dere, Jagua?' He lunged forward to retrieve the case which contained his passport. 'Jagua, be careful!'

But the maddened woman only turned on him and he felt himself torn asunder as by a lioness. Jagua kicked open the suitcase, rummaged among the clothes till she found the precious document. She took it in her strong hands and tore it to shreds. The document that had cost more than six months of forgery and bribery. Freddie felt the tears tingling under his eyelids. He tried to intervene but she sprang at him, all claws and teeth. A Jagwa woman could be fire. He felt the scarification from the flames. She lifted the suitcase and threw it outside. It fell and split open and his things scattered. A penny rolled away and lodged under the stairs. Freddie started at that penny. 'Go Englan' now, let me see!' She pointed at Nancy. 'Go with her, and lef' me in Lagos. I jus' an old woman, and you got no use for me. So take your sweetheart Nancy and go!' She took an axe and ran outside. She could wield it with dexterity. Nancy clung to Freddie while Jagua split the boxes open.

All the tenants came down from their rooms but Jagua dared them to come within the range of the axe. She had now belted a cloth across her middle and stood like a fighter when the 'seconds out' bell has just been rung.

'Ah will chop you head if you touch me!' Her magnificent bosom heaved as she stood with eyes burning anger.

'Jealous mad woman!' Freddie hissed. 'You done gone craze with jealousy.'

Everyone watched her in utter silence. She stamped upstairs, locked her front door and caught a taxi, driving furiously away in the direction of Central Lagos. Just then a policeman showed up within the compound but finding no one to answer his questions and confronted by hastily retreating backs and rapidly closing doors, he swore under his breath and went back to his beat.

Freddie turned to Nancy. 'I beg you, 'bout all dis. Is me own fault. Das de kind of Jagua woman who love your Freddie. Love done turn to sickness! She gone crazy and she kin kill anybody now. God 'ave mercy!'

'No worry, Freddie! I goin' back home. I leave de passel wit' you?'

'Yes. If everythin' spoil and I don' go, I kin return de parcel. She already tear de passport now, so I wonder.'

Nancy slipped away. Freddie sat on his bed. People came to the door, but seeing his thinking attitude, slipped back. He heard them mumbling and talking about him and his heart was heavy. Some of the things they said, Nancy had already said more pleasantly.

The thought of not going to England any more was most unwelcome: after all those noisy send-offs! Though he had applied for a Government Scholarship what chance had he of winning one of the three hundred being offered? Thousands of people must have applied and it would be foolish to deceive himself.

He went to the Passport Office with the fragments of his passport. As always the office was crowded and after considerable jostling with housewives wanting to join their husbands in England, a Lebanese who had naturalized as a Nigerian, Freddie found himself seated opposite the Immigration Officer.

The polished brass buttons on the khaki uniform did not put him off, but when he saw the disarming smile, the greasy weapon of men in key positions, his heart sank.

The officer rubbed his hands. 'Bring me Freddie Namme's file!' A police constable clicked his heels and disappeared.

When he came back he was carrying a file marked POLICE DEPARTMENT. The officer thumbed through it, shouted some more and a pile of forms arrived.

'Fill these!' he said.

Freddie took them. 'Is that all?'

'Yes.'

He took the forms home and filled them. He continued to go to the Immigration Office and when he had gone one hundred times he could have drawn an accurate map of the officer's moustache set against the bare walls of the office. Nothing had developed. They were 'looking into' his case. If Freddie had only heard this once, it would have meant something; but now he was beginning to hear it in his dreams, and Jagua was in the centre of those dreams.

On his way out one evening, Freddie again saw one of the three '.been-tos' with whom Jagua had gone away for one night. He had parked the car outside and was asking Mike where 'she' had gone. Freddie hung around. Mike said he did not know when 'she' would return; she had left no word. He pointed at a notebook hanging against the door and invited 'been-to' to use it but he would not consent to scribble his name in Jagua's Visitors' Book. He left, muttering something about coming back later. Freddie guessed that Jagua must have gone to live with some man – probably one of the other two 'been-tos'. She must be very comfortable where she was and might not even be thinking of coming back.

He was torn by wild imaginings. Jagua had grown into some essential element in his make-up. He saw now that he enjoyed being molested by her. He missed her violent fits of temper and impulsive actions. Just as the *Tropicana* had become a drug in her blood, so also she had become his daily dose of anguish, lust, degradation and weakness of will. Under all manner of pretexts he went to her room and stared at the heavy Union lock on the door. He avoided the people who lived in the same compound because he knew they would ask him questions he would not like to answer.

At night he dreamt. His eye had become enormous and it could see through the keyhole and into the room. She lay among the disorderly lingerie, pouring perfume on her breast. Her face was no longer old, but had become a mask – like the idealized female dancing masquerades of the Ibo country. It was not a smiling face or a serious face: just a face – small nose, pointed like a Greek's, thin lips, cheeks so fair as to be non-African. As this huge eye focused Jagua, she turned and gazed back at the keyhole. Apparently she did not see the eye for she rose and walked towards the wardrobe. She stood in half-shadow and her eyes became luminous black, focusing with suspicion on the keyhole. On her lips a smile lingered but the eyes never wavered. He saw her lips move.

'Freddie . . . I seen you . . . Freddie . . .' She scarcely opened her lips but the voice was rising and swelling into an echo that filled the room and hit back at her. 'Freddie, so you cheatin' me? You choosin' anodder woman, because Jagua done old? . . . Jagua done old? . . . Awright, Freddie . . . I goin' to borrow anodder face . . .'

The eye, inexorable, riveted her nakedness in that half shadow, studying every detail. Her body had been caught in a greenish spotlight and she did not care to move away from it. She took out a luminescent brassiere and fixed it over her breasts. But her hand could not reach the clip at the back. She flung it away, threw back her head and laughed. Then she took out a knicker and got into it, raising her legs to the top of the wardrobe and gyrating her hips to force in the knicker. The eye photographed her. Then Freddie felt his whole body melting and flowing upwards into nothing else but the eye, greedy, peering, inquisitive, jealous.

With a sudden effort, he tore himself away and fell against the cement floor. The eye burst and the juice squelched against the door. Freddie sat up in his bed, trembling and wet. The clothes felt damp and gummed to his body. He realized he had been asleep all the time and this was one of his nightmares. He reached under the pillow and produced his torchlight. He shone it on the clock. The time was 2 a.m. Since Jagua left, this new habit of going to bed early had not ensured trouble-free sleep. Could it really be – as Nancy had suggested – that Jagua was resorting to black magic to torture him? Was she a witch with black powers over his soul? Only that morning he had been telling the pupils at the College that there was no such thing as black magic or witchery, only the imagination. Scientific facts, he held, could be demonstrated; but these extrasensory qualities depended too much on vague circumstances and conditions.

He listened to the night sounds. At this time a mysterious hushed stillness lay over Lagos. Only in the distance could he hear the faint note of a saxophone, a melody in the wilderness. The *Tropicana* must be busy now: 2 a.m. – their brightest hour. Would Jagua be there, he wondered? He sighed and lay back in his bed but could not sleep because of the ache in his head, lashing out at his temples. He pressed his fingertips to his brow.

'Freddie . . .' came the low voice. 'Anyone in de room wit' you?' He looked about him in the darkness. 'Answer me, my loving Freddie! . . . Anyone in de room wit' you?' Could it be Jagua, calling out to him from the other side of Devil's Island, bewitching him with all her magic? This woman had become a bug in his veins. He felt the terror running through his bones. He remained still, he wished he could shrivel up and shrink and disappear into nothingness.

'Freddie . . . Anyone in de—'

He became instantly awake and suspicious. He must still be dreaming. He tried his voice. 'No one in de—' but only a croak issued from his lips.

'I beg you; I want to come inside, Freddie. Is Jagua here – your woman.'

He thought it over. 'You come to fight me or to make frien' with me, or to kill me?' He was sure now. His voice was coming back. This was his Jagua. Violent and crazy one moment; calm and repentant the next.

'Open firs', Freddie! I beg you open firs'. I standin' at de door an' is late.'

She may have come to kill me this time, Freddie thought. But what was the sense in being afraid? He found a stool in the dark and placed it against the door. He climbed up and peered down on Jagua. She was alone, standing against the door in a white cocktail dress. A dark mantle was thrown over her shoulders. He felt a sudden twinge of pity for her.

As soon as he let her in, she began to cry. He could never stand her tears and he sat on his bed, lonely and confused. He let her weep for some time, gazing at the rising and falling bosom inside the low-cut blouse, at the eyes, heavy and puffed and red; at the hair, glamorous and, no doubt, specially done up to please him. He saw then that in some way Jagua lived for him. She was bright and full of verve when they loved, but when they quarrelled the light went out.

'You forgive me, Freddie? I sorry for everythin'.'

He yawned. 'But Jagua, you surprise me as you act. You take axe, you wan' chop off my head – like craze woman. Suppose de polis catch you again? Anodder big case.'

'Is love, Freddie.' She dabbed a handkerchief against her eyes. 'I tink about all dis and it pain me.'

Freddie remembered all the trouble he had been taking at the passport office and he became angry. 'Me who hear about you behavin' in de *Tropicana* and in de street I never chop you head off with axe.' In spite of all his need of her, Freddie found himself getting more and more angry now that she was before him.

'You hear story? What kin' story? Tell me – quick!'

'Ah hear dat you use to walka on de road for night time. Den white man will pick you up and you follow him an' sleep. Is not de firs' time ah hear de story, but ah never try chop you head off wit' axe.'

'Freddie, you come again! Make we forget dat one. We awready go into dat matter an' I tell you is a lie. De Lagos people keep on poke nose. So you no wan' to see me back?' She rose. 'I goin' back, den.'

Freddie held her hand. 'Wait, Jagua.'

'No. Ah see dat you still vex wit' me, Freddie.'

'Not so, Jagua. Awright, jus' leave de matter, siddown.'

She sat on the bed, and he sat beside her. His anger was still there and that meant that pride had seized his hands and rendered them heavier than an elephant. He sat awkwardly not looking at her, unable to touch her.

'What you waitin' for, Freddie? You just a proud boy who got spoil by woman.'

She put out the light and folded him in her arms kissing him. 'Freddie, when I get de chance I will visit your hometown. You never one day take me to Bagana, because your fear say Jagwa too old. Your Papa won't 'gree for you to marry me. I want to go and know dat Bagana and see your modder and fadder. You will take me before you go Englan'?'

'If I still goin',' Freddie said. He remembered Nancy telling him that she too would be visiting Bagana. No doubt his parents would be astonished to receive two successive visits from two strikingly beautiful women, one just over nineteen and the other nearly forty-five.

She began to unbutton her dress. 'So you will take me to Bagana?' She could be good, sweet, loving, delicious and satisfying, this mad woman. In spite of himself the tightness of his anger began to slacken. He felt an agreeable warmth creeping up his spine. She put her clothes over the arm of a chair and came and knelt beside him, looking up into his face, seeking a smile in the half-light. She smelt sweet.

'Since I lef' dis place, I never sleep one night.'

'Yes. Because you always go to *Tropicana*.'

'Not so, Freddie! Because I thinkin' about you. I keep dreamin' day an' night.' The expert fingers were feeling him intimately. The low vibrant voice struck chords in his very fibres. He felt her fingers on his cheeks and the warm flesh on his face. He was engulfed. He was sinking into the soft abyss of this erotic woman. He hated himself but her breast was pushing against his face and he reached out and seized the nipple with his lips.

In the morning the tenants saw Jagua emerge from Freddie's room after her long absence. They saw her go up to her room which had remained locked up all the time. No one showed any surprise or asked any questions. There was a law about Jagua and Freddie which was too big for them to understand, and this was it – operating before their eyes.

9

It was one of those nights when the *Tropicana* was poor company, and Jagua was bored. The chairs were empty. The girls sat still as anthills, their eyes trained on a gate that brought in no customers.

For many of them it was going to be a lonely night without a man, and a hungry day without a pound in the purse. It was just past midnight when Jagua decided to walk home.

She walked up the road between the waiting taxis and the lustful eyes that leered after her dancing hips. The noise of passing traffic surprised her at this hour of the night. She was forced to pick her way on the edge of the road among the petty traders selling bread, matches, cigarettes, tea, fried bean cakes. She felt not merely on the edge of the road but on the edge of a world totally different from the *Tropicana*, the real Lagos, noisy and confused, speaking the after-midnight language. She was more preoccupied with the tiny naked lights set on little tables than with the big moon-shaped glares from the cars and lorries. The woman sitting behind the tables flashed her white teeth and beckoned at Jagua. Some of these traders must know her now – as Jagwa. She heard the growling trumpet floating above the noise and hesitated. If she had gone back then, what happened that night would have been avoided. But she walked on because she knew that nothing had changed since she left the *Tropicana*. Nobody had arrived. The trumpet was merely warming the air.

She walked consciously, dangling the bait. The women in the Club had told her that if 'trade' was bad, all she needed to do was walk along this road and the men would stop their cars and start up some conversation. This night would be the third time she had tried and failed. It was the wrong time of the month. Payday was usually on the twenty-sixth. By the twentieth of the month, no Lagos man had any more spending money. This was the time when the men resorted to credit buying and the women trekked across the bridge instead of going by bus. There was no more question of rushing to the big Department Store; instead, everyone sought out the cut-price markets and bought tinned foods from dubious sources. Jagua knew all this, and yet she walked. She passed the roundabout and for some reason, she suddenly remembered Freddie lying in his bed but quickly dismissed the picture from her mind.

A car had stopped. A white face was peering at her and horns were sounding all round. One of the men inside the car began to wave and to shout at Jagua. She walked on. The white man's car had held up the traffic and now the horns were blowing louder and the air became a loudspeaker from the rehearsal of the giants. To make things worse the road was 'one-way' and one part of it had been dug up. The other side had been piled high with huge pipes for the Public Works Department. The white man simply had no choice but to drive straight on till he found a clear space – some hundred yards off – or obstinately hold up the traffic till he had spoken to Jagua. He had swallowed the bait completely. Jagua smiled to herself.

'Going my way?' Jagua heard him yell from the din.

She shook her head. The white man leaned further out of the car, his hair darker than the gleaming black limousine. 'Come with me – to *Tropicana* – come for a drink!'

She could well go and it might represent a victory – something to show off to the other girls, especially on a dry night like this. 'No sah! I jus' comin' from dere. Drive on! You soon meet odder women plenty!' She was tickled.

The car revved up and slowly moved away. Another girl who had been standing in the shadows came out and looked with some surprise at Jagua. She was small and sweet and rather new to Jagua. 'What de white man tell you? Why you don' follow am? He be rich man, you see de car? He for give you plenty money.'

'Lef' me. I tire.'

'Person who findin' money cannot tire in dis Lagos. De month done reach twenty-hungry. You got boy friend who jealous?'

'Boy frien'?' asked Jagua. 'What boy frien' got to do wit' dis one?' She looked at the face of the girl; heart-shaped it was very beautiful. She was entering the trade young. 'Ah never seen you before. You use to come *Tropicana*?'

'Sometime . . . My name be Rosa. I use to see you in de *Tropicana*? Not you be Jagwa Nana?'

'Yes. Rosa, my dear; ah use to be careful about dose men with car. Dem too fool woman.' The wind had begun to stir and she looked at the sky. 'I hope de rain no go fall because I wan' to take foot reach house. De night still young.'

Rosa studied the sky. 'No. Rain no go fall. Jagwa, I sure dat you let dat man go because you be rich woman. If is me—'

As they stood arguing, another car stopped within reach. Both of them saw the blaze of red rear lights. The man at the wheel pointed instantly at Jagua and Jagua walked towards them, feeling strangely elated.

'Rosa, excuse me. Ah goin' to see what dem want.'

She thought at first that she saw two heads but when she approached she was certain it must have been the shadows and the poor light playing tricks.

'Good evenin'.' She leaned into the car.

The man's bow tie was dark and his hair odorous in a manly way. He was a Nigerian of some class, she could see that. The lights of passing cars shone on his dark eyebrows and strongly defined nose. 'I – I always see you standin' here – every night when I'm going home. I work at the airport . . .'

Jagua laughed. 'I waiting for somebody, das why ah standin' there.'

'Every night? Who you be waiting for? Not me, I hope? Well, jump in, le's go.'

She did not answer for a moment. She had seen another car stop in the distance. The other girl – Rosa, was racing towards it.

'Where you live?'

'Ikoyi.' He held the door open. 'Get in, we go there.'

She drew in her breath. 'Ikoyi.' That was the Government Reservation where the white men and the Africans high up in the civil service lived. Ikoyi where the streets were straight and smooth, where they played golf on the open sands: a reservation complete with its own police station, electricity base, motorboat beaches, a romantic place. This man must be set high up on the ladder, because an Englishman she used to know lived there in a flat by the lagoon.

'I got mah own place,' Jagua said. A gentle wind began to stir carrying with it a damp smell. 'If you wan' to see me, you mus' come dere. I never sleep in anodder man house.' In that interval she could hardly understand the reason why she hesitated. But the novelty of the strange man's house was there: perhaps he was some youngster whom she could bewitch and sap, draining the pennies out of his purse. Certainly his new car suggested a possible victim. If he insisted she would go to his flat, but she would not remain there till morning. She might on getting there, discover that he was a married man whose wife had gone away for a holiday. Then Jagua would see his wife's wedding picture on the radiogram. She would wear his wife's dressing gown, bathe in the same bath, be fussed over by husbandly hands. In that brief interval the make-believe would be sweet and when the morning came she would be paid off; discreetly or degradingly depending on the finesse of the man. In the cold streets she would once again revert to what she was, and who cared? The real wives were no better than she was. In her make-believe she could claim these various men as husbands for a time. The wind blew dust against her skirts and into the car. Better to go with this man, poor though he looked (the good-looking Nigerians were always poor, she knew) than to hang about and earn nothing this night. She thought of the countless girls now in the *Tropicana*, showing off, casting aside offers until the rain came as it did now, pelting down, hurrying them off to their empty beds.

The door opened wider and she went inside. The car moved forward. She looked at the young man, but he only smiled and said: 'Get up, Freddie. You owe me ten shillings! I won the bet! I think I told you I saw her?'

Jagua nestled closer to him. 'What you say?'

'Freddie, get up now! You owe me ten shillings!'

The truth dawned on Jagua. She stared about her. From the back seat came Freddie's voice. 'Wait. You'll get your money.' Jagua saw his head rise as if actuated by a spring.

'I told you I knew her beat,' the young man went on. 'But you never believed.'

'You were quite right, oh God, you were! Now I should chop her head off with an axe.'

Cold chilling streams of sweat ran down Jagua's back. She could not look back because her eyes no longer focused. The young man beside her, the instruments in the car, the street lights, all swam in circles. Her head was splitting. Why had Freddie humiliated her so? Freddie, the one man who must never see her in so shameful a light.

They must have talked to him; egged him on till he took to sneaking on her. These Lagos people would never mind their own business. The car stopped, but the circles still swam before her eyes and she did not even know that it was not Ikoyi but the front of where she lived in Lagos. She got down. She saw Freddie get down too and thank the driver. She followed Freddie into the room. He sat on the bed. She was too terrified to sit beside him. He held his head in his hands and massaged his eyes and cheeks the way he always did when anger blinded him.

'Jagua, I sure say you know I don' want you again.'

She sat silent.

'You never tell me true word one day. One day, jus' one day! Only lies, all de time! You say you love me, but you sleepin' with any man you see and you takin' dem money. You cryin' you cannot conceive chil', but you keep spoilin' you blood with rotten nonsense. You say you wan' to be my woman. And you run after any man with car or money! True, I no understand all dis. Me, young man like me! Is no wonder dem say dat you take magic and witch-craft to hold me. Dem say you give me *juju* to chop. Das why I can't see anodder woman but you. Das why you treatin' me like boy who got no sense.' She saw genuine tears in his eyes and she knew that when that happens to a man, the wound has gone deep. But she could not go near him. She had become unclean. For once she actually felt unclean and he was to her a god with the power to pass judgement. 'What you wan' from de worl', Jagua? You jealous, but you no fit to keep one man. You no fit take your eye see money in a man hand. You mus' follow any man who give you money. Whedder he get disease or not. So far as he got money. You mus' go to *Tropicana* every night. You must feel man body in your belly every night. Any day you don' see anodder man private you sick dat day. If dat be de kin' of life you choose, why you wan' me den?'

He talked on and she resigned herself to the lash of his derision and the acid of his condemnation.

She could not get herself to leave Freddie until well into the morning hours and when she tried to lie beside him on the bed, he jumped down and spread a mat on the floor and lay there. 'Don' come near me, Jagwa; you smellin' anodder man smell!'

She was afraid. Never had she known Freddie to refuse her. She got out of the bed and looked at the long-limbed but tense body on the floor. 'Freddie! . . . Freddie, I beg you . . .'

She saw him stiffen. 'Don' come near me.' The words terrified her. She threw herself on him. 'Kill me, make we two die together – now!' At that moment, she meant it. There was nothing she could have wished better than for Freddie to shoot her or stab her or in some violent way shatter the degradation on her head. Even as she thought of it, she received it – in the face.

Freddie had struck her. It was deliciously painful. Freddie ripped open her dress and pushed her against the wall. She yelled for help, opened her mouth wide and screamed – at three in the morning. The piercing note carried farther than the whistle of a railway engine. No one came. Freddie's hands had become claws trying to tear out her windpipe. Other hands had begun pounding on the door. She heard the stampede on the other side. Help had come. She screamed, but it was not a scream that came out. Freddie was crashing her head against the door now. But the door was caving in, and suddenly it burst and there were strangers in the room. She was whimpering and she was gloriously naked. She clung to her rags.

Before they could say anything she had slipped away and climbed the stair to her room. She heard Freddie ordering the strangers out of his room. With her door bolted behind her she listened to the chatter. But after a while it died down and she presumed that everyone had gone to bed. She sat in an armchair, rolling her head from side to side. The bitter side of a woman's life, she thought. Young Freddie – twenty-five – trying to discipline her, a woman of forty-five, simply because they had shared the same bed. She could go now to the Police Station and report and he would be charged with assault. She could even say he was trying to rape her. She rolled her head from side to side, and the tears rolled off her cheeks. But what would be the result? She still loved Freddie. He had the right to be jealous. He had the right to flog her – it was her choice. She must take all it implied, and not only the sweet part.

In the early hours of the morning, just before she dropped off to sleep, she heard a car parking outside. A man came to her door and knocked and later on she could hear his footsteps on the stairs, going out.

When she awoke, she heard not a sound in the whole house. She yawned and rolled out of bed. Yesterday seemed so far away, and her throat was as uncomfortable as a blocked pipe can be. She felt thirsty, but knew she could not drink. She slipped her painted toenails into slippers. She could see her own oily face with the swollen lips and black eyes in the mirror opposite the bed. This mirror which she had placed in that position in the room, gave her an exciting view of her own feet and of the feet of the men as they made love to her. And when she rose she would turn first to the left, and pat her wide buttocks and turn to the right and pat her tummy. She never failed to revel in the beauty of her body. The superb breasts, God's own milk to humanity, the lovely shoulders, and the skin, olive-orange, in the manner of the best Eastern Nigerian women. But on this morning, the stiffness was in her joints and her temper was strained.

A sudden glare of light reminded her that Lagos had been awake for a long time. The men were already at work. Freddie must have gone to school too. Freddie. What had come over him last night? She must find some way of making amends. She would go and cook him a nice meal, and when he returned from school she would dress herself well and tempt him into lying with her. After that, she would beg him to forgive her.

She went downstairs. The air was thick with the smell of diesel oil from the buses; cycle bells were jangling, and the trains were shunting away at the railway yard; in the streets the hawkers were yelling their wares, weaving songs around simple commodities. Freddie's door was open, but this was nothing. He usually left it open when he went to school.

But when she got to the door she found nobody in the room. No furniture, not a sign that the room had ever been tenanted. She looked round for Freddie's servant.

'Sam! . . . Samuel! . . .' And when he did not answer: 'Mike! . . . Michael! . . .' Her servant came and she asked: 'Mike, where's Freddie and Sam?'

'Dem done pack away, Madam.'

'He tell you where he go?'

'No, Mah. When he come back in de mornin' he call one taxi and de taxi pack all his thing and go. You been sleepin' all de time, Ma, so I no worry you because I think say you mus' know. But, Ma, I hear say he gone to meet him brodder.'

Jagua held on to the wall. 'So Freddie done gone and lef' me, like dat? Oh, Lord! . . .'

She kept walking round and round the corners of Freddie's room and crying but the room could tell her nothing.

She tried to trace him in Lagos but failed. In desperation she went to the school where he taught, but the Principal of the National College told her he no longer taught there. He had resigned some time ago. The rumour was that Freddie had begun to teach in some night school in the suburbs of Lagos while preparing for an important examination. She came away feeling that she had been done. Obviously, with all his silence, and his gentlemanliness, Freddie had been planning this move for a long time.

One day she heard his name mentioned. It was in the *Tropicana* and they said his name had appeared among the three hundred names printed in the *Daily Sensation*. He had been awarded a Government Scholarship, and the flying date was put against his name. She felt like one betrayed, the victim of an incalculably mean trick. At that particular moment, if Freddie had confronted her, she would gladly have shot him.

She ordered a double whisky. She had begun to drink furiously again. Her body wanted fiery drinks at this time. She lit a cigarette – one of the chain, endless and enslaving. The burning weed smouldered, the fumes of smoke issued from two nostrils like the twin exhausts of some ancient car. The whisky came on a tray and she heard the waiter call her 'Madam'. She knew the hypocrisy behind it all. He wanted some of her money. She picked up the change which he had carefully arranged on the tray, leaving him the shilling. Immediately she had downed her double whisky, she ordered another. Life was short, she told herself. Lagos was full of men. Even if Freddie fled to England, eventually he must come back home to Nigeria – to Lagos. They must meet face to face. He could not get away from his own spiritual beginnings in this simple manner. Only young men deceived themselves they could. She had lived almost twice as long as Freddie and she knew that the process was not as simple as he imagined.

She could not think of him without bitterness, and the bitterness carried nothing but depression. She must get away from the *Tropicana* atmosphere. The 'beat' would be a good place to go now. She collected her bag and slipped away.

As she approached the roundabout she prayed that a white man should stop his car and hail her. She would not hesitate to enter the very first car that whistled at her. She walked, dancing her hips, flexing her breasts. And whenever she heard an engine sound and saw the approaching beams of light, she deliberately crossed the road, turning her smile into the headlights and crying: 'Leeft!' The exercise liberated something in her. The blue mood lifted. She thought of Freddie at the airport on his way to England. How revealing it would be if she went there – uninvited – and found Nancy Oll in tears, and Mama Nancy, and Freddie's 'good friend' who had planned the trick of catching her on the 'beat'.

She would go; and she would go, dressed to kill. Another car was approaching. She crossed the road, smiling and crying: 'Leeft! . . .' But the car accelerated, and Jagua melted back into the hedgerow.

10

Jagua had been standing at the bus stop for over thirty minutes, and no bus passed her way. She saw a lone man snorting along in a Pontiac and waved. The big red lights glowed in the tail. At the wheel was a man whom she had often seen at the *Tropicana*. She knew he was some kind of Party Agent, but little else.

'You wan' leeft?'

'I goin' to de airport. Ah don' know whedder you kin—'

He held the door open for her. 'I know you're Jagwa. You may not know me, I'm Taiwo, Secretary of OP 2. But they use' to call me Uncle Taiwo.' He roared with laughter and said, 'Jump in!'

'Tenk you, sah.' The seat enveloped her in comfort.

He drove very fast because the night was coming and the airport was some twenty miles off. By the time they got there a belt of blue smoke was creeping down from the mountains. Jagua knew that soon it would smother up the planes and darken the faces of the petrol boys.

Uncle Taiwo parked the Pontiac under the mango trees. There were already over three hundred cars parked in rows, from little two-seaters to the eight-seater limousines used by Party People like Uncle Taiwo.

Jagua was wearing a very tight skirt and when she got out a group of jobless boys whistled. Some shouted, '*Jagwa!* . . .'

She pretended not to notice, though inwardly she felt pleased. She knew there was nothing very *Jagwa* about her bright printed cotton blouse, although her breasts were almost half exposed. She was very conscious of them. She always wore blouses which showed the skin above her breasts and on her arms and shoulders because she knew her best points. Her skirt was split half way up the left thigh, so that when she walked, much of her leg showed. She had taken care to sweep back her hair and knot it at the nape of the neck. This 'hair' cost her 30s. at the Department Store.

Uncle Taiwo locked the car and came after her. She wiggled her hips as befitted a woman walking side by side with the Party Secretary of OP2. That pleased the boys and they yelled: '*Jagwa!* . . .' more loudly than before. Uncle Taiwo said something to them under his breath and waved them off, but Jagua guessed he was flattered. Jagua no longer thought of her ability to tense her hips independently as she walked. High heels and tight skirts tended to emphasise her efforts, but even when she was wearing *Accra* – that is the cloth tied *sarong*-wise – men would feel the woman inside as she walked past.

This occasion, she felt, was not the right one for hooking men. Freddie was leaving for U.K. and the airport was humming and her ears were full of aeroplane sounds and goodbye chatter. She walked towards the passengers with Uncle Taiwo beside her. Names were being announced on the microphone all the time, but none of them seemed to concern Freddie Namme.

Then she saw him, already dressed in an English wool suit. He had become an 'Englander'. At the *Tropicana* they had warned Jagua: 'You takin' big risk by lettin' Freddie go. He goin' to U.K. to forget you. Soon as he reach Englan' he goin' to see all de white gals, and he'll hook dem and come home wit' one. So what you goin' to do? Eh, Jagua? When Freddie go an' return wit' one of dem white women, what you goin' to do? I think you jus' wastin' de money you kin put in trading business, Jag!'

She could not be sure now that Freddie would want to speak to her after their violent quarrel and his flight; but she walked up to him where he stood, coat in hand.

She said to him, 'Freddie, kin I speak wit' you?'

He came away with her to a part of the lounge while Uncle Taiwo and his friends walked towards the freight forwarding shed.

'Freddie, why you eye look so distant from me? Because you goin' now on scholarship?'

'Who tell you dat?'

'I hear say you win scholarship, and—'

'Nonsense!' His eyes flashed. 'Dese Lagos people!'

Freddie told her how he had managed to recover his passport after endless visits to the Immigration, and how his father had sent him a small sum – barely enough to pay his passage and to look after him for a few weeks. His father was in the middle of a Chieftaincy dispute and he was surprised that he had been able to do so much. Freddie said he was not going to England to live like an aristocrat. He was going with a purpose: to suffer and to achieve, to grow into a man.

There was no time to ask him now how he finally managed to obtain his passport, and what would become of all the money she had advanced him. At that particular moment the subject appeared to her out of place. Uncle Taiwo came up then, flamboyant in his velvet fez, jingling the keys of his Pontiac. Freddie smiled at him and he smiled back.

'You got fine weather for flyin',' he said.

'Yes, the weather's fine. Not too hot, not too cool. Is always good to cross the Sahara in the night. No bumpin'.'

'How long you goin' to be?'

' 'Bout' two years,' Freddie said. 'I'm goin' to study law. I suppose Jagua already tol' you. I already done the Intermediate.'

Uncle Taiwo's eyes twinkled. 'An' you leavin' dis beautiful lady behind?' He glanced at Jagua and roared with laughter.

Jagua cut in: 'Uncle Taiwo, he not leavin' me behin'. You and de odders will take care of me. Not so? You approve, Freddie?'

'How do you 'xpect him to approve?' Uncle Taiwo roared with highly infectious laughter. 'If is me, you tink I'll approve. Anyway, Mr Freddie, you got nothin' to fear from me. My three wives will look after me – and your Jagwa!' He held his sides again.

Jagua said, 'Freddie 'll soon return. Him brain open. Is a clever young man who know de books.'

'Ah wish you luck, young man.'

'If de gals allow him,' Jagua added. She remembered Nancy. 'Freddie, where Nancy? Or she already come and gone?'

A ghost voice interrupted before Freddie could answer. 'Passengers for flight 23416B Nigerian Airways . . . Please collect your hand-luggage and proceed to the aircraft . . .'

She glanced at Freddie's face. It still wore the stern look which told her he had not yet forgiven her.

'Freddie, no time to fight now. Forgive me, I beg. Forgive everythin'. You goin' on long journey; is better you go with clean min'. Den God will look after you. I wish you well; you will come back safe and meet we all in dis Lagos.'

His sigh hurt her deep. She saw the wrinkles on the side of his face and the fine gleam of his teeth, like a man who has been struck a wicked blow. She loved Freddie's good looks. When she looked at his face, something turned in her womb and she was hot inside, because she wanted to give him babies. They had tried for eighteen months and failed. He blamed it on her lapses with other men with whom she went but she must go with those men. That was the law of her survival. After all, Freddie was only a teacher in the National

College. His salary was not sufficient to buy her one good cocktail dress. He had no money and he knew it. He was living in one room with his houseboy Sam before he packed away. How could she reserve her body for him alone? In Lagos it was not possible. She had tried to be discreet, but instead of letting her alone, Freddie had allowed the busybodies to lure him to her 'beat'. And he had not been able to stand the shock.

She took his topcoat and held it close to her. His brows were knitted firmly together again as if he did not want to be near her.

'When you reach Englan', Freddie . . . try hard!'

'I goin' to try, Jagua. I not goin' dere to joke. Is a land of tradition and culture and I goin' to see if I kin bring back de Golden Fleece.'

'Pass all de exam quick quick, and come back as lawyer, so we kin enjoy our life. I gettin' old, Freddie.'

He sucked in his breath. 'Lord, you come wit' dat kin' talk. I already tell you, you still Jagwa!'

When Freddie said that, it was something. She longed for him to embrace her. But she knew he was much too reserved for that kind of display. He took his coat away from her and moved off. The lights had been put on now all over the airport and when he broke away he waved at her from beyond the hibiscus fence and walked among the petrol boys with their yellow caps, and the passengers holding their coats, mostly Englishmen.

She saw him climb the stairs into the plane, pausing to look blindly back. Then they removed the stairway and there was a moment of quite unbearable suspense. A man stood before the big plane and pointed one by one at the engines till they all started, to his satisfaction. It was a ceremony Jagua had seen often but every Sunday she came again to see it afresh. The big plane crawled away, swaying as it went.

She watched that plane. She fixed her eyes on the nose as if it would kill her not to look. And all the while the tears were running down her cheeks and into her lips so she tasted them. The plane lumbered to a standstill about one mile away among the palm trees by the yellow mansion. The belt of blue smoke had reached there now and she could not see the plane very clearly. The air seemed to explode when the engines began to summon forth all the power they required to hurl the monster 4000 miles in ten hours. Jagua was terrified for Freddie.

She remembered the disaster at Kano Airport when so many Nigerians and Europeans had died in an exploded aircraft, meeting their end within walking distance of the airport. She never imagined that a man so dear to her would have to travel in a jet. She'd been at the airport once when the plane brought Her Majesty Queen Elizabeth, looking majestic in the sun, and again when a jazzman Wilbur de Paris stepped down in a panama hat, holding a bright trombone. It was true no disaster befell those VIPs but there was no predicting Fate.

Freddie was in one of those windows, perhaps staring and waving at her. But which one? He had become like a prisoner, shut away from all who knew and loved him. He could not wave, and thought it looked stupid, she was waving at him – and crying. Then the plane began to move, heaving itself clumsily at first like some Nightmare Creature from the depths of the jungle, like some mermaid from the River Niger; on – along the tar strip – gathering power, groaning faster and faster till – in one wink – she saw the wheels tucking themselves into the belly of the plane. She sighed. The boys were chattering all about her.

'Goodbye-O! . . . Goodbye! . . .'

'Tomorrow morning, they'll be in London!'

'White man power; nex' to God power.'

'Tomorrow morn', before you wash de sleep from you eye, dem done reach London, shaking from de col' . . .'

Her eyes had not left the sky. The stars were out but the plane seemed to be carrying its own stars. They winked – in colour too – from wingtip and nose and tail, as the plane pointed its nose at Kano, 800 miles away and even hotter but much less humid than Lagos.

'Goodbye, Freddie!' She could only murmur the words. 'Now, I goin' to Bagana to see you people.' She had lost him to the ether. The emptiness was coming to her now, and her spirit was hollow and thin.

Freddie had talked a good deal about his father and mother,

about Bagana his hometown. She wanted to go there and know his people and his place. Her own hometown of Ogabu was not too far away, once she crossed the River Niger. She could also touch Ogabu and see her father and mother whom she left ten years ago.

How would Freddie's father take it, when he learnt that she, Jagua Nana, a woman of forty-five, had fallen in love with his darling boy Freddie Namme? That she had spent her own pocket money freely so that Freddie would obtain a passport, and having obtained it, might then be able to go to England and study. The fact still remained that she had paid for Freddie's dinners and his accommodation long before his father ever thought of contributing the passage money.

She heard the jingle of keys beside her. It was Uncle Taiwo. 'Where you wan' make I drop you, Jagua?'

She did not care where he dropped her. The jobless ones had gathered round the Pontiac, admiring the layout of the instruments. This time she remembered how very low the seats were and took care not to expose her slip beneath the too-tight skirt. Though the jobless ones fixed their eyes tightly between her knees, they saw nothing.

11

Jagua had to admit that at first Freddie's letters came. She did not know then that the loneliness of cold England was at work. But it made her happy and she concluded that Freddie had forgiven her and renewed his love. After the first three months the letters began to trickle in, till she heard no more from him. She had always known Freddie to be studious, so she was not surprised. But during those first few months, Jagua was almost certain that he was thinking of her much of the time. He wrote to her again and again and at last she went to a letter-writer and paid him two and sixpence to write a reply.

This happened on the Marina just beside the bank, near the public lavatories. She sat on a bench and behind her the canoe boys peddled their ebony carvings to the men in the ocean-going liners anchored in the deeper reaches of the lagoon. In her elegant *Accra*-style blouse and *lappa*, Jagua sat on a packing case, crossed her dainty shoes and held a sparkling yellow-green sun umbrella above her head. She had been speaking to the rusty-haired old man for a while when he looked up and beamed through his glasses. He handled her words like a priest at the confessional, each one with a sense of the power to save or perish the soul, to shower with happiness or flood with sorrow. The letter-writer had developed the benign air of forgiveness for youthful intrepidity – a quality which attracted Jagua and made her confide intimate stories to him. At the end of the session, Jagua realised that she had told him nearly everything there was to know about Freddie. At the same time, a sharper definition of her relationship with Freddie emerged.

'Gently, gently, I soon write dat one down.' The old Letter-Writer dipped his pen in the ink-bottle, waved it about in the air, in diminishing circles till the point of the nib made contact with the paper. 'Eheh? . . . Eheh? . . . And den . . . Go on!'

Jagua was short of ideas. 'Read what you got down.'

She could not fully understand the whole of what he read, but she knew when a letter sounded right, and this one did. The beautiful words, she felt, fully conveyed her feelings and she loved the Letter-Writer for his cleverness. Before he read it out to her, he took off his glasses, polished them, and replaced them. He put the sheet of paper a good distance away and read:

'My Darling Freddie,

I remembered the very day you left me for England, I was charmed by your beautiful face which took me to a land of dream at the very night; you know where hearts agree there joy will be, your love attracted me; my heart and soul were aflame, the love in you cannot be abolished by any human creature except God the Almighty. I last night dreamt of your beautiful and your smiling face which seems to me like vision.

Look, dear one, I am specially moved by feelings from heart to heart to love you always dearly and I hope you will have some love for me through your long stay in that cold firmament the United Kingdom.

I will be always loving you and adoring you with all my heart till you return. There's nothing lives longer than love, which sends perfect happiness to the soul, therefore will you summon your beautiful strength and body to me as I am dreaming on my side. God's ways are mysterious, nobody knows Him or His contemplation on the end. Therefore let us live lonely and happily as you know, you are a nobleman and charming among your fellows, don't you see God creates you apart of them? And I am proud of you in all respect, for God knows the way we must treat, and could not hope for a finer example.

With all my heart-soul love and hoping to hear from you again as early as possible.

With true love and affection wishing you happiness till once more I look into your heavenly eyes and hearing your sonorous voice . . .'

Hand on chin, Jagua listened, sighing, nodding.

'Das all I got down.' The old Letter-Writer looked up.

'I got nothing more to say, sah. Tell him Cheerio. May God Bless am wherever he may go. Den I kin sign.'

She posted the letter herself and drifted into a trance about the streets for the writing had taken something out of her. A part of herself had gone into that envelope and was now on its way out to Freddie 4000 miles away. She felt exhausted and exposed to some remorse, some discontent she did not understand. It dogged her footsteps which now led her into the big Department Store. As she entered, noise reared itself and slapped her ears. She saw the girl in the photographic section leaning against an instrument – an enlarger, perhaps – smiling at her. Shop-girls must smile at total strangers, Jagua thought, passing on. She wandered past the Chemists, and was struck by the odd sight of a sunburnt white man, over fifty at least (he must have seen the tin-rush of World War I, a real veteran) parading a gorgeous Nigerian girl proudly along the shopping lanes. The Nigerian girl was so young and buxom with her turgid breasts bursting through the tight-black cotton-lace blouse, and her lips red, her black skin oily and alluring in the fluorescent lighting, that everyone turned to gaze at the strange pair though the hubbub still went on and the cash registers jangled their bells.

'Jagua!'

She was passing by the outfitting department for ladies. They knew her here, for this was where she spent her money. But it was not the shop assistant who had hailed her, but Ma Nancy. She was dressed, Jagua noted, in an expensive off-the-peg dress with pleats. Nancy wore a Swiss blouse that revealed her dazzling smooth shoulders. The *lappa* which she folded around her waist was green with strange fascinating patterns and it came down to her manicured toes. She had thrown a sling bag carelessly over her left shoulder. This girl Nancy was charming and young and Jagua envied her, the way the Department Store lights loved her skin. Jagua wore a fixed smile.

'Mama Nancy! . . . And Nancy too. What you buyin'?'

'I tryin' to buy Nancy some col' clothing!'

Here in the Department Store, Mama Nancy could afford to sink her grievances, because on this occasion she happened to be doing the buying. It was all bluff, but Jagua, out of curiosity, also pretended to have forgotten everything: the *Tropicana* fight, the smelly prison, the magistrate's court.

'Nancy goin' anywhere?'

'U.K.' Ma Nancy spat out the words and looked aggressively round the section. Everyone knew it was something to be going to U.K. 'But not yet, you see Jagua. De whole thin' cost damn too much. We tryin' to save de money . . .'

As she spoke a slow anger began to burn inside Jagua. It glowed and in the redness of the light she saw clearly where her own discontent lay. She was discontented with the Lagos atmosphere. She would welcome a change now. She too must travel.

'Oh yes, Nancy travellin' abroad. You hearin' from Freddie Namme?' Mama Nancy's voice faded to her consciousness.

'Jus' now, I post a letter to Freddie.'

'Das awright,' Ma Nancy said. 'By de way . . . dis two cardigan, which one better pass?'

Jagua could no longer escape. She helped them choose between the pink and the yellow cardigan and later on down the corridor some warm underwear and then told herself it was time to be getting out of that store and away from Nancy, Mama Nancy, the *Tropicana* and Lagos as a whole. This would be the right time to visit Bagana. The more she thought about going there, the more anxious she became. Suddenly a picture of her father flashed across her mind. It was the last Sunday she had spent at Ogabu before she ran away from home. Her father had just come out of church in his ill-fitting black suit, and the red edge of his bible glistened in the sun. Beside him stood her mother in a flowery gown, wide panama hat and thick-heeled shoes she reserved for Sunday wear. They were waiting for her to catch up with them and her brother Fonso in a white-cotton English suit was shouting at her: 'Nana! . . . What you doin', playin' after church; don't you know Papa's waitin' for you?'

Her father's love was a great prize and after ten years of having betrayed it, she knew she would go back to him and still be welcome.

She turned to Ma Nancy. 'Excuse me, but I mus' have to be goin'. I goin' somewhere important.'

'You done well, Jagua.'

Jagua turned her back on them. It was a back at once insolent and flamboyant, with a narrow waistline, wide hips and well-shaped legs. The rhythm she infused into her walk awakened men's staring instincts and she could see the startled looks on the lifting faces. As long as there were men in Lagos who knew what that walk promised, she knew she would always be Ja-gwa.

12

Jagua stood in the middle of her room staring at the floor. Half-open trunk boxes, basketwork packed full with linen, crockery, kitchen utensils, chairs, an unmade bed, all added to her confusion. Mike came in, asking questions which only served to heighten her irritation. How she would ever get some order into the room, what she must extract and what she must leave behind, she found it impossible to decide. If she could have known how long she would be away, packing might have been easier.

She put some of her best clothes on the bed. By evening she was still puzzled but had managed to extract a few other clothes which she felt would impress people in Onitsha, Ogabu and Bagana. She had a five hundred mile journey before her and with all the risk involved she chose to travel by Mammy Wagon because it was much the quickest way.

They did not set off until the following evening. In the early hours of the next morning the Mammy Wagon in which she had been travelling broke away from the trunk road and swung into a forest track. By this time Jagua was the only passenger left in the lorry, and after the four hundred miles from Lagos her hair was matted and her eyebrows caked with dust. She knew that her home town lay some six miles inside this track and the thought of getting home brought her some comfort.

Though she was travelling 'first class' which meant sitting beside the driver, a muscular young Ibo from Onitsha, her bones were aching. On the door of the lorry, the licensing authorities had painted the words, DRIVER AND ONE PERSON ONLY. This 'one person only' was not meant to be a woman, least of all Jagua; but she had – with her own comfort in mind – argued her way to the front seat and was determined to keep it. Once on the road the driver did not mind for it was early dawn and he told Jagua that he wanted to take her home quickly and return to Onitsha in good time to catch the 8 o'clock ferry crossing back from Onitsha to Asaba and Lagos that morning.

The lorry turned a bend and travelled along a lane. She told the driver to slow down as she peered at the sign boards and tried to decipher the lettering. Much of the forest, she noticed, had been cleared of undergrowth and there was a new space of many acres where the builders were beginning to work. The palm trees still towered skywards. As they drove ahead the tree tops cut off the sun. Jagua was the first to see the tree trunk which bore the sign: DAVID OBI, Pastor.

'We done reach!' Her cry was jubilant. Before the lorry came to a stop she jumped down.

The smell of wet humus and damp undergrowth brought back memories of her girlhood days when she ran errands along this same lane for her mother. The hot tears filled her eyes and blurred the forest. She saw her father's house, roofed with zinc, standing at the end of the courtyard. The waterhole in front was new to her, but not the carpenter's bench standing under the iroko tree. Ten years! And this tree where she had played see-saw with the children was still standing there.

A woman came along the road and met Jagua as she was coming towards the house. She said, 'Welcome, our daughter,' and wiped her hands on a big cocoyam leaf. She stared at Jagua without recognizing her until she said, 'I am the daughter of the Pastor,' and then a loud jubilant cry went up. The cry was taken up and soon all over Ogabu it was known that the daughter of the Pastor had come from Lagos. Little boys, black and naked, wheeling their hoops and carrying their smaller brothers and sisters on their hips, ran away from Jagua because she looked strange in those down-to-earth surroundings.

In Ogabu the people tilled the soil and drank river water and ate yams and went to church but came home to worship their own family oracles. They believed that in a village where every man has his own yam plots, there is much happiness in the hearts of the men and the women and children; but where it is only one man who has the yam plots there is nothing but anger and envy; and strife breaks out with little provocation. Jagua knew that the men thought only about the land and its products and the women helped them make the land more fruitful. So that her city ways became immediately incongruous. The film of make-up on her skin acquired an ashen pallor. The women fixed their eyes on the painted eyebrows and one child called out in Ibo, 'Mama! Her lips are running blood! . . .' Jagua heard another woman say, 'She walks as if her bottom will drop off. I cannot understand what the girl has become.'

They all followed her through a cluster of red mud houses. An old man sitting by the fire in one of the mud rooms looked up and called, 'Bingo!' to a skinny dog which immediately stopped whinnying at Jagua and came and lay at the old man's feet. This old man was the watchman and he told Jagua that David Obi and his family had gone away, packed most of their things and gone visiting to the districts round Onitsha, some fifty miles away. He could not tell

Jagua her father's itinerary, but if Jagua went to Onitsha, to the mission, she might find out from the Bishop.

Jagua asked him about her father's health. News had reached her in Lagos that he was ill, had he recovered? The old man told Jagua: 'Your father is not a young man any more. If he can get someone to stay with him and look after him, he will feel better. Your mother is sickly too. Them both, them need young people about them.'

'You hear anythin' about my brother, Fonso?'

'He's trading in Onitsha. You fin' him in de market, where dem sellin' cycle parts; and his wife, too.'

So Fonso had settled down with that girl, after all the protest from their father. Jagua vowed that if she found the time she would visit Fonso in Onitsha. In the meantime she decided to spend the rest of that day in Ogabu. Tomorrow she would resume the journey, but instead of going back to Onitsha to ask after Brother Fonso and her parents, she would continue forward to Bagana, Freddie's hometown.

The air in Ogabu delighted her and she took deep whiffs of it holding her hips and raising her nostrils to the palm trees. It had the mixed scent of palm fronds, wild flowers and humus. The old man showed her into his room. Here were no spring mattresses, terrazzo-tiled floors and decorated walls. Jagua had to stoop to enter because the roofing of the house swept down so low. Inside, a shaft of light illuminated a spot in the gloom.

The old man showed his gums. 'Our daughter, if you wan' sleep, put a mat dere. We soon fin' you sometin' to eat.' Already the boys had arrived with fat bananas and a basket of oranges. One of them held out a small keg of wine which the old man took from him and tasted.

'Good wine,' he mumbled, and handed the keg to Jagua.

Jagua shook her head. Her bones were heavy within her, and her head soggy. She lay down on the mat. 'I travel long way,' she said. 'Am tired. Perhaps I better sleep small.'

When she woke it was early afternoon with the sun throwing shadows on the banana leaves and the fowls no longer scratching the humus but lying in the shade. The boys lay, swollen-bellied in the shade, faces turned away from the glare, snoozing and snoring. They seemed content with the little that life offered them. They read their books to the rhythm of a swinging cane wielded by a school 'Miss' very much like the one who came home here to Ogabu to be with her widowed mother every Friday evening. Jagua did not want to think too hard now or to question things. Ogabu was restful enough for her.

She asked for a sponge and a calabash of soap and took out a towel from her portmanteau. On her bare feet she padded down to the stream. The sand was hot, but it should not be, if her skin had grown the protective cuticle so prevalent in these parts. How Ogabu had changed. She now discovered that the wide area which had been cleared beyond the church was being planned for building a college. She learnt that Government had not yet approved the funds necessary for the project, but the people of Ogabu had started off, optimistically, on their own. When she got to the stream the women washing clothes looked at her with curious eyes. Some of them were washing cassava for foofoo, others had children on their backs and were beating the linen against stones.

She went up the stream where the water was limpid clean and waded in. It was ice-cold and her skin contracted in thousands of gooseflesh pimples. She knew well the art of bathing in the river in the public gaze. She began by sponging her face and neck, her breasts, belly and back. When she raised her arm, the men on the other side of the bridge looked at her armpits. She was glad she had shaved off the hair, though she knew the men here did not like bald armpits. Without removing the girdle from her waist she sponged her hips, down to her thighs and knees, looking round the stream with semi-aggressive eyes, quelling all seekers. But this was a part of the world where Nature prevailed and nudism was no stranger; human bodies were not concealed with the art of non-concealment.

When she felt clean she sat on the riverbed and ran her hands over her body massaging it well until it was no longer slippery. Then she walked to the bank where her clothes were and putting a cloth over her shoulders took off the girdle and went back to the stream to wash it. She was singing gently now and enjoying the very rare luxury of being free. This was what the city woman meant when she told her friends, 'I am going home.' No men ran after her in Ogabu, none of them imbued her with unnecessary importance. Here she was known, but known as someone who lived with them and grew up with them. She was not known as a glamourite, someone to be hungered after for sheer diversion.

Things were now in their right proportion. She was glad and she washed the cloth and sang and then she went to the bank and began combing her hair. In the evening the girls danced and sang in the clearing and told folk tales. The moon which she glimpsed between the trees, was big and lazy. How many years now, since she had had the time to look up at night and see the moon? In Lagos the street lights were so bright that no one ever really saw the moon. She surrendered herself to the idleness and voluptuous feeling of laze. The hard earth bruised her body with all the fervour of an ardent lover. She was too lazy to care and too deeply asleep to feel anything.

Next morning the bicycle-taxi came. While she ate boiled yam dipped in oil, her suitcase and other paraphernalia were tied on to one bicycle which departed for the main road. As soon as she had completed her breakfast and bade her host goodbye, she climbed into the seat at the back of the second bicycle and the rider set off, wheeling through the compound. The forest road was six miles long and as he pedalled forward they met and overtook other bicycle-taxis coming down the road. Little boys with shiny bellies ran after them for a while, raising dust. The road was populated all the way with pigs, fowls and sheep. This was indeed the land of the bicycle-taxi where the people did not in the least depend on four wheels for their transport.

On the main road, they did not have long to wait. It was market day and the market was situated at the junction where the forest road met the tarmac. The bicycle-taxi wheeled straight into the market and before Jagua had dismounted they were mobbed by lorry drivers and motor-park touts.

'Port Harcourt! . . . P.H.! . . . You dey go P.H.? Enter mah own. I soon go quick, quick. Dis way for P.H.! . . .'

She looked up at the lorry and saw the emblem: a huge eagle labelled GOD'S CASE NO APPEAL. In fact the lorry was packed full and looking as though ready to depart that minute. Jagua felt herself lucky. She would not lose any time, she thought.

'P.H.! . . . Dis way for P.H.! . . .'

'Is not P.H. am goin',' Jagua said. She tore her arm from the vicious grip of a tout. 'I goin' to Bagana.'

They laughed. 'Den you mus' reach P.H. firs', Madam. From P.H., you join canoe in de wharf. Canoe will take you reach Bagana in four hour.' The speaker gripped her hand once again. 'Follow me.'

'All right! How much you charge to P.H.?'

'Only three an' six!'

A new face was thrust between them, dark, bearded. 'Enter mah own. My own cheap pass.'

More faces appeared. More arms gripped her, pulled her this way and that. It was a nightmare of confusion, indecision, treachery and robbery. She yelled.

She broke away from them all and made straight for a brightly painted lorry with the sign TRUST NO MAN. It was now a choice between TRUST NO MAN and GOD'S CASE NO APPEAL. But from what Jagua could see GOD'S CASE seemed a trifle more ready to set off than TRUST. She soon discovered her folly. The men and women seated on the benches in GOD'S CASE had been hired to deceive. They were not travellers but had been put there to fill the benches and to convey an impression of readiness to unwary travellers. TRUST NO MAN. She should have heeded the sign. One of the men seated in GOD'S CASE got up to make room for her and she never saw him again. The other men and women were no less ready to get down, every time the touts hooked a new passenger and led him into the lorry. She sat there for hours watching one benchwarmer after the other vanish into the market. She had already paid her fare and her money was well beyond her reach now. She shouted angry epithets at them. This could never be GOD'S CASE but in spite of it, she knew there was NO APPEAL.

*

At Port Harcourt Jagua mingled with the newsvendors, canoemen, merchants, timber workers and travellers who floated around the wharf. A canoe labelled SWEET PEACE was filling up with women carrying yams, vegetables, oranges in big baskets, for it was said that Bagana was a village of fisher folk living on a tiny island. There was very little farmland, and unlike in Ogabu, their food must be purchased in the city of Port Harcourt.

SWEET PEACE did not depart for another hour and again Jagua knew the frustration of waiting. When the engine started rattling and they floated down the creeks, Jagua tried to visualize what Freddie's home would be like. The long stilt roots of the mangroves, the mud-skippers sheltering in the squelch, told her nothing. Women paddling canoes thinner than paper smoked pipes and hummed strange tunes. Jagua's canoe crossed many such women who had the same ease on the water as birds had in the air. They were said to know the mysteries of this Niger Delta. The birds and crocodiles never attacked them for they were part of the habitat.

Bagana came in sight after two hours steady drumming of the outboard diesel engines. What stood out clearly above the skyline was a church steeple and it remained sharp and clear for one hour. When it disappeared they were practically at Bagana. The covered tin houses which she had noted fringing the island she was told were defæcating houses, and this was why Bagana smelt so sweet and clean. She found she could have walked from one end to the other in twenty minutes. It was quite true that she would not meet any motor cars, only bicycles. There wasn't the space, and the vehicles would only clutter up the beautiful island.

It was impossible for her arrival to remain hidden. There were boys and girls who trooped down to the beachside every time a canoe landed, having sighted it a good hour ago among the creek waters. One such group led by a tall boy in shirt sleeves and bright wrapper, seized Jagua's suitcases.

'De sister done come! De sister done come!' He was shouting at the top of his voice and soon other Baganans arrived.

Jagua, embarrassed, saw them trooping down towards the beach. Among them she picked out a woman in city-type dress, a frock with a broad belt in the middle. She could not believe her eyes.

'Mama Nancy, you here?' She let the anger lash out in her voice. 'Not you I meet in de store buyin' cardigan for Nancy? And what you tell me in Lagos? Dat Nancy goin' abroad, not so? So you deceivin' me?'

Mama Nancy smiled. 'Welcome, Jagua. Oh yes, you meet me in de store and I tell you Nancy goin' abroad. But I forget to tell you we comin' to Bagana firs'.' Her smile was triumphant as though there was something glorious in her forgetfulness.

13

Jagua could not help admiring the girl standing beside Mama Nancy. She looked smart in her tight yellow T-singlet and green-flowered *lappa*. Her breasts jerked restlessly under the singlet. It could be the sun, but Jagua thought that the girl's skin seemed to have become several shades fairer. Mama Nancy noticed the look in Jagua's eyes.

'Nancy, you won' say welcome to Auntie Jagua?'

Nancy smiled at Jagua. 'Welcome, Ma.' For all her sweetness Jagua felt a deep sense of betrayal.

She had never loved these two: plotters, whom she had already fought and knew she must fight again. But she tried to smile back. 'Nancy so you come to Bagana too? You come see Freddie home-town. I tink you tell me say you goin' to U.K.? How you manage reach Bagana?'

'Yes, I still goin' to U.K. But my Mama, she say is a good thing if I see Bagana firs'.'

'Oho!' Jagua felt terribly late about something. 'Is your Ma Nancy idea, then. Not your own?'

Jagua walked along the sunlit streets of Bagana in the clean air, tramping on the gritty periwinkle shells which paved the ground. She noticed that many of the buildings in Freddie's hometown were old and decaying. They had a peculiar decorative style that did not look Nigerian. She pointed at one of the buildings, typical of so many, raised on stilts.

'Dey call dem Deckin',' said Mama Nancy. She spoke with authority and Jagua was irritated.

'How long you bin here, Ma Nancy?'

'Today make four day,' Mama Nancy said.

'You only been here four day. How you manage know all dis?'

'Because David Namme, Freddie's papa, he tell we everythin' before he travel. You jus' too late to meet him. He gone to Port Harcourt. But you will meet Uncle Namme, de brodder. You just miss Freddie his papa. He lef' here yesterday for Port Harcourt, he gone to attend Council meetin' and dem will be dere for about fort-night. But Freddie's Uncle, you will like him.'

Jagua shut her ears to the historical stream with which Mama Nancy was now flooding her. At every turning Mama Nancy had something new to show her. In the olden days, she said, sometime in the 19th century, Bagana was a great trading base. It used to be the centre of the oil rivers and palm oil was the chief commodity which brought British Merchantmen, German Traders, French Colonialists to Bagana. They traded gin with the ruling houses of which the Namme household was the most famous. The Portu-guese came too, and it was they who left the 'Deckin' '-type house. These houses, Mama Nancy said, were brought – every plank of them – direct from Spain. As a result of all this presence of Europe-ans all seeking the same things, there had always been fighting in Bagana, between the white men and other white men, between the ruling houses, and also between Baganans and other tribes. Mama Nancy pointed out the cannon rusting on practically every street corner they passed.

'So you see, Freddie come from royal family, though he never one day say so.' She paused for breath.

Nancy said, 'Mama, we nearin' de palace now. I think tha's Uncle Namme standing at de entrance.'

Jagua saw a tall man wearing a silk top hat in the Victorian man-ner. His hands were folded across his chest and he was smiling. When Jagua began ascending the steps he stretched out his hand.

'Ah, welcome! . . . My name is Namme, and Freddie calls me Uncle Namme and so I am. Welcome. It's a pity, David – Freddie's father – is gone to the Council Meeting at Port Harcourt. Freddie's mother went with him. You know what those meetings are like . . . Sometimes they last three weeks! And accomplish nothing.'

He took Jagua's hand graciously. She liked him instantly. She began to see in him signs of a more mature, more distinguished Freddie. How different it would have been if she could embrace Freddie here – this night – in his own hometown; by day she would like to link hands with him and be shown round by him as a kind of special privilege.

'Me own name be Jagua.'

'Jagua?' He squeezed her hand warmly. 'Freddie wrote me. He said how much you helped him in Lagos with passport and other things. God will bless you.'

Jagua was delighted. 'I come from Lagos to know de home of Freddie Namme. He talk so much about Bagana. Now I seen de place I like to live here – with Freddie.'

'Oh yes,' said Freddie's uncle. 'Bagana is a fine place. Everyone who visits it says so.' He chose his words carefully, giving them their full value. 'Even now – at this very moment – we have an Englishman from Cambridge. He's studying our customs, so as to write a book about Bagana. He's in a little room by the water.' He pointed over the housetops.

Jagua noted how Nancy moved about in the Namme household. Nancy appeared so confident, Jagua almost concluded she had become one with the Nammes. And so she must have, they appeared so kind. It was discouraging indeed.

Uncle Namme ordered a girl into the room with Jagua's suitcase. He waved at a chair. 'Sit down. I'll bring you some of Our Home Made Stuff. That's O.H.M.S. gin, which we distil in the creeks. The Government calls it illicit, but Governments have no imagination. You wait! When we start making our own gin, they'll see! How long shall we depend on imported stuff? For five shillings I can get a bottle of O.H.M.S. You know what that costs in the shops? Thirty-five shillings. And it's the same thing. The only trouble is, and I'll tell you this in confidence . . . our distillers are too impatient. They don't give the stuff a chance to mature. Gin must ripen . . . Too much hurry makes it harsh, like acid. A man distils out a bottle of spirit and he expects to drink it the same day. Pure fire! No wonder it kills. All O.H.M.S. in this house comes from a cellar. At least it's five years old.' He clapped his hands and a decanter was brought, a decanter in the most royal tradition. Indeed everything about this place struck Jagua with its quiet dignity. The sitting room, she noticed, was adorned with three portraits one of which she immediately identified as Uncle Namme. Though the print was old and faded, the high collar, bow tie, top hat and gold chain added a dash of sportingness to an Uncle Namme not unlike Freddie at his best.

Jagua wanted to know about the other two gentlemen.

'The one in the centre – that's David Namme. Freddie's father. He's in Port Harcourt as I told you, at the Council Meeting. The other man –' he paused for a moment and Jagua saw his face flush. 'Well, there's a story about him. He's one of us. He's got Namme blood, I mean. But we disagreed and he went to Krinameh to live – that's the island on the other side of the creeks.' Uncle Namme pointed through the window. 'Chief Ofubara is his name.'

Jagua looked closely at the picture. Chief Ofubara's brow had an obstinate set and his manner was that of a dandy. His gloved hands rested on a gold-headed cane. Jagua liked him. 'Why he lef' Bagana to go an' live for Krinameh?'

'It's a long story.' Uncle Namme sipped his O.H.M.S. 'It's all about who should rule in Bagana. You know – Chieftaincy dispute. By tradition, Bagana is ruled by the *Yaniba* of Bagana. Now when the reigning *Yaniba* died thirty years ago, Freddie's father was to succeed him. But Chief Ofubara strongly disputed his right to the throne. He took the matter to court. For five years the case dragged on. During this time I was appointed to act as Regent in the absence of a *Yaniba*. Later on, Chief Ofubara withdrew from the case. I believe he found it too costly. He and his supporters packed their canoes with their belongings and paddled over to the island of Krinameh. They planted their fish-traps in the swamps and cut down the trees in the fields. They tilled the ground and today they have their own village and Chief Ofubara reigns over them.

'I still have great respect for Chief Ofubara; after all, he's a cousin of ours. But we have no dealings here in Bagana, with the people of Krinameh. They are enemies. When they catch our people, they kill them and put the body in a canoe for us to see. And we also, we retaliate when we get the chance.' He laughed harshly. 'It happens to this day, as I stand here. We are always very careful when we go to the stream to draw water or to bathe. That's where they get us, you see. We never cross the line into the Krinameh creek-side. Some have tried it, and the crocodiles ate them and their spirits went to the promised land. That was better than being captured by Krinameh men. They will take you to Chief Ofubara and there you will be tortured. All men from Bagana who come into his hands are tortured, unless they promise to become his supporters and to live there. I tell you all this, Jagua, because it is good that you should know. Not that you will go swimming there, but if you do – know where is safe for you.'

Jagua poured herself some more O.H.M.S. She sipped it allowing the slow fire to glow in her chest. 'But how ah will know which part of de water belong to Krinameh?'

'That's easy. A guide will show you.'

'Tell me one thin', Uncle Namme! How de Government allow Chief Ofubara to do all dis without checkin' him?'

Uncle Namme smiled. 'What can the Government do? Our islands are so small and far away from Headquarters. They can't spare the police force required. We Baganans always have been peace-loving. Of course, sometimes the police come down. They make some arrests. There is quiet for a while. But it soon flares up again. It never ends, this hatred. Any small thing can start it. You see, we in Bagana still hold that Namme was the original founder of the Bagana nation, no matter where they may be scattered. Chief Ofubara claims, however, that there is no Royal House of Namme, but a Royal House of Ofubara . . . But the fact is that we have evidence that Namme did found Bagana. It is commemorated in the bronze carvings. Our Namme was a brave fighter who learnt how to use cannon which the Portuguese presented to him.'

Jagua said, 'Dis be big palaver! So because of dis, de two cousins lavish all dem money in de court.'

'Oh yes . . . But don't you get depressed over the matter. It is always with us; I only mention it to a stranger like you. It has ceased to worry us in Bagana. When David Namme goes to P.H. for the Council Meetings, he consults lawyers, you see. Because once his status has been recognized as *Yaniba* of Bagana by the Government, Bagana will be a happier place. At the moment we are without a ruler of our people; I mean a ruler officially recognized. Don't you see how they build houses, haphazardly? How can anyone settle here, with all the trouble? So while you're my guest, for your own sake, Jagua, keep on this side of Bagana. Have no dealings with Chief Ofubara, or any Krinameh man. I have already told Nancy and Ma Nancy. Now, I've done my duty.' He rose. 'I'm sure you want to go and wash and change. Then I shall give you a guide who will take you round Bagana – unless you prefer to rest.'

The maid appeared and took Jagua to an outhouse, where a room had been swept and polished for her. The linen on the bed smelt clean and sweet. She began to take off her blouse. 'Freddie come sleep wit' me on dis bed,' she whispered. 'Come we sleep togedder in you own fadder house.'

Next evening Jagua, Uncle Namme and Ma Nancy made for the courtyard where the drummers had already assembled for a performance. The guest-of-honour seats had been laid out: locally woven from the coconut, facing the half-moon of dancers. Uncle Namme went over and stood near one of the three men with torsos hewn out of tree trunks. Jagua counted nine drums in all. The King drum stood high above one drummer. The second drummer held the medium-size drum between his knees and flourished the two hooked sticks that created the rhythms. The third man was a wonder. He alone sat facing the remaining seven drums of varying size, presiding over them with the tense air of an expert.

As Uncle Namme appeared the drummer with the seven drums welcomed him with an intricate patter. The King drum nodded, the medium-size punctuated. Jagua's blood glowed. Uncle Namme raised his hand. He turned to his visitors. 'This is what the war-drum said: it said, when I talk like that all the villagers assemble together and I tell them why I summoned them.'

Uncle Namme was a tall man but the nine-foot drum dwarfed him. He was stroking it as he spoke. 'You see, our fathers came here to settle long ago. They settled here, and founded the island of Bagana. The Namme family is the ruling house. Never mind what Chief Ofubara may be saying. He can remain there in Krinameh. But the Namme family is the ruling house in Bagana.'

The drumming resumed. Jagua felt the urge to take off all her clothes and shake to the rhythm. She sat near Uncle Namme who offered her a bottle of O.H.M.S. Jagua filled her glass and watched the women pouring into the compound from the palace gate. Mama Nancy was sitting on Jagua's left, but neither of them spoke to the other. Nancy was nowhere to be seen. So much noise was being made that to speak to Uncle Namme, Jagua had to shout. She saw the dancing group at the far end, coming to the centre of the stage. When they performed, their movements were acrobatic, rhythmic, demanding muscular contortions fit for real athletes. Watching them in their yellows and reds, the men in shirt sleeves and georgette *lappas*, Jagua thought of the girlhood days in Ogabu when she used to dance in the moonlight; she and a dozen other girls with virgin breasts.

Jagua gripped the arm of her chair. There was a girl in the troupe, and she had virgin breasts. She wore a garland round her neck and flowers in her hair.

'Who's de gal?' Jagua asked.

'Is me daughter, Nancy,' Ma Nancy informed her, though the question was not addressed to her. 'Since we come here she been rehearsin' with de dancers.'

Envy swelled in Jagua's heart. Her eyes were so wide open with surprise that she saw two Nancys. The two of them, out of focus, were leading the dancers, performing with an elasticity which drew cheers. Beside her, Jagua heard Uncle Namme cheering, saw him waving his glass. The double pictures became one. She sighed.

'I kin dance better dan dat.' Jagua said the words calmly.

'Oh, your daughter Nancy can dance wonderfully,' said Uncle

Namme smiling across at Mama Nancy. 'Jus' like a Bagana girl. The more I look at her, the more I see why Freddie fell for her.' He laughed loudly, then rose and went into the ring where the dancers were.

Jagua saw him take something out of his pocket and plant it on the brow of Nancy. It was some coin – a shilling perhaps. But to a dancer this was the highest honour she could win. The *Yaniba* Regent himself, gracing her with a trophy. As Uncle Namme came away, the cheering that greeted him sent the onlookers frantic. Only Jagua did not cheer. She realised that Nancy had made a great conquest of the Bagana people. Already they must be thinking of her as one of them.

Jagua turned to Uncle Namme. 'Excuse me. I just goin' to de house.' She was not sure what she wanted to do in her room, but the air here had become suddenly unbearable. She saw Ma Nancy watching her with a sneer on her face and this sneer infuriated her.

'Sit down, my dear; the programme is only just beginning. We're here till midnight!'

'I know. I comin' jus' now.'

Uncle Namme stared at her. 'You're not going to change and join the dancers? Jolly good, if you do! The more the merrier.'

The mere fact that he had guessed her thoughts took away the element of surprise. 'No, I only goin' to easy myself.'

It occurred to her then that just as Nancy had won over the Baga-nans by exercising her youthfulness, so she too must endear them to herself by showing her experience of life. She knew that as an older woman she must aim at something infinitely larger than excelling at Bagana dancing. But try as hard as she would no ideas came.

Nancy's group had cleared off the stage, and now another group came in, the masqueraders. Jagua sat down and watched.

Jagua got up early and went down to the stream to bathe. She had spent a sleepless night, unlike her Baganan hosts who had not yet turned over once. To her surprise Nancy was already there before her and undressed. Jagua looked round the creek, silent and completely deserted. On the other side beyond the rocks Krinameh rested, a village in sleep except for the few fishermen perched on their canoes, slithering from one fish-trap to the other in search of a catch. She watched Nancy Oll on the water's edge, coldly and without the slightest hint of admiration: the satin-smooth skin and elastic flesh, firm and young. Nancy was fuller in the hips than her clothes suggested. She was no innocent.

Jagua tiptoed to the water's edge. She saw Nancy wade into the water, then stoop and feel the coldness. The water was not more than three feet deep at this end, but beyond it the treacherous rocks of Krinameh lurked. She kept her voice low but threw out the words.

'Nancy what you doin' on de waterside dis fine mornin' when de birds never wake?'

Nancy turned and faced her. The morning light, foggy and vague, shrouded her in swirling mists. 'What you think am doin', Auntie Jagua? You think I come 'ere to make juju sacrifice, like some people use to do?'

'Who use to make juju sacrifice, Nancy? You modder?'

'Ah don' call anyone by name. But some woman when she love some man, and de man don' love her, she kin come to de waterside in de mornin' an' kill chicken, so de man kin love her.'

'You got anyone in min', Nancy? I comin' to talk with you. I wan' to hear what you got to say about dis interestin' palaver. Sometime you kin explain what you done about Freddie Namme. Or sometime your modder got some idea?'

'Don' call me modder, Jagwa. You kin curse me as you like, but don' call me modder 'cause she better'n you in every way.'

'She better'n me?' Jagua waded into the water after Nancy. 'Wait me, dear. I comin' to talk with you, so you kin tell me how Ma Nancy better than Jagwa Nana.'

'You jealous of young gal like me. Me modder keep to man of her own age. She don' run after small boy whom she kin born for herself. You only followin' Freddie because you think he kin give you some young blood. But when person old, de remedy is differen'. You mus' act old, so people kin respect you. My modder got respect, you got none. You wan to dance young like I do. You take corset an' pull up you breas' so, he kin stan', so you kin deceive person who don' know. But all dese thin' come from Nature as blessin', and person no get power to make dem. Ah better tell you now, you wastin' your time about Freddie. He already choose me. Freddie's goin' to pay you back all de money you spen' on him. I goin to slave with him too till we pay all de money!'

It was not so much what she said, as the smile which angered Jagua. The cheek in Nancy's manner penetrated all Jagua's self-control. Jagua began quickly to take off her clothes. Nancy's taunts enraged her, drove her into a fit of wildness. 'You goin' to learn a lesson in de water today, Nancy!' She was taking off her clothes as she spoke.

'Come now!' Nancy waved at Jagua. 'Come here an' I will tell you what I say. I will show you how to move in de water!' And with that she dived into the water.

Jagua was naked now. She dived into the water after Nancy. Nancy swam faster than a crocodile and Jagua pursued her with anger welling within her. Occasionally Nancy's head surfaced, only to vanish again and when it appeared it was some fifty yards away. They were approaching the rocks now, in the direction of Krinameh, and although Jagua knew this to be the area which Uncle Namme had spoken about she dared not turn back but must catch Nancy and show her she was not all that old.

She paused for breath, steadying herself by lashing slowly out with her legs. Nancy had disappeared again. When her head reappeared, she knew that the girl had entered the Krinameh half of the creeks. Like a conjuring trick a young man appeared on the rocks. Jagua had not seen him there a second ago. He raised his arm and flung something at Nancy. Then he dived after her. Nancy saw him too, and tried to swim towards Bagana. In that fraction of a second other young men—at least ten of them—dived from various parts of the rock. Jagua saw the intentness in their eyes. She knew they must be killers. The water was full of young men who had circled the helpless Nancy, some of them swimming with jaws split open like crocodiles about to strike.

Jagua turned quickly and swam for the Bagana shore. On the water's edge she felt a sudden cramp and a wave of paralysis shot through her body. She gritted her teeth and with a last effort gained the shore. Her clothes were scattered on the beach some fifty yards away. There was more light on the beach now, and as she walked towards her clothes she saw a woman standing completely still, regarding her with an accusing eye. It was Ma Nancy. She must have seen everything. Jagua hated her.

'You ol' witch woman, Jagua. What you done with Nancy? What you done with my daughter?' She gripped Jagua by the wrist, but Jagua broke free and raced for her clothes with Ma Nancy in pursuit.

Ma Nancy was yelling like a woman gone mad. 'Jagua done drown my daughter! . . . Jagua done kill Nancy Oll. You done kill am!'

She began to run towards the palace. Boys and girls on their way to the wells crowded the path and stared after her. 'De ol' witch done kill my daughter! . . . Lord 'ave mercy! I come for Bagana to lose me daughter. Jagua done kill Nancy! . . . Give me my Nancy, de only daughter I got! . . .'

The anger had gone from Jagua; in its place grew fear. If indeed Nancy was killed by the Krinameh people and her body floated down in a canoe, the blame would be hers. But she had not meant to drown Nancy, or to kill her, only to teach her a lesson. Her fingers were unsteady. She managed to fix on her clothes, and then she began running back to the palace. Never had it taken her so long to get there.

14

Jagua saw Mama Nancy waiting in the lounge. Presently Uncle Namme, eyes reddened with sleep and swollen by O.H.M.S., came out. He pointed at Jagua.

'What have you done? Didn't I warn you? You went and pushed Nancy into the river? You drove her into the hands of the Krinameh people . . . Lord!' He held his head in his hands.

Ma Nancy shouted. 'De ol' witch woman mus' be hang. Bloody harlot!'

'Uncle Namme, ah never dream of dat. We only quarrellin' an' I follow de gal to teach am sense. And den—'

'Oh, dear me!' Uncle Namme paced up and down. His sleeping clothes were rumpled and his eyes were shining large. 'They will torture her. They will kill her. Is too late now. And she's my guest: such a good dancer! . . .' He saw a man passing in front of the palace. 'I say there! Go at once! Beat the war drums!'

The man looked startled. 'This morning, Your Highness? Wha's de matter? We going to fight anybody?'

'You heard me! . . . I said go and beat the war drums! And don't stand there arguing!'

The cry was instantly taken up. 'Beat the war drums! . . . Beat the war drums! . . .' In the courtyard there was a fever of movement. Men and women were rushing about in all directions, while the goats bleated and dropped faeces as they vanished into safe nooks. The war drummers came, the same three men whom Jagua had seen the evening before. They beat, but this time, the sound of the drum was hollow and carried a grim loneliness.

All over Bagana men were yelling and diving into their houses only to emerge flourishing cutlasses and dane guns. They were answering a call to war. They came to the palace, bare torsoed, in shorts. They came ready to fight. Uncle Namme stood at the door of the palace. He spoke harshly to them, pointing at the tallest of them, who now came forward. He was speaking to the Bagana people and Jagua could not understand what he said, but she gathered that the tall man had been made the leader of the expedition against Chief Ofubara of Krinameh. Their duty was to capture Nancy Oll. The men were receiving orders to fit out the war canoes, to bring them out from hiding, to arm and to sail for Krinameh. Uncle Namme clapped his hands, and the men briskly disappeared. Jagua could see that he had become a different man, no longer the genial host. He was tense, distant and she could not dare to look him in the face.

Ma Nancy was cursing her aloud. 'You harlot woman. You not goin' to die well. You goin' to die in de gutter. Vulture will chop you eye!'

Uncle Namme raised his hand. 'Be patient. Ma Nancy, I know how you're feeling. Nancy's a fine gal. D.V. nothing will happen to her. We all love her. The whole of Bagana.'

When Uncle Namme went into a room, Jagua followed him. He was still pacing about like a man in a dream. In the courtyard the women had assembled and were dancing and yelling, working up the heat. They carried staves which occasionally they flung at the wall facing Krinameh. Jagua knelt before Uncle Namme.

He looked haughtily beyond her. 'Don't come near me! You started all this nonsense! I should take you up now and lock you inside. Yes, we have a prison. Better still, I should take you and fling you into the waters of Krinameh. Then you'll know what it's like.'

'Pardon, Your Highness. I want to go there. I want to go for dis Krinameh. Me one.'

Uncle Namme stopped walking. 'What?'

'I beg you not to sen' man-o-war canoe to Krinameh. Or dere goin' to be plenty people kill. Uncle Namme, is me who cause all dis palaver. So let me go an' see Chief Ofubara.'

Uncle Namme glared at her where she sat, meek and repentant.

'What d'you think you can do? Suppose Chief Ofubara captures you also; that will make two. No! I refuse!'

Jagua began to cry aloud. 'Uncle Namme, ah beg you for allow me. Ah will go dere an' ask Chief Ofubara to take me, instead of Nancy. I prepare to make de sacrifice. I prepare for take de risk.'

Uncle Namme held his sides and laughed. He laughed with his throat and tongue, and then sat down. 'You're joking! You don' know Chief Ofubara. He's my own blood. Wicked man! You don' know him. Ha, ha! . . .'

But Jagua was adamant. 'Ah don' mind, Your Highness! Me begin all dis trouble. So, if you kin let me. Ah goin' dere an' ask Chief Ofubara to kill me, if he like, but to lef' Nancy. I wan' you to give me good canoeman for take me dere. When ah go an' I don' come back quick or you don' see Nancy, den you kin sen' your army.' She looked up into his eyes and saw the faintest flicker of indecision. 'You goin' to waste innocent young men. Dis not matter of force or power. If you sen' your men with power, den Chief Ofubara will fight with power too. But when he see a simple woman like me, what he goin' to do? He goin' to laugh . . .'

Uncle Namme looked at the kneeling Jagua. He lifted his eyes and looked right ahead of him and said with decision. 'Go and make ready. I shall get my best oarsman to take you. But if you are not back, or if I don't see Nancy within twenty-four hours, there shall be smoke and blood in Krinameh Creek.'

Jagua prostrated flat before him. He looked down at her and smiled. 'Rise now. Time is going!'

'God go bless you, Uncle Namme.'

Jagua rose and walked towards her room, scowling at Mama Nancy who was still waiting in the lounge.

In less than an hour she had made herself really Jagwa. The effect pleased her. It was like bringing the *Tropicana* chorus girls in a helicopter and dropping them among the mud-skippers, the stilt roots of the mangrove, the paper-light canoes that skidded on the salt water. They would be objects of wonder and speculation. Jagua felt like a hunter who has smelt out the lion in a forest, wounded but concealed. All her wits must be about her, for there was no knowing when the enemy would strike and what his latent powers were.

When she appeared before Uncle Namme the look in his eye was a reward. All men looked at her like that when she was really Jagwa. It compensated for all the polishing, scrubbing and brushing that resulted in the Jagwa gloss, characteristic of racing steeds.

'De canoeman ready, Your Highness?'

'He's been waitin' some time now.'

She walked down to the beach with them gazing about Bagana in her sunshade and caring little for the looks which she received. She had chosen the brightest lipstick in her bag, her blouse was sleeveless and cut so low that only the tips of her breasts were covered. The skirt was so tight she could not take a stride of more than six inches at a time. It was a grey skirt with three big buttons down the front and a big split down the back. Her olive-skinned calves were fully on show and her feet were barely kissed by openwork wedge-heeled shoes. She carried a plastic handbag and wore a wig which almost succeeded in altering her into a Malayan or an Indian lovely.

On the beach, two men were glad to lift her into the canoe. Although Krinameh was clearly visible from Bagana in the afternoon, the journey took over an hour. The canoeman sang as he paddled but maintained his distance. Jagua sat stern and stately, a *Tropicana* princess in the mangrove creeks of Krinameh.

On Krinameh beach the youths treated her with the deference she had seen reserved for royal persons like Uncle Namme. She was surprised to find that they took it for granted she had come to see Chief Ofubara. They showed her into his lounge where she sat looking at the identical portrait which she had seen in the Namme lounge at Bagana. When he appeared in person, Chief Ofubara was not quite so young as in the picture. His eyes had grown fairly puffy and his manner less debonair. He wore a silk shirt, tied a georgette *lappa* about his waist and carried a fly whisk. An attendant – a boy of about fourteen – stood beside him.

'You from where?'

'From Lagos, Your Highness. I come to spen' my leave in Bagana, an' das where I see your picture in de house of Uncle Namme.'

Chief Ofubara smiled. 'Welcome! You are very fair, my lady.'

Jagua smiled and acted shy. 'I like dis Krinameh very much.'

Chief Ofubara beamed. 'It's a fine place. We're still trying to build. We've had our troubles, you know . . .' He talked about the rift between him and the Nammes, about the prospects of education in the island of Krinameh, and about trade. 'All the agencies are in the hands of the Nammes. But we shall make a headway. We are working slowly . . .' He clapped his hands in the Namme manner. A decanter arrived, and he offered Jagua some O.H.M.S. 'Is what we drink here, to forget the world . . . Tell me about Lagos. Are they still dividing themselves into smaller and smaller political parties? . . . We shall never progress that way, you know! We need to unite!'

'You believe in unity? Den why you separate from de Namme family. Why you don' work with dem?'

He fixed his eyes on her. But she was certain he was not looking at her, but beyond her. 'You got it wrong, my dear. You're a stranger. You only go by what you hear; and you've heard only one side.'

He poured out the story of Bagana, and when he had finished Jagua saw Chief Ofubara in a new light. She saw that he was not a man who wanted strife. It was he who had withdrawn from the case, because he felt that too much money was being wasted while the people suffered. He still valued the love and friendship which had always existed in the family. He wanted education, trade, development for Krinameh and for Bagana. But as things were, no one would make the move. There was suspicion between the two families and unless an outside force united them, they could never come together. Instead of coming together they kept on circulating tales and these tales became distorted and served only to widen the gap.

'We are all Africans, and we must come together. There is no time for petty squabbles. As for me, I never go anywhere. I remain here in Krinameh and help my people. But if anyone seeks me out and puts his finger into my eye, then I must fight.' He talked loftily, and Jagua was impressed. He had been described to her as wicked, but she found him sober and of progressive views.

Not once had she mentioned her mission. She let him talk, and as he talked an idea began forming in her mind. It would be a very daring thing to accomplish, but she would try.

'I got somethin' to tell you,' Jagua said.

'Plenty of time.' He went on talking about the future of Krinameh, Bagana, and the Bagana people who were split and scattered by petty strife and as a result were living in exile. 'I like talking to you. We agree on many things.' He smiled. 'I've never met so intelligent a lady.'

Jagua remembered the twenty-four-hour limit which Uncle Namme had given her so as to produce results. She remembered also that rushing Chief Ofubara might produce the wrong kind of result. And in the meantime, Nancy must be languishing in the hands of her captors.

To fill in the time before lunch Chief Ofubara suggested he showed her round the palace. He took her to the museum, the oracle house, the office, the dining room with chairs which he said were presented to his grandfather by the Portuguese. Finally they came to a special room. It was lined with silk and smelt strongly of rich forest woods. Spanning the middle of the room was a huge four-poster with enormous spring mattresses and a velvet bedspread with decorative patterns.

87

'Very fine room,' Jagua said.

'The bedroom,' Chief Ofubara told her. 'Fit for a queen, eh? My wives come to me here. I have only three wives and they each got their own place. My wives come to me here when I send for them.'

Jagua took out a fan and waved it in front of her bosom. A sigh escaped from her parted lips. Impulsively she flopped into a chair. 'Oh, am tired.'

Chief Ofubara leaned over her. 'Is my own fault. Come and rest here.' He took her by the hand and led her across to a sofa.

'Thank you,' Jagua said. She was carelessly sprawled on the sofa, and one of the buttons on her skirt had come off, showing her thigh. She tried to inject into the look she gave the Chief, a feeling of intense desire for him.

'May I sit down too? Am also tired.' He shifted her and sat down. It was very silent. A curious light glowed in the room and wild incenses haunted her blood. He was a very big man, and though she was by no means small, he made her feel small. 'You must sleep in this room . . . We got a lot of fine women in Krinameh. But they're not like you. You're fine too, and you got refinement . . . You've seen the world . . . ' She felt his breath on her ears, alcoholic, stirring the blood.

'I don' come here to sleep, Your Highness . . . I come to beg you some favour.'

'You are very fair, my lady.'

'It is a big favour. And I am afraid to start.'

'Go on.' He took her hand. He leaned over the hand and kissed it. He had wild moustaches that tickled her skin. 'Where you come from? I mean your home?'

'My hometown is Ogabu,' Jagua smiled. 'I be Ogabu lady.'

'All the women in Ogabu fine like you? I must get my next wife from there.'

Jagua giggled. She shook her shoulders in the reckless laughter of a bad woman wanting to be seduced. Chief Ofubara took the hint and put his arm on her shoulder. She let it rest there but when the hand touched her breast she pushed it away and gave him a reproving look. 'Excuse!'

'You look like queen, Madam. Your husband is a lucky man.'

'Why?' Jagua giggled and spoke in a very small voice. 'But suppose I got no husband. And I jus' by myself?'.

'You'll still be nice.'

Jagua swung to her feet, but the Chief held her back. 'You're too hot-tempered. Have I said anythin' rude?'

'You only jus' know me today, and you tryin' to sleep me. Suppose, if your wife come and meet we inside here now?'

He glanced at the door. 'They never come to my bedroom unless I send for them. I've told you!'

Jagua spoke in her sweetest voice. 'I no come for dat. I only come to Bagana on visit. Den de accident happen dis morning and your boys catch de gal from Bagana.'

'Accident? Tell me about it. I hope you were not wounded?'

'Das what I tryin' to tell you all dis time.' She gave him the full details of the adventure with Nancy Oll. She told him what she feared might have happened since then. 'I want you to use all de power you have to release de poor gal. De fault is from me.' She threw herself at his feet and began to cry. 'De gal done nothin' to you or David Namme. She's not from dis area. Now de young men catch her and goin' to kill her, like she done dem somethin'.'

'No, no, no, my dear lady! Rise.' He helped her to her feet and rested her on the settee. 'I give you my word. No one has any right to punish the girl. They usually show me anyone they capture. I'll go now and have her released. I'm sure they're waiting till I come round and see her. Excuse me! I'll not be long.' He left her and she felt very excited.

He did not come back for about an hour. Jagua slackened the buttons on her blouse and skirt. She relaxed her legs across the settee, and with her head on the armrest, shut her eyes and feigned sleep. Through half-shut eyes she saw him come in and there was a triumphant smile on his face. He tiptoed to where she lay and leaning over, tickled her lips with his moustache. Then he went back and shut the door.

'You sleepin'?' He was standing over her. She lay still, eyes shut. The Chief knelt beside her. She felt his hand on her skirt button, the central button. But it was too tight and his fingers were too clumsy to undo the catch. Slowly Jagua rose and yawned. She pretended not to know what had happened.

'Sorry, sleep catch me. I too tire. You done return?'

'Come to the bed!' His eyes were blue and his manner urgent.

'No, Your Highness. Dis place is all right. I don' feel sleep any more. What about de gal?'

'I've sent her back in a canoe to Bagana. You happy now?'

'God bless you! I know dat you're a good man. No matter what dem say 'bout you. Is only enemy talk.'

'Lissen Jagua . . . I like you. I'm going to give you a wardrobe fit for a princess. Just something, so you can remember the day you met Chief Ofubara of Krinameh—'

'Tenk you, Your Highness; but you only know me today!'

'Today's enough. Life is too short, Jagua.'

She could see that he had become infatuated with her. She saw through his loneliness for David and Uncle Namme, his need for someone with whom he could exchange ideas. He was looking at her with adoration in his eyes. She knew exactly the type of man she was dealing with: a Provincial, who was more readily infatuated with the idea of Lagos, of the *Tropicana*-type woman than with the woman herself. In her estimation he was becoming like a man in a daze. Confronted by the headlights of Jagua's glamour before which all his wives and all the women he was likely to come across paled, he was becoming like putty in her hands.

He held her breast and she let him squeeze it. 'You can stay in this palace with me – as my guest.'

'No, Your Highness. You see, Uncle Namme he tol' me to return back before de night come.'

'I'll send a messenger to tell him you're well and happy.' He stroked her cheek. 'Jagwa, wha's your reply?' His eyes burnt into her cheeks.

She sighed. 'Ah tol' you before, Chief Ofubara. I tol' you dat I got somethin' to beg you. You already done one. You release Nancy. But dis one is somethin' I want to beg you for myself.' She felt his hands slacken. 'When am leavin' dis Krinameh, I want me an' you to go togedder to Bagana. I take God beg you dis. We will go togedder to Bagana, and you will shake hand with Uncle Namme. Das all I beg you.'

Chief Ofubara sat straight up on the settee. 'I got my pride, Madam. Why they themselves can't come to me? They know the way!'

'But you tol' me jus' now dat you love me?'

'Yes.'

'An' you promise to give me wardrobe. An' I know dat if you ready to give me money, it will be somethin' . . . But I don' ask you for all dat. I jus' ask you to come with me to Bagana an' shake hand with Uncle Namme. Den you two kin talk. Lissen, Chief Ofubara. Your country people, dem suffer because of dis foolish proud you showin'. You proud. David Namme proud. Uncle Namme proud. Well, I got no proud, so I beg you for my sake.' She saw that he was listening and went on: 'Just now you talk with me. You say you wan' unity. Well, I goin' to give you de chance to get dat unity! . . .'

She got down and began to unbutton her skirt herself. His eyes widened. She was wearing silk undergarments frilled with the finest lace. She knew how clean her body was and how beautifully groomed. When he talked now, his voice was trembling. He was hooked.

'So that's all you want from me? Just that.'

'Oh, God bless you! . . . I know you're better dan dem all. Dem only talking word. But you doin' de deed! . . .'

'I like your shape, Jagua . . . I wan' to marry you.'

'Am a business woman; I can't marry no one, Chief.'

One part of her felt intensely sorry for the Chief. He was still under the Jagwa dazzle and she knew she could have got anything out of him. She asked for some more O.H.M.S. which he quickly provided and they sat drinking. She strutted about the room in her high heels and jutted out her hips. His eyes were getting redder and redder with every passing moment. He slapped her bottom and pulled her to his knees, kneading her breasts.

He took her to bed and she gave him herself with an abandon calculated to shock and delight him. The feigned noises, practised over the years, the carefully punctuated sighs and cries of pain, the sudden flexing of thighs and neck . . . All these she performed with a precision which surprised herself. It was a long time since she had played her true role.

Chief Ofubara went mad. 'I mus' marry you.' He rose and walked to another room. She heard him rummaging in a cupboard. When he came back he was holding a green canvas bag. 'We got no use for this here . . .' He threw a wad of notes on the bed. It was marked one hundred pounds. 'You say you're from Ogabu. The bride price there is about one hundred and twenty pounds.' He dipped his hand into the bag and threw on the bed another bundle. It was marked fifty pounds.

Jagua sat quite still. She felt rotten, loose and awful. She knew she could never really abandon her past life and settle down with someone like Chief Ofubara in a village like Krinameh. But the money would come in useful. She reached out her hand and clasped the two bundles.

'Come lay down, Chief. You never satisfy me. I hungry for your love.' She guessed that none of his wives would dare talk to him as an equal. He came and lay beside her. She took off his clothes for him and kissed him.

'Hol' me tight. I goin' to teach you 'bout de worl'. I goin' to show you how young man use' to loss his head when 'e sleep Jagwa woman.'

He was mumbling incoherently and sucking at her lips like a child of six months. She stroked his hair tenderly and laughed the submissive laughter of the practised whore, brassy, with an eye to the gold coins in the trousers pocket.

Jagua Nana remained in the palace at Krinameh for ten days. And every day a canoeman from Bagana came searching for her in the palace at Krinameh, but she always sent him back to tell Uncle Namme that she was well and would soon return.

The wounded lion had been caged. Jagua felt the proud glow heroes must feel on their return, victorious, from the hunting ground, carrying the vanquished animal on their shoulders. When the people of Bagana saw the Royal Canoe of Krinameh with Chief Ofubara gloriously seated in it, they stared. They crowded the beach. The canoe landed and stalwart arms lifted Jagua and Chief Ofubara and planted them on Bagana soil. Chief Ofubara took a handful of the soil and tasted it and Jagua heard him mumbling like a man at prayer.

Jagua showed him Uncle Namme standing in the group further away from the water's edge. He was flanked by his councillors. Mama Nancy and Nancy stood on the fringes of the group. Nancy was wearing a maroon T-shirt with a white bow above her left breast.

Jagua whispered to Chief Ofubara. 'Go meet Uncle Namme now. Remember how you promise me? I take God beg you: don' show any proud. Go meet Uncle Namme. Salute am like you brodder an' let everythin' finish today!'

Chief Ofubara tottered and hesitated, but Jagua gave him no respite. She prodded him in the back. One step at a time he advanced on Uncle Namme and his Councillors, holding out his hand. Jagua saw the muscles tighten in Uncle Namme's jaw. He must be struggling with himself. Instead of taking the proferred arm, Uncle Namme opened out his arms and the two men embraced. The tears came in a flood to Jagua's eyes as she watched the scene.

Many times in later years Jagua saw this happy moment in her dreams. It was evening and the sun was peeping for the last time over the tops of the mangrove trees. The bars of gold etched out the red and yellow robes of the two royal men who had been in strife for over thirty years, but had now come together. Fussing around them was an amateur photographer, focusing his lens on the great Bagana picture that was later to hang on every wall in Krinameh and Bagana. While the men embraced drums of Bagana sang out the joyful news. Men ran after goats, and capturing them slashed off their heads. Fowls were taken and their blood spilt on the family altars. The news went round and round that a great thing had happened, that a woman from another land had brought with her the good luck they had prayed for all the time. Jagua beamed with joy. She knew that her victory in bringing the two feuding villages together was far greater than Nancy's mastery of the Bagana dance. She did not deceive herself into thinking that the problem had been solved. Wounds inflicted many years ago, she knew, still festered.

But she was glad. The first step had been taken; and there was goodwill on both sides.

She could hardly see clearly for tears as she joined the procession to the palace, mumbling the joyful song with the crowd.

'When David Namme returns from Port Harcourt,' said Uncle Namme, 'we shall rejoice – properly. Oh, this is a great thing.' He turned and looked admiringly at Jagua. 'So this is what kept you, eh? You did well! You should be made a queen of Bagana for this!'

'I already ask her,' Chief Ofubara said.

'And she refused, of course!' laughed Uncle Namme. 'She promised Freddie Namme, but I don't know about that young man. He wants Jagua, he wants Nancy! He must make up his mind . . . I don't understand these modern people . . . But Jagua is a sincere lady.' He winked at Chief Ofubara. 'If you're serious, perhaps she will change her mind. Personally, I believe Jagua will suit you fine, eh?' He was in a happy mood, Jagua could see that and she smiled and sang even louder.

The mention of Freddie shot through her a stab of remorse and pain. She knew she must not wait any longer in Bagana. She must be on her way back, through Ogabu and Onitsha. Her mission in Bagana was accomplished. She had known Freddie's people and become known to them. No matter what her enemies thought and said, she felt she had contributed something to the happiness of Bagana.

That night, in the middle of the drumming, with the hurricane lanterns etching out the muscular outlines of the dancers, Jagua went and touched Chief Ofubara. He lifted his face and his eyes danced with admiration. For his benefit she had shampooed and curled her hair and from her earrings down to her dancing shoes, the colour was violet. The hurricane lamps caressed the skin above her breasts, her bare shoulders and arms. She had accentuated her eyes with discreet applications of antimony. The total effect pleased her: that of the well-groomed and happy woman, mature and independent.

'Tomorrow, I mus' be goin' back . . .'

He jumped in his seat. 'Nonsense! You not going anywhere! Not while I live. Don't you like it here? You must follow me back to Krinameh. I've already paid your bride price!'

'You can have de money back.' Her fingers sought the catch of her handbag. Chief Ofubara restrained her.

'Wait!'

'Is all you thinkin' about! You think you kin buy me with money? Am a free woman. An' I already sleep wit' you ten night an' give you experience of Lagos woman dat you never dream! . . .'

'I'm sorry, Jagua! . . . I'm only jokin' . . . Now, Jagua, what are you going to do about your fiery temper?' He held her arm tightly. The drumming and the laughter, the shouting and the cheering insulated them in a private world.

'You kin have your money back, Chief Ofubara. But you mus' promise me about Bagana.'

'That's settled, Jagua. David Namme's going to be *Yaniba* of Bagana. We're going to draft a letter to the Government and recognize him . . . already the people of Bagana promise they'll give me some trading agencies and financial help with education and medical work.'

Jagua sat on the edge of his chair. 'You see now! I already tol' you. Is pride dat killin' you two family. If to say you still prouding, where you will get all dis?'

'I have you to thank, Jagua.' He tapped her arm. 'Come with me, Jagua, and let's talk seriously.'

'You done gone crase about me?' She giggled, showing all her teeth. That night, Jagua was looking as beautiful as she had ever been in her life.

She walked beside him. The moonlight had a yellowness that gilded everything it touched. He was talking earnestly as they approached the beach-side but she manœuvred him to the bathing-place where she had forced Nancy into the lagoon and pursued her into the Krinameh rocks. The coconut palms spread their dark fronds into the face of the moon. She looked beyond the haze and saw Krinameh. She remembered the silk-lined bedroom, the O.H.M.S. evenings, and the days when the Councillors came in and Chief Ofubara introduced her to them as 'my special visitor from Lagos'. How the men laughed and told Chief Ofubara not to deceive them, to speak up like a man if he had married a Lagos queen, so they could come and drink his O.H.M.S. She would gladly go there and live with him. He seemed to see things in her own way. He listened to her advice; he appreciated her. He would solve the problem of her life. But was there sufficient urge?

He broke into her thoughts. 'That's Krinameh over there; and you can join me and be very happy there . . .'

She knew he had the money to lavish on her. If he could casually fling away one hundred and fifty pounds he also had some gallantry. She leaned against him.

'I confuse. I don' think I fit to say anything till ah reach Lagos. After!'

'Then you'll come back to Krinameh?' He gripped her hands. 'You're not deceiving me – you're speaking the truth?'

'Ah goin' to come back.' She walked away from him with a wiggle of her hips, striking a pose. 'I think you wan' me – not so?'

He came towards her, hands outstretched. Jagua walked into his arms and he lifted her joyfully.

'You'll come back to me – promise.'

'I already tol' you. Or you don' trust me?'

He set her down. In silence they walked towards the palace. A chorus of female voices came floating towards them on the thin veils of the night. Jagua remembered that she must go to bed early, so as to leave early tomorrow morning. She would not be able to keep the all-night vigil of the joyful Baganans.

At the entrance to the palace gate, Jagua saw a woman who seemed to be waiting to speak to them. It was Mama Nancy. She must have watched their going and now was making sure of seeing their coming.

'De harlot woman!' she said aloud. 'De shameless harlot woman! She sleepin' with de Papa, an' she lyin' to de Pickin', and she don' care nothin'. De harlot woman! You goin' to die wretched! Vulture will chop you eye!'

'Ma Nancy, you talkin' to me?' Jagua flared, leaping towards her enemy. Chief Ofubara restrained her.

'Try to act like a queen! Ignore her!'

Jagua struggled, but the Chief's grip was unshakeable. She could do nothing but yield. Mama Nancy's curse followed her, rising louder and louder but the drumming suppressed the vitriol in her words, neutralizing their sharpness.

15

By now Bagana had become a chain of rusty-red pan roofs on a horizon dominated by a church steeple and set deep beyond the flat waters of the creek. Jagua's canoe swung into one of the wide arms of the Niger Delta, heading towards Port Harcourt. It was her way home to Ogabu and Lagos. It was goodbye to Bagana, goodbye to Chief Ofubara, Uncle Namme, Mama Nancy, Nancy Oll, Krinameh, the war drummers. The swarthy face of Chief Ofubara had become even darker as he told her: 'Remember your promise, Jagua. I already paid the bride-price.' His voice had been dead earnest.

Jagua held her breast as if that would ease the pain. Now that the canoe was taking her away from Bagana and Krinameh, she began to think of the fishing people with a touch of nostalgia. She would come back to Krinameh, to the spot where the youths had dived in and captured the naked Nancy Oll. This one desire – to come back – kept expressing itself. She could not suppress the montage of jutting rocks, and salt-creeks, and Chief Ofubara's moustachios and O.H.M.S. decanters and the intertwined legs on the bed, the finger-tips on unshaven jaws and her whispers of 'I goin' to teach you about Lagos woman, to make you loss your min' . . .' Now it was she, strangely enough, who was on the verge of losing her head over the Chief.

Suddenly she was seeing Chief Ofubara as the outcast of Kri-nameh, as a man who was infatuated with her, as a man of her own age and attitudes. She could see that he had never really experi-enced the sensation of African woman as equal. Jagua treated him as she would treat a brother or a precocious lover in modern Lagos. Her glance stripped him of his title, and he became a man lusting

after her; her temper made him her slave, willing to obey her mad-
dest whims merely to restore the smile on her lips.

When the canoe turned the creeks she stood up, nearly upset-
ting it. The other passengers protested, but Jagua was waving at a
Bagana vanishing in the rising heat. 'Goodbye, Chief! . . . Expect
me! . . . I mus' surely come an' see you again!'

In Ogabu she kept the mammy wagon waiting in the forest lane and
ran to her father's house. The barking of the old watchman's dog
welcomed her. He came out of the hut and brought the dog to heel.

'Daughter. You back? You stop there long time.' The sun caught
the angles of his shoulders and elbows, the criss-cross wrinkles on
his bare skin. His eyes were dancing with delight.

'Only three week I stay. Where's Papa an' Mama?'

'You're to be feared!' He clicked his hands at her, in a gesture of
reproach. 'You won't even bring down your load, you begin' ask
about Papa an' Mama! Your Papa still on tour.'

'I go an' see dem for Onitsha!'

She ran quickly back to the lorry and jumped in beside the
driver. The old man called after her. 'If you don't see them, you find
Brother Fonso in the market.' He waved at her. 'Go well!' By this
time, his children had appeared and were waving and yelling.
Before the people of Ogabu gathered to make a fuss, Jagua's lorry
was well on the way to Onitsha.

She found Fonso in Onitsha Market sitting among bicycle parts,
poring over an account book. It was just as the old man had said.
He did not appear to her different in the least. If anything he
appeared a little paler, like one whom the world has treated none
too gently.

'Ai, Sister!' He looked up and shut the book. 'You come to our
Onitsha? Is it in a good way?'

'I jus' from home; I returnin' to Lagos by de ferry, so I say let me
come an' see how you gettin' on.'

Fonso folded his book and talked to his helper, a young man in
khaki. He talked earnestly while Jagua waited.

'Le's go,' he said. 'De ferry can cross you today, but you mus' stop and eat pepper with me. Is a long time I seen you.'

Jagua followed him into his little house by the waterside. Onitsha, the market town, she thought as they passed along the streets with the noise of bicycles, the blaring of gramophone records, the tooting of horns, all slamming at her eardrums. Onitsha was busy in a fiendish way, minting the money. By the riverside she saw the yams and the cassava, the newly-killed fish and the long canoes, vying for the merest space in which to squeeze and make a stand against the customers. The riverboats and launches were drenching the market with soot. Jagua felt caught up in the unbelievable atmosphere of trickery, opportunism, intuition, daring and amazing decisions. People who lived here, she was sure, did not care what happened elsewhere; they were hard-headed and complete strangers to laziness.

Brother Fonso pointed them out to her triumphantly. She sensed a sharp reproach in his manner, though as yet he had said nothing direct. He talked about their father, how ill he was and how neglected. 'One day, you'll just hear he's dead.' Was Jagua doing anything in Lagos, and when Jagua said she was trading in cloth, Fonso laughed. 'Let us hear somethin' else, Jagua. You deceivin' no one. My dear sister, is time you stop your loose life. Is a shameful thin' to me, your brother. I got a beautiful sister like you. God made you with dignity; an' when I think of your kind of life . . .' He was not looking at her face, and he walked so quickly that she found difficulty in keeping up with him. 'So what I say to you is this. My sister, come home and stay in the family. You don' wan' to marry. Awright. Nobody forcin' you. Den keep yourself with respect.'

'You won' let me reach house, before you start, Brother Fonso.' This was one reason why she dreaded meeting him. He was always trying to lead her to a righteous life. 'But I tell you, brodder. One chief in Krinameh wan' to marry me. An' he already pay my bride price.'

'So they always do; and when them sleep with you finish, no more talk about marriage.' He walked faster. 'Jagua, come out from deceivin' yousself.'

If it was money she wanted, the money was there in Onitsha, Brother Fonso told her. For instance, she could remain with him now and try to become one of the Merchant Princesses in the town. Fonso talked about one woman who made a monthly turnover of £10,000. The Merchant Princesses, he boasted, were independent women; and he knew that his sister loved independence. And they were free. They turned their minds to business, not frivolities. They were grown-up women.

Brother Fonso's house by the ferry waterside was ill-lighted and musty. Jagua knew that her brother was worth a good deal of money, and in her turn she upbraided him for living so drably. What was the use of making money and not finding time to enjoy it, Jagua asked him. But he was more interested in making the money – first. He was living alone now, he said, because his wife had gone home to her own people to have a baby. He scrambled her a meal, but kept pressing her to stop in Onitsha, not to cross any more with the ferry. She must stop with him and try her hand at trading – in the Onitsha manner. He was sure she would soon pick it up. Jagua suspected Brother Fonso of unhappiness and loneliness, of wanting to detain her for company. Certainly she felt he made the whole thing sound easy. He made no reference to his loneliness but she saw it in his wild-eyed look and in the breath of wind his cry brought.

She listened to him because he was her brother and she wanted to show him that she was not a 'useless' woman. In the morning they went together in search of the Merchant Princesses. Brother Fonso took her to one of them who said she sold £2,000 worth of exercise books a week during the boom period. It was she alone who distributed exercise books to three million schoolchildren. She owned a fleet of lorries which travelled north and east, distributing bicycles, soap and cement. Jagua sat in her shed and listened almost mesmerized. She could find nothing at all unusual in this money-spinning woman who did not know how to write in English. She came away feeling like one who has been offered a new path to salvation.

When she had seen all that Brother Fonso would show her, she wanted to be one of them. Fonso took her to the secretary of the woman traders who had an office at the market entrance. He looked at Jagua through his heavy-rimmed glasses and told Jagua that she was new and must 'prove herself'. He could not take her before the white agent who supplied the women with goods, until she had proved herself. To prove herself she must take out goods and pay cash first. Then – if she did well – she would be trusted with credit facilities, and the amount would gradually be increased to a worthwhile sum.

Jagua consulted with Fonso. With his permission she decided to use the £150 she had and Fonso added another £50 to make it a round £200. The Union Secretary told Jagua that £200 worth of goods would only bring her a profit of £2. There were women taking £10,000 worth of goods, and getting £100 commission. 'You need not really sell. All you must do is move the goods. Get people to come from the jungles and buy them. It doesn't matter where they come from. Push the goods to your sub-customers who will then take them deeper inside. Nigeria is a big country, there's plenty of space. Then, you bring back the cash to us: and take out goods worth more money. And so on. But mark you, you must study the market and know what you can push. You must always buy goods that move. D'you know something?' He stirred the snuff in his palm with a stick. 'You don't even need a shop or a stall to succeed.' With the stick he scooped the tobacco into a left nostril and inhaled.

Sitting in her own stall, Jagua was miserable. It rained, and when it was not raining, the customers came, but not to her stall. She saw them in the stalls of the other women traders. Once she saw a dark man holding a canvas bag. She watched him: he walked past her stall to the nearest stall and began counting out money from the canvas bag, waiting while the woman trader in the stall checked it. 'God, if I kin get lucky like dat woman,' Jagua thought.

But it was not to be. Her stall seemed to repel the buyers. She was new, she had to 'exercise patience'. Fonso told her that a trader must be a patient animal. Jagua found herself quite unable to learn this new quality of patience without glamour. She loved showing herself off, but sitting in the stall gave her no time to preen herself, to strut about the alleyways of Onitsha. She spent her time in the bleaching sun, from morning till six at night, with a meal snatched behind the goods she was selling. It was not her idea of living her life. At night she moaned. Yet when she saw the merchant princesses in the evenings, sitting in the owner's corner of their limousines, she envied them, and longed to own hers. She told Fonso and he reminded her of the one hundred rungs of the ladder. According to him her foot was scarcely planted on the first rung. He told her to 'have patience' but already her stock was exhausted. She was glad Onitsha had given her an insight into the big money business. But she was realistic enough to know that she was not yet equipped to partake of the loot. Though she had lost her money in the first venture she could still go, Jaguaful, down to the riverside in the evenings to watch the canoemen bringing in the day's catch of the best-tasting fish in Nigeria.

It was from the beach-side that she caught a glimpse of the ferry launch packed full with Lagos-licensed cars. The wind blew across to where she stood, snatches of a familiar jazz tune from the *Tropicana*. It must have come from one of the car radios. She saw a young man, Lagos-tailored, talking to a dashingly dressed girl with a heavily made-up face. The two of them must be coming from Lagos, going eastwards. Those two young people seemed to tell her she was in some danger of losing her chic, of becoming more provincial and less Jaguaful. This was the last thing she ever wanted to happen to her. The suppressed desires came rushing to her stimulated imagination.

She gave the fish-seller a pound note, but it was when she got home she realized she ought to have waited for her change.

16

Someone told her once that if she ever left Lagos for one week, no one would remember her. But Jagua soon discovered that leaving Lagos as she had done for more than three months meant – in addition – not recognizing the city on her return, it was changing so fast. The lorry park had been cemented and paved and they had now built a proper entrance and exit but the lorries and the touts and small quick-quick buses were still there. If anything they were flourishing more vigorously.

A taxi took her back to her lodgings. She was glad she still retained her rooms. Try as she would Lagos still remained her natural habitat. The memory of Chief Ofubara and Krinameh still lingered, but the pressure to go back was already becoming less urgent. This time was perhaps the best hour to come back unnoticed: sunset fading into a short twilight that dazzled the eyes and confused the senses. People were mere forms, hazy and ghostly but identifiable. No one knew just when Jagua got back to her room. She remained for a moment in the room, smelling its mustiness. At last she had reached home. Ogabu was the home of her father and mother; Bagana was Freddie Namme's home where Uncle Namme lived as Regent; Krinameh was the home of Chief Ofubara who was infatuated with her. Jagua thought of all these places and tried to fit herself into one of them. There was none quite like Lagos and the *Tropicana*. She opened the windows and without putting on the light, she began to unpack, mainly foodstuffs, yams, oranges, plantains. She would not need to spend her money on expensive Lagos food for some time at least. Back home. She breathed in the air of freedom.

While she took off her clothes, Michael came in and beamed over her, telling her how well she was looking. He had kept the place remarkably clean in her absence. She examined her body in the mirror as she talked to him. Going east had made her fairer of skin, more rounded on her face, younger looking, more desirable to men, she hoped; something different from the usual dried-up bones of the *Tropicana* girls.

'Anybody ask of me?' She covered her hips with a cloth as she talked to Michael. He was only a boy and she appeared naked before him without any hint of self-consciousness. What always amused her was the way he averted his eyes from her breasts and hips when she confronted him, but she had often caught him stealing very grown-up looks at her from behind.

'One man come here plenty time.' He rushed downstairs and produced a small notebook. 'He come here, till he tire. He use to wear long dress and cap. He get money plenty. He never come 'ere before you go home.'

With the help of a neighbour they were able to decipher the

scrawl. 'Taiwo,' it read. Jagua immediately remembered him as the man who had taken her to the airport the day Freddie was leaving for Britain.

'Finish, de man who come?'

'Dem too plenty; but dis man get money pass all!'

Jagua smiled. 'How you know he get money?'

'I know, Ma. I see de money for him face!'

Jagua laughed, with her head thrown over her shoulder. She had not finished admiring herself in the mirror. JAGWA. She gave herself the title now, whispering it and summoning up in her mind all the fantastic elegance it was supposed to conjure up. JAGWA. It was like an invocation. She was sure the men would like her much more now. Men, she discovered, found a strange appeal in a woman whom they knew but who had been away on holiday. Again she thought of Freddie and only managed to repress an impulse to go downstairs and ask of him. So Freddie would not be coming to her rooms, crashing into her secret life and starting his jealous quarrels. His jealousy was tough to bear; but Lagos for her also meant Freddie and his quarrels.

She heard the stirring throbs of jazz from a neighbour's radio. A new record, too. She must go to the *Tropicana*. Wonder 'bout dem. Mama Nancy still at Bagana. Wish her all de best. She kin marry Uncle Namme if she choose. Must go to *Tropicana* to forget de worl'. De trouble wit' de worl' is dis: people too take life serious. Life is serious, mark you. I don' deny that. But you mus' take life easy sometime. Yes. Mus' go to *Tropicana*. Dis night too. I know I only jus' return, but Brodder Fonso not here to stop me an' talk all him serious talk about Papa an' Mama. After all who in de fam'ly suppose to look after dem? De men or de women? Am only a woman. Ah marry an' loss by name to anodder fam'ly. De man name must remain. Is only 8 o'clock now. Time never pass.

'Jagua? Hel-lo! . . . Welcome! . . . You look so well. You enjoy yerself at home? What you bring back to us?' The girls would want something from her, the hungry sluts. They dug their claw-like fingers into men's pockets and smoked men's cigarettes and drank men's drinks and took men's money, but they would always dig their hands into their colleagues' pockets for the odd copper to buy kola nuts to keep them awake and the odd scraps of food to keep them from collapsing. 'Borrow me your brooch, Esther! Borrow me your shoe, Mary! I wan' wear am go dance, repairer never return my own. I give am to repair he never come back.' *Tropicana* women. She hated them. Yes, they would want her to bring them something; they who had been rooted in Lagos enjoying the limousines and the silky tenor saxes of Jimo Ladi and his Leopards.

She stored away the food, then she took out her towel and went to the bathroom, but when she knocked a man answered her from the inside and she went instead to the lavatory. The same old bucket, piled high; the floor messed about, so she could see nowhere to put her silver sandals. It was all done by those wretched children upstairs. Why blame them when their mothers did not know any better. Where was the landlord? Where was the Town Council Health Inspector? This inspector was supposed to come here once in a while, and whenever he came he made notes in his black book but nothing ever happened. She would talk seriously to him the next time. The unpleasant side of Lagos life: the flies in the lavatory – big and blue and stubborn – settled on breakfast yam and lunchtime stew (they were invisible in a stew with greens). But Jagua closed her eyes and shut her nostrils with her towel.

The bathroom was free now, slippery and green, but thank God for the shower. She was through in a few moments. She stretched her hair, oiled her skin and wore her print dress. Something provincial was there in her get-up. She must find out what it was and eliminate it. This was Lagos and she was Jagwa.

She found the *Tropicana* much the same: entrance through a hole in the wall. A smile from the proprietor standing dark-haired in his shirtsleeves under a harsh light. She bought a kola-nut from the Hausa hawker who had a pitch inside, near the manager. Jimo Ladi and his Leopards had not begun to play yet, but they were all there on the bandstand. The women smiled at her.

'Jagwa. You return? Welcome! How's home?'

They flocked round her and teased her and she was glad. They said she looked young and fine. She told them that 'one man wan' to marry me, one Chief!' And when they expressed surprise, she reeled off the whole story, down to the detail of the reconciliation she had brought about. This story made her feel important. Unlike so many of them, she was not coming to the *Tropicana* out of necessity, but because it had become a part of her. She knew from the silence on their lips that she had succeeded in putting across that impression. The loudspeaker began to scratch out a tune. The girls went to their tables and sat with eyes trained on the door. But there was one girl who lingered.

Years later, Jagua remembered this particular night. It was the memorable night on which she saw more closely the young woman called Rosa. Rosa had a ready smile and a charming way of speaking. She said she had come to Lagos, from the East. She had nowhere to stay in Lagos. Could Jagua help her? Jagua took pity on her and promised, rashly, to do something. 'If you come to my place, sometime I kin fin' somethin' for you.' She quickly dismissed Rosa from her mind, but later that evening it flashed through her consciousness that Rosa could well live with her. Rosa could be her companion, in Freddie's absence. Lagos then, might have a new meaning. Rosa could pay something towards the rent, help with the cooking, washing and cleaning. The idea was worth considering.

At the moment, Jagua was far too occupied with shaking her hips to Jimo Ladi's *High-life*. Everyone was on the dance floor stomping and rocking with complete abandon.

She walked along the front of the *Tropicana*, among the taxi drivers and sellers of soap, candles, matches, sardines, toasted corn and peanuts. The lights played with her and she was glad. Glad to have been at the *Tropicana*. She heard the steady sound of footsteps behind her. Without glancing back she whispered to herself: 'Dem done start to follow me, awready! Ja-a-gwa!' The sensation of being followed brought with it a new kind of self-importance. She tried to guess from the rhythm of the steps what kind of a person it was. Not an old man, certainly. The steps were light, but hesitant. When she stopped, the sound ceased. She looked round and saw him: a young man.

He had one hand in his trousers pocket. 'Ma'am, I see you for *Tropicana*.'

Jagua looked at him, young, arrogant, smart in his open-neck shirt. 'You see me?' He could not be older than Freddie Namme, and she thought: 'Dese young men, dem never use to get money. Only sweet-mouth.'

'I see you for *Tropicana*, an' I say, even if I die, I jus' mus' speak wit' you.'

'How? I no understan' you.'

'I don' mean to offend you, Madam. I get some plan.' The hand stuck in the trousers pocket came out in one swift movement. He was holding a small packet and Jagua watched him open it. She drew in her breath.

'Gold?' she said. 'Who get de trinket?' She could hardly control her excitement. The trinkets were worth at least one hundred pounds. She recognized them as a complete set, suitable for use with native costume on special occasions only – funerals, naming ceremonies.

'I only wan' ten poun' for de whole. Cash. You kin do what you like wit' am, I no care. Melt de whole ting down and make new set, if you no like dis one.'

The chance was not one to be missed. 'Follow me,' Jagua whispered. 'I no hold de money here. Follow me to mah house.'

She took him to her room. He sat on the edge of the chair, the young man, nervous. She talked to him while undressing carelessly and then she left the room and went and showered her body with cold water and scented her armpits with something Oriental. When she came back she was wearing only a transparent chemise. She sat on her low carved stool with her little mirror propped between her bare knees, gazing at her wet hair. Her arms and shoulders were bare and she sat with the chemise bunched between her thighs so that the mirror bit into the skin between her knees.

Jagwa. She raised her arm and ran the comb through the wiry kinks of hair and her breasts swelled into sensuous arcs and her eyes tensed with the pain as the kinks straightened. And the hour was not less than three in the morning, with everywhere a dead quiet, and the light in the room low and sleepy. The young man sat on the nervous edge of the seat, gazing at her killing him off with temptation and he sat tense and said nothing.

'So you say you wan' ten poun' for de trinket?' she murmured, injecting a secretive note of intimacy into her voice. 'Eh?'

'Yes . . . er . . . oh, yes!'

'But you know de whole thin' don' worth more than five pound. I only goin' to give you five pound. Das all I got.' She smiled up at him, tilting her face upwards to gaze into his eyes. He was nervous. She saw that.

She rose, put aside the mirror and came and stood near him so that he could see all of her and smell her. She came and put her hands on his ear lobes and stroked them. 'You good lookin'. You wan' to cheat poor woman like me. I only goin' to give you £5.'

'Madam, I been like you so much. Das why I follow you from de Club. I mean, I like you so much. If you wan' de trinkets . . .'

'You be fine boy. Wha's your name?'

'Dennis. Dennis Odoma. I got a group of frien'. We use to do business togedder. You know what ah mean. Business. Sometime we can get trinket like dis three times in one week, is all by lucky. One of my frien', he's de taxi driver. And de odder three, dey are de business men. De agent.' He laughed and struck a pose. 'When we get somethin', sometime dem can travel far to Port Harcourt or Onitsha to sell de thin' and return for Lagos in two-three day. And de Police will be wastin' de time here for Lagos . . . Am de leader. When I get somethin' like dis dat I like I keep it for myself . . . I also got one gal frien', Sabina. Phew! She's too fine, but I like big woman like you, to keep for outside. I never seen wonderful woman like you. As you walk, is wonderful. As you dress, is *Jagwa*-ful.'

Timidly he placed a hand on her left shoulder. She put her hand over his and lifted it to her breast. She could feel the shiver of fire run through him.

'You like me, so? You like Jagwa-woman? Jagwa woman cos' plenty money. You be only small pickin' of yesterday. Jagua woman is for men in de Senior Service. For Contractor and Politician. You ever see Jagua woman with young man like you who don' put on tie? You just put on shirt and trousers and you don' wear robe, or gold chain round your neck and you come to me and say, I like Jagwa woman. Dem don't like Jagwa woman with sweet-mouth. I already got one boy who talk sweet-mouth. You just come late, so you mus' bring somethin'.'

'I like you, Ma. You fine too much.'

'I fine, but I mus' pay mah rent! I fine, but I must chop and wear fine cloth.' She leaned against him.

'I love you, Ma.' She felt his hot hand, massaging her left breast. He leaned on her hair, smothering it with kisses.

'Gently, don' rough me. Senior Service man never use' to rough lady. Contractor never use' to rough lady. Jagwa woman must be handle' gently, with respect.'

'Yes, Ma. But your breast stand like dat of virgin.'

'Like your gal frien' breast?'

'Fine pass! Fine pass my gal frien' breast. I love you, Ma. Since I seen you . . . Since you comin' to de *Tropicana* with one young man.'

'Freddie, my darlin' Freddie. He gone to U.K. for study de law.'

'Since dat time, I been like you, but I fear—'

'What work you doin' in Lagos?'

'Ah got no work. Am an independent man.'

'And you got money to give Jagwa woman?'

'I love you, Ma. God kin help me fin' somethin' to please you. If you like de trinket, Ma . . . You kin take am.'

'I tenk you,' said Jagua. She took out the box again and ran the tips of her fingers over the glittering surfaces. She put the earrings on and admired them in the mirror. 'Tell me, Mr. Dennis. I no understan' de kind of business you say you an' your friends doin'. I mean, you tell me about your frien' who drive taxi and the other frien' that he got, and you tell me about your gal friend, but . . . I begin to wonder. Tell me true, Dennis.' She took his head in her hands and kissed his lips. 'What kind business you doin'? If you breakin' house, is no shame. I know plenty people who's in de business. Dem gather in de *Tropicana*. Yes, I use' to see dem. If is so, den when you got gold like dis one, you kin bring and we kin do business. You see?'

'Yes,' murmured Dennis, seeking another kiss.

'You kin come here. I will give you small sweet somethin'. I know what you want! An' you kin get am from me, sweet pass your gal frien' who got no experience of de men. I will give you sweet somethin' to turn your head, you kin almos' drive your gal frien' away! Have no fear, you safe wit' me. Your gal frien' will not know. Even self, your wife! She kin see me and we pass an' salute, and she kin not know. Das what Jagua woman is for. She kin keep de secret of de men, and nobody fit find out. You hear dat. You safe with me, if you give me what I want.'

'Ah promise.' She kissed him with fire on her lips. His hand went limp under her chemise for a moment. Then the strength returned and he tore it open and saw the Venus of a body. 'God done make you Jagwa.'

'Gently!' whispered Jagua. 'I been dancing dis night. I jus' return from travel, an' I tire. I tell you, I be woman for Senior Service men; and Contractor and—'

'I won't handle you rough, I promise. True!'

She liked the dark frown on his face. 'Freddie never rough with me. Freddie's a gentleman.'

'Who's Freddie? Oh, you mean de man in Englan'? Yes, I use to see you and him in de *Tropicana*, and I always jealous.'

'He's in England now, reading de law. And you kin taste what 'e use to chop every night before he come back an' marry me proper.'

'You be real Jagwa,' said young Dennis, and the words were sweet in her ear. 'You deal with men who got class.'

'Is late now,' she said. 'You sleepin' here? Or . . .'

'No. I only stoppin' with you for some time.'

'Why you not sleepin'? You want to scratch me, den when my body get up you lef' me an' go? Is because of your gal? Why you tell me you don' love her? You fear her! . . . One day I mus' go and see dat Sabina. I wan' to know what she like.'

She felt his eyes like two hot loaves of coal from a blacksmith's forge. The white-hot eyes of desire followed her as she bolted the door and slipped behind the mosquito net.

17

The day Rosa came, Jagua was sitting in the kitchen turning over a huge lobster in the frying pan. The kitchen was enveloped in grey suffocating smoke and anyone who passed by caught a whiff of the peppery and appetizing aroma of the lobster. Jagua liked showing off her cooking. She had just come in from the once-in-four-days market by the lagoon, and the greens and tomatoes, the fresh fish and the plantains, were stacked in a basket at her feet. She heard a noise, and looking up, saw this young woman heaving her suitcase up the stairs.

'Ah wait, wait, wait. I don' hear no news from you, so ah come. Am never get any place yet. Remember as you promise to fin' me place when we meet in de *Tropicana*?'

'Ah remember. Put your box in de parlour. I busy cookin'.'

Without ado, Rosa pushed her suitcase against a wall, came into the kitchen, took the knife from Jagua's hands, and began cutting up the meat. Then she ground the pepper, and the egusi, the tomatoes and the krafish for the stew, wiping her hands on her cloth and singing to the rhythm of the grindstone. Jagua liked her cheerfulness instantly. Rosa could be arrogant – with the looks she had. But instead she chose to be friendly and to show respect for someone older and more experienced than she was. Jagua smiled at her. True, she did not look very attractive now – in the kitchen and without make-up. But she had a certain elegance and Jagua had seen her at the *Tropicana* and she knew that men liked her small, rather slim figure. At first, Jagua was shamelessly jealous of her. But soon she began to see her as someone who could be a useful partner. She visualized something akin to 'retirement' and 'pension' on Rosa's work.

After one week, Rosa was still trekking the streets and searching for lodgings. Jagua did not complain because she had always wanted a companion since Freddie left, and Rosa seemed to her to be the right kind, though she could not always trust her women friends.

Sometimes Rosa brought in a man – in the afternoon, when Jagua was away. Jagua had often seen her flourishing the money which she took great care to put away because she had not yet collected enough to 'advance' a landlord with six months' rent on a room. One of these young men Jagua observed again and again – always in his college blazer, no matter how stifling the heat.

One afternoon, when Jagua was at home resting, she heard Rosa coming in with the young man in the blazer. Jagua slid down from the bed and put on her clothes. The young man looked to her like one of the Lagos intellectuals. She could have sworn that he attended the British Council Lecture Freddie had taken her to hear. He wore his hair high and talked grammatically. Jagua had grown to know his face now and to accept him as Rosa's young 'steady'. Nervously Rosa sat with him for a while and Jagua could feel that Rosa wanted her out of the way.

What to do, Jagua wondered. Yes. She would go and see a young man, herself. Young men were becoming the thing, and with Freddie 4000 miles away, Dennis Odoma of the trinkets would serve. She would go down to Obanla where Dennis lived and see his group – the taxi driver and the gorgeous gal frien' and the whole group he had talked about. She felt a new thrill in knowing that young Dennis who called her Ma and bedded her, giving her trinkets, was perhaps a dangerous criminal. But she could not see him with a policewoman's eyes. To her, he was a strangely disturbing young man with grandiose ideas of his attractiveness and power. Thieves usually rested in the afternoons, so she might just be lucky to meet them at home.

She got off the bus at Yaba and walked through a grove of trees to Obanla where in a derelict unlighted part of Lagos, Dennis lived. When she knocked at the door, a girl, slim, in tight jeans and tighter T-singlet, answered. Jagua guessed that this must be the girl Dennis had talked about.

She was chewing gum, splitting it with a rhythmic click so that her teeth – big pearls – flashed periodically. 'Who you want?' Her skin was oily with cream and her hair had been newly dressed and glossy black. She was all lips, soft, aggressively kissable.

Jagua instantly felt an outsider. 'I wan' Dennis.'

'He busy. What you want him for?'

'Jus' to see am.'

Jagua stood looking beyond Sabina at the long corridor which all the rooms faced. There are places in Lagos City where any strange person – black or white – may not go without being instantly identified as a stranger and his movements watched minutely until he leaves. Obanla was one such place. As Jagua stood there she saw doors opening and shutting all along the corridor. Heads peeped out and vanished once again. All was silence. She was the stranger here among Dennis Odoma's thieves. Yet she had been told that Obanla was the home of a number of highly reputed practising barristers, engineers and business men. These were the men who shrouded the underworld character of Obanla in a respectable cloak. She had been told that no one living in Obanla had ever complained of losing anything to the thieves. In fact, the story went that any of them who dared to steal in Obanla was punished by the gang for breaking the code. The corridor seemed to get darker with the silence.

'Wait me,' said the girl.

She turned her full back on Jagua. It was a back filled with lust. She did not have big hips, her hips were merely out of proportion to her slimness. The jeans clung tight and when she walked, each tremendous lobe of her buttocks contracted against the garment, just failing to rend it before the weight shifted to the next foot. She walked slowly, elastically and with enraging self-consciousness. Jagua felt a rush of jealous blood to her eyes. Oh, for youth! When she was younger, girls like these could never dare hold a candle to her in looks or in lust appeal. But she had to admit that Dennis had made a juicy choice, someone from the new generation.

A moment later, Dennis appeared, smiling. Behind him were three men. 'You come to see us today, Ma!'

'De gal sed you busy.'

'Oh, Sabina? Don' min' her . . . Come inside.'

He wore a texan shirt, very narrow trousers and Italian shoes. He had grown whiskers since she last saw him and his breath smelled of home-distilled gin, reminding her of Bagana and

Krinameh without the decanters of the Victorian showpiece. The room in which he led her smelled even more strongly of O.H.M.S. At first she could not see clearly but soon her eyes grew accustomed to shapes and objects and it was like being in an expensive shop. She made out the radiogram standing in the corner and saw one of the men loading ten records into it. Soon the craziest *High-life* record began to blare from the instrument. A drink was pushed into Jagua's hands. The girl in the tight jeans began dancing, contorting her body into lascivious postures, her lips agape, her eyes shiny and transported with ecstasy. She was wriggling alone and Dennis paid no attention to her. One of the men shuffled towards her and seized her, himself contorting to her rhythm.

Dennis bowed over Jagua's hand and with his fingertips took her and danced with dignity and respect. 'Me and my friends, we talking when you knock.'

He showed her his special group of friends. One of them was the taxi driver. He pointed at him, sitting dazed in a corner, a mere shape. He had been out all night, Dennis told her. This taxi driver had a wife who was extremely beautiful. She had once won a beauty contest, she had seen the world; but now she decided to settle down with a taxi driver. Was that not funny, Dennis asked her? A beauty queen marrying a taxi driver, he laughed.

'We jus' passin' time, till night come.'

At that moment they heard the sound of a police siren just outside. Instantly the boys dispersed into their various rooms. Jagua saw Sabina leap into the next room and pull up a ladder from somewhere. Up the steps she climbed, lithe as a cat, and vanished through a hatch in the roof. Even the record player had stopped, the record jammed in it.

The sliding panel glided with precision into place and the ceiling assumed its normal shape. The rooms were all empty and the luminous eyes were trained expectantly on the door. Only Jagua and Dennis remained in the room. They sat tense while police boots thudded on the pavement outside. There were at least twelve uniformed men and they showed Dennis the search warrant. The whole village had come to the door to watch them.

Jagua admired the nerve of Dennis. He remained calm and completely unflustered. 'Upon Information Received' the policemen had come to Obanla to search the lodgings of Dennis Odoma and his friends. They took down all the boxes, opened them and looked inside, threw around the photographs, asked questions, then all went back into the Black Maria and drove off.

Before the van had turned the corner, panels began to slide. The taxi driver was the first to come into the room and hand over a small packet to Dennis who handed it over to Jagua with a smile.

'Das what dey lookin' for,' he said. 'You know what to do with dis.'

Jagua tore away the wrapping. The gold trinkets sparkled even more elaborately than those Dennis had given her the other night.

'Wonderful! I goin' to take dem to goldsmith to buy an' melt. An' you kin have de money.'

'Das alright! You don't charge me commission?'

Jagua laughed. 'Plenty time. Make we sell de thin' first'.'

The taxi driver gripped Dennis by the arm. 'Masta . . . Masta, what about tonight? What time you wan' me for bring de taxi?'

'Is better we leave after twelve o'clock night,' Dennis said.

The taxi driver looked anxious. 'Is too early. I tink de bes' time is two o'clock midnight, so dat de shop kin close and de night watchman begin feel sleep. You know dem use to keep late in dat area of Lagos. Plenty pub-houses.'

Jagua realized that they were planning a raid. She gathered from their talk that it was a shop they were going to burgle: not for goods, but for money. The taxi driver kept reminding Dennis that he had actually seen the shop owner put away at least £1000 in notes, in a strongbox and that he was sure the strongbox 'slept' in the shop. They talked cold-bloodedly, not minding the presence of Jagua.

Jagua had the sensation of a man who has suddenly opened the door of a strange room and found a man and woman in bed, naked and intertwined. The difference lay in her being unable to shut the door quickly enough on what she had seen and heard. Consequently she remained with her self-inflicted embarrassment.

From one of the rooms, a woman was shouting abuses at the taxi driver, projecting her voice so that it came vividly into the room and became a presence. She was calling him lazy and useless, threatening to pack her things and leave him. It was the taxi driver's wife, Dennis explained. She was in a fighting mood because she had been wanting to buy an outfit costing £100 but the taxi driver could not find the money. The outfit had been described as a funeral-ceremony dress, and the woman was bound to attend as she was the most important relation of the dead man.

'Thief that you are!' came the abusive words in Yoruba. Jagua looked at the face of the taxi driver. She saw on it the fear of a man who feels too small for the woman he has taken. 'I left all better men to come and marry you, you're not glad! You should rejoice! . . . This is how you make me go naked every day while other women dress up and I feel shame and cannot show my face where they are. Rogue, that you are! You must get me that £100 if not go to the shop yourself and buy me the *Asho-Ebi*. If you don't buy it, there are men who will, you hear that! Don't think you're the only one I hope upon, you idiot! When a beauty queen like myself come to this wretched house and sleep with dirty man like you, who get nothing in his pocket, you think my life is finished . . .'

Dennis turned his face in the direction of the noise which had become unbearable. 'You there, Bintu! . . . Shut up there, you hear? We got a decent lady here. You disgracin' we before her!'

'Useless man!' went on the voice. 'You drive taxi from morning till night! You carry women free and dem give you no money. You're only splitting their legs in their rooms. When you do that whose going to buy de petrol? Useless ass!'

Jagua saw the manner in which Dennis left the room. She heard a door slam, heard the sound of blows and the whimpering of the woman. A moment later, she raced out in her chemise, her face swollen and the Obanla crowd again gathered at the door to see. The taxi driver held Dennis by the arm. 'I beg you. Leave her. If you follow de mouth of woman, you will commit murder. Let her talk! Is good for her. She's me own wife, and is me she cursing.'

'Come on! Get back into de room!' shouted Dennis. Jagua saw him in a new light, as one to whom all the gang showed respect. 'An' if I hear anodder word from you, I come inside an' kill you!'

Sabina came towards Dennis, wiggling her full hips. She slipped her hand under his arm and rubbed her small hard bust against him. She led him back to the room where Jagua waited patiently.

'As I was saying,' Dennis began. 'Now, where was I?'

Jagua put the packet of trinkets in her bag. 'I got to be goin' now. I goin' to take dis to de goldsmith an' see what I kin do.'

Dennis frowned. 'Jagua, I sorry about all de noise. Dat woman tryin' to bring confusion for our business. She trying to drive we to do what we not ready for. Everythin' person do in dis world got to be done with sense.'

'Don' worry,' said Jagua.

'You treat her well!' Sabina giggled. She was sitting on the floor, Indian fashion. 'You flog de okro soup out of her mout'. Nex' time she mus' know how to talk!'

Jagua said: 'I goin' now, Dennis. When you come to de house, I goin' to tell you what de goldsmith say.'

She got out of the taxi, slid past the market that stank of decaying leaves and fish. Leaving the noise behind her, she entered the goldsmith's shop, a dark alcove between a tailor and a barber. The goldsmith had been working for some time and now he got up as she entered. She produced the packet and handed it over, sitting in the musty office.

He unwrapped the packet with careful hands, and examined it. 'Not gold!' he said, folding it back and handing it to her. 'Ordinary pan. Not gold at all.'

'Nonsense!' said Jagua, indignant. 'Jus' say you go' no money to pay.'

'Who say I got no money. All right, bring let me see.'

Jagua handed back the case. The goldsmith looked at it carelessly, then said: 'I give you ten poun'.'

'You think I need money so much? You don' see de clothes I puttin' on? If you don't give me £50 I go with my thin'.'

The goldsmith went outside and consulted with three of his friends. Jagua saw that she had something valuable. She sat tight while the men talked. Then they took the trinkets indoors and were there a long time. Jagua knew that this was the best time to get a good sum for them because the ram festival was nearing and women would be looking for such jewellery. All the smith needed to do was melt them and bring them out in new designs.

She heard a murmur and they came into the shop. 'All right,' said the goldsmith. 'Twenty pounds, last!'

Jagua did not so much as look at him. At one point they shouted abuses at each other. But two hours later when she left the shop, she had thirty-five pounds in her bag.

18

Jagua did not see Dennis till two days afterwards. As soon as he came into the room, Rosa slipped out. There was something terrifying about his looks that evening.

'Wat happen, Dennis. Your face dark like you loss some big money – or person.'

'Our taxi driver,' Dennis said. 'He go out las' night. Dem kill him, throw way his body for gutter.'

Jagua held her head in her hands and shrieked. Rosa ran back into the room post-haste. 'Why you cry so, Ma?' She walked on tiptoe as if to still the noise she brought along with her. Jagua and Dennis were silent, looking at the carpet.

'Wa's wrong, Ma?' Rosa asked again. She sat down. 'Wa's wrong, Ma? Somebody die? You cry like somebody die! . . .'

Dennis turned to her. 'Dem kill our taxi driver.'

'Lord a' mercy!' Rosa folded her arms over her bosom.

Dennis talked quietly, telling how it had all started with the taxi driver's wife, nagging him about money. There was to be an outing for a dead relation, the end of the period of mourning for the widow. Custom demanded that a dress be prescribed for all the women. The widow's relatives assembled and they chose an outfit costing one hundred pounds each. It consisted of damask and velvet, nylons and gold trinkets. The taxi driver had no money. His wife, who was the most important relation of the widow, would not hear of it. She threatened to leave him if he did not find the money within two days. One hundred pounds within two days. She was always threatening to leave him, anyhow. Always Dennis had to settle their quarrels. Jagua had seen him try to discipline her because the driver himself was so weak where she was concerned. She kept up her nagging the whole of that night and finally the taxi driver pressed Dennis to let them go and raid the shop where he had seen the woman stowing away £1000 in a strongbox; but Dennis did not feel like going, and finally they went without him. They did not know the woman employed armed men who slept inside the shop. The taxi driver was stabbed and thrown into the street-gutter with the open drain. And there they found him in the morning.

That was the story Dennis had to tell. Lagos was 'hot' for them now because the police were alert and hungering for an arrest, around Obanla.

'Wat of de taxi-driver wife?' Jagua asked.

'She pack her thin' and run, quick-quick.' He smiled. 'But Sabina tell me she know where de woman's hiding. De two of dem be proper enemy.'

'You mean Sabina and de taxi-driver wife? . . . So she won' come back?'

'No, she say she don' want any trouble.'

Jagua sighed. 'She born any child for him?'

'Yes,' said Dennis. 'Dat woman born pickin' like fowl. Every year she mus' born one child. She already born three pickin' for him. Before dat, she born anodder three pickin' for odder men who she marry, or some lover man. But she no care for de pickin', only to dress herself. She run away now and hide, but my gal kin fin' her out. Anywhere she see clothes, money, and chop, she don' mind. She will live there. When she an' de taxi driver begin, de man use to make about £10 a day. She chop all him money finish and begin talk rot. Das why I vex las' time and beat her. Am sure she mus' go dis burial ceremony. She mus' fin' some man to give am de £100. Dat gal! She don' care at all, for anythin'. Only to dress herself, fine! And to look man face.'

Jagua gave Rosa a meaning glance and Rosa left them alone. From under the pillow Jagua took out a bulging envelope and handed it to Dennis. 'Count de money. Is £35; das all dem give me.'

He took the money from her and as he began counting, she looked at the determined and angry set of his brow.

Dennis, I wan' to tell you somethin'. Dis kind of life dat you follow, you think is a good life.'

Dennis smiled. 'What you wan' me to do? To go an' be clerk? Awright! I already try to find work. Dem ask me to bring bribe-money. I give one man ten pound, and he chop de money and he no fin' work for me. How I go do? I mus' chop. Myself and de taxi man who die, sometime we kin make one hundred pound by Saturday. Sometime, we don' see anythin'. But we live happy. I got my gal, Sabina, and she love me well. She say dat any day de police catch me, she goin' to kill herself. Before I meet her she never know man. I disvirgin' her. She don' believe any odder man live in dis worl' only me. She love me. I got dat whole house. Me and de taxi man who die, and de boys, we rent de place and we pay our own rent, regular. We never look money in de face, an' say "dis money is too much". We jus' spen', to get anythin' we want. Anythin'. So why I worry? De day dat de policeman catch we, we go. Is all de same, whedder we live in cell or outside de cell.'

Jagua watched his expressive hands. Somehow she felt that this young man's philosophy was intricately bound up with hers. He lived for the moment, intensely, desperately. He had no use for conventional methods of thinking. 'What you say is true,' she told him. With her elderly woman's heart, she could not bear to see this young boy who could well be her son, sacrificed on the altar of recklessness. For she was sure that he must die – and swifty too – if he kept this life up. 'Wat you say, is true, Dennis. But I beg of you to stop dis business. Take de taxi driver case as warnin', you hear me? Stop and go do hones' work, so you kin live long and help your modder in her ol' age. Is plenty work in Lagos, though de money not like de kind you use to. But suppose dem kill you one night, take knife open you belly so de breeze rush inside, what your modder goin' to say?'

'Is jus' my bad luck, das all,' Dennis said.

'You been in de army before?'

'Yes, I go for Burma campaign, but I desert.' He gave a short laugh.

Jagua was staggered by his detachment. 'Dennis, I beg you. Take dis as warning and stop. Plenty fine work for Lagos. I already tell you. My boy frien' Freddie, is in England. He got no money, but is ambitious. Is an ordinary teacher. He try, try, till God give him luck and he fin' way to go U.K. Is in England now. He soon return as lawyer. I like man who try to go forward in de worl', by honest way. For de sake of dat gal Sabina who love you, you kin try to be good.'

Dennis smiled. 'Sabina no min' at all. She know everythin' and she like de fas' life. You ever seen her dance in de *Tropicana*? I don' mean, in de house. Dat one is small thin'. I mean in de *Tropicana*. De white men use to crase for her. But I don' let her mix her blood. Sabina love me, because of my 'business'. She love me because I young and wild and I got no fear of anythin'. She too, she got no fear in her blood. She fear nobody; and she strong like leopard! God!'

He had been carried away, and now Jagua saw that it was useless trying to make him change his mind. 'Is all right – O!' she said in desperation. 'We live to see.'

Jagua said to him, 'Dennis, you better go now. I jus' remember de man keepin' me soon come now.' She was terrified of him now. He could easily contaminate her with his frightening life. She knew he could spoil her chances with men who mattered. 'De man keepin' me in dis house soon come, Dennis. He use to come here in de evenin' time, like dis. So I beg you, no vex. You kin come anodder time.'

'I see you again,' Dennis said. But he was still standing there when 'the man keeping her' came into the room.

Jagua immediately bridled and swung her hips to delight him and winked at him intimately. Soon after she returned from Bagana Uncle Taiwo had become so taken with her 'provincialness' and marvellous skin that he spent first one night, then two nights with her and now she saw him daily in her room. He said he liked her because she was 'not like Lagos women'.

'I mus' go now,' said Dennis.

And when he had left: 'Jagua, who's de young man?'

'Jus' my brodder, Uncle Taiwo.'

'Your brodder who sleep wit' you on de same bed, not so?' And he roared with laughter.

Uncle Taiwo was not a young man. He had seen life and in his fifty odd years he had developed a manner she liked. He was not stingy with money. She knew him as the Party Agent for O.P. 2, one of the big political parties in Lagos. He rode a Pontiac and lavished a lot of campaign money in the name of the Party. Although the elections were still far away, he told Jagua that this was the time to do all the groundwork; and therefore he gave himself little or no rest, save when he came 'here' to see her.

She came near and caressed his cheeks. 'You too jealous, jus' like young man. What I will do wit' small boy like dat. Is my brodder, I swear. Don't you trust me?'

'I glad say he be your brodder. God save 'im if he's not. I go jus' kill am one time. Ah go make trouble for 'im till he ron away from dis Lagos. You tink I goin' to pay rent and furnish dis house for small boy to come when I turn me back? No fear!' And again he roared with laughter.

'Is only me brodder, Uncle Taiwo. He come an' tell me say our Senior Brodder done die for we country.'

Uncle Taiwo's face did not soften and she knew he did not believe her. She was almost certain that men she picked up in Lagos usually knew nothing about her near or distant relations; but Uncle Taiwo knew about Freddie because it was he who had taken her to the airport when he left. At first when he began coming to her, he asked questions about him; whether she heard from him, how he was . . . but now Freddie's name seldom came up for discussion. He was beginning to regard himself as the rightful lover, always jealous. She got around him by mothering him. She went over now and sat on his knee, rubbing her thinly clad hips into his thighs. She threw one arm over his shoulder, so that her left breast snuggled close to his lips. Presently she felt his thick, rough lips close on the nipple. 'A dog with food in his mouth does not bark,' went the proverb.

She felt the powerful arms binding her towards him, smelt the vapours from the voluminous robes that now swallowed her.

★

In the middle of the night she heard a knock on the door. She would not get up till the caller shifted to the window. She glanced at Uncle Taiwo. The weak blue bedroom light rested on the globular blobs of fat, the face like a baby's unlined and innocent looking, the thick rough lips parted and snoring, revealing large front teeth. He was gone, transported to another land. She had mothered him well.

She slipped out in a single cloth tied under the arms and went to the door. Dennis Odoma was standing there. She placed a hand over her mouth to avoid shouting at him. He even tried to push past her into the room, but she pressed him back with her bosom.

'Where you goin? You don' know my man is in de bed?' She was hissing like a cobra.

'Always some man in de bed!' Dennis growled. 'Some man in de bed! You will die with some man in de bed one day. Look me!' He raised his arm then, and her glance caught the silver bangle on his wrist. Jagua recognised the handcuffs.

'Dennis! . . .'

'De police catch me, an' I ron away from dem. Das all. I come to warn you, sometime, dem will come here, come to ask you 'bout me. You mus' tell dem, you know nothin'. You hear?'

'God!' breathed Jagua, not daring to raise her voice for fear of waking Uncle Taiwo. 'You wound de policeman? Tell me true word, Dennis!'

'Ah knock 'im down. I don' know. Sometime he wound, or die. Not my lookout. All policeman be thief, so I don't use to sorry for dem. If to say ah give am small money, he for lef' me.'

'Is officer of de law you wound, Dennis; das serious you know. De Government no go let you go free, however!'

'I don' care.' He came nearer. 'Lissen, Jagua. Since dem arrest me, I don' see Sabina and she take de gun.'

Jagua recoiled. 'De gun?'

'Only small revolver dat we tief from army barrack. I hide am for some place an' when I go look, is gone. Only Sabina know de place.' He frowned, then began talking intensely. 'I know dat gal goin' to do somethin', das why I fear. She tell me dat if ever dem catch me she goin' to take her life. Lissen, Jagua. I beg you if she reach here to ask of me, tell am not to worry 'bout me. Try to keep am happy. De gal never reach nineteen year. She too young to die.'

He turned and was off into the darkness. She broke down then. The tears came. She leaned against the doorpost and let them flow. Then, with her cloth, she wiped her tears and went back to the bed, bolting the door firmly behind her. Uncle Taiwo made some protest, and Jagua told him she had gone to ease herself. But she was unable to sleep any more that night for worry. If the police came, what would they ask her? Would they want to take her to the station? What had really happened between Dennis and the police officer? Had she not warned him to give up this reckless kind of life? Now it was too late. An officer of the law! The Government would never rest till they had got Dennis. He could never escape with this one because the Government must protect the policemen who never carry arms.

She had been sure all along that it was coming to this. Why, why had she got her fortunes entwined with those of this dashing but tragic young man? She knew now. She knew that if a girl went to *Tropicana* every day, that girl was a pawn; a pawn in the hands of criminals, Senior Service men, contractors, thieves, detectives, liars, cheats, the rabble, the scum of the country's grasping hands and headlong rush to 'civilisation', 'sophistication', and all the falsehood it implied. She turned over in her bed, and every time she turned it seemed to her that the meshes twined even more remorselessly. Dennis. Jagwa. Rolled into a ball of steel and nylon cords, inseparable, confused.

Uncle Taiwo had left in the morning when the police called. Jagua's room with the unopened windows smelt a man smell with erotic odours.

'Where's Dennis Odoma?'

'Why you askin' me, you tink I know where he live. Go find him in his own house!'

'We gone there, we don't see him. Tell us where we kin fin' him. We got information he use to sleep here.'

'He don' sleep here. But what happen? Why you findin' him so hot-hot?'

'Dem go tief. When dem reach there, policeman catch Dennis. We been findin' him for long time now. At las' de policeman catch him and know him; to make sure he don' ron away, de police hand-cuff him to hisself. Dennis wound de policeman and run away with handcuff. The policeman is in hospital now, on danger list.'

They brushed past her into the room as if the picture of the law officer in hospital had awakened a new flood of vengeance against the thieves. Jagua watched them turn up the carpet and shift the radiogram. Then they stamped out.

Jagua flung after them. 'Go an' ask Sabina; she mus' know.'

'Sabina?'

'Him gal frien'.' Jagua felt no qualms of conscience in betraying the girl she envied so much. 'Dem live togedder for de same house. Sabina's de name.'

The policeman laughed. 'So you never hear?'

'No, what happen?'

'Why you think we lookin' for Dennis so hot-hot? Sabina take revolver. She go to de place where dem makin' some ceremony for somebody who die. She shoot one woman dere, den shoot herself. She say is de woman who make Dennis thief. I think dat Sabina crase. Such fine gal, an' so young: go waste her life for nothin' sake!'

'Sabina, kill . . . woman – and kill herself, for Dennis?'

This is a dream, Jagua told herself. A mad dream, a nightmare. She saw Sabina again in her jeans with the pendulous buttocks, the face overlaid with too much cold cream, the lips sensuously kissable, with a blot of too-bright lipstick. A girl who was content to live her life among bed-springs, surrounded by fast drinks and chains of cigarettes. Sabina arriving at the funeral ceremony, incongruously dressed. The other women would be in their deckings of gold and gossamer nylon, winking from made-up eyes, holding the cocktail glasses with the tips of their nails. Then the one she sought, coming in – the ex-beauty queen. A momentary exchange of words, and then 'Have it, now! . . .' The recoil of the gun, the sudden diving for safety. And Sabina, alone with the overturned chair and tables and the writhing wife of the dead taxi driver, standing in that wreckage like a messenger from Lucifer's fold. And the next instant turning the little weapon on her breast.

'You people, you get strong mind! I don' fit, at all!'

From the day when the twelve policemen came to search them and Dennis and Sabina showed no fear – even though they had the missing trinkets – Jagua lived in awe and admiration of them, especially of Sabina, the iron-nerved girl in her teens.

When Uncle Taiwo came back in the evening, he told Jagua that if she called herself his woman, she must do her best in every way to help win him votes from the women. She could go round now and begin to give door-to-door talks.

Jagua was in no mood now for such talk. 'Uncle Taiwo, I beg you. I receive bad news from home. I'm not in de mood.'

'I goin' to teach you everythin' about politics. You think you know nothin' about politics; and you call yourself Lagos woman!' He roared with laughter, and roared again and she was embarrassed because his laughter told her that it was a shameful thing not to be interested in the fortunes of the city. He promised to take her to campaign meetings so that she could see for herself, and afterwards they would go to the *Tropicana* to dance.

They went the following night and afterwards they sat in the *Tropicana*. It was too early but the chairs and tables were rapidly filling up. Someone who sat with them was talking about Freddie and he was certain Freddie had returned from England, with a white wife. Jagua's heart leapt uncontrollably. She could not contradict him. Anything could happen to a young man who left Nigeria and went to stay in England for eighteen months.

'He only been gone eighteen month,' she said. 'How he manage return so quick? I don' think is Freddie you see.'

She downed her beer and turned her attention to the guitar and the big drums which dwarfed the drum-beater of Jimo Ladi and his Leopards. Men and women on the dance floor were wiggling as though they wished to propel their hips away from the rest of their bodies. A girl broke away from her partner in a heated improvisation. She placed a hand on her navel and began gyrating her hips back and forth. She had big hips, rendered out of proportion by the huge bundle of velvet she had tied. The men formed a ring round her and cheered. She threw her head back, far back, forming almost a wrestler's bridge and how she maintained her balance, Jagua could never tell. Oh, it was good to be young. The men loved her. They were conquered.

'De lates' dance,' remarked Uncle Taiwo. 'Well, how you like our campaign meetin'?'

'Is nice. Plenty people come; and you give dem plenty money so dem kin vote for you. But if dem don' vote, how you kin know? Dey jus' chop your money for nothin'.'

'Dem will vote. Sure. And for me too. I goin' to win de seat in Obanla Constituency, easy. Out of all de sixty seat, das de one we sure of in O.P. 2.'

'I wish you good luck.'

They did not leave the *Tropicana* until three in the morning. They were heading for the gate when suddenly the rhythm changed. No more trumpets, no more guitars, no more saxophones. Drums. Drums only. The whisper went round. The *Tropicana* was going to put on a little show. Jagua – when she heard it was going to be a masquerade dance – begged Uncle Taiwo to let them stay. She dragged him back to their seat. He had been complaining of sleepiness and now he began grumbling aloud. The dance would be primitive, not the thing for the *Tropicana*, he told her.

Jagua was all ears. Everyone had sat down, gazing at the stage. Brisk, came the drumming. Brisk, rhythmic, fantastic, driven, impelled by some crazy devils. Relentless, brisk: and suddenly, the dancer was there. No! Not a dancer; just a thin bamboo screen, an elliptical screen, painted, stamped with all the existentialist badges and the cubist doctrine. A bamboo screen that hid a secret and stood in the middle of the stage. Two masquerades in chalk-red and blue, surrounded the screen, chanting to it, waving horse-tails. Brisk, came the drumming. Brisk. Incessant, impelling the screen into a sweeping whirlwind of movement, sneezing along, occasionally freezing, dead stop. The masquerades staring with fixed eye and gaping lip, bewildered. What was this? Neither male nor female, a screen, a bamboo screen of reeds in yellow ochre and dabbed with all kinds of weird colours. Only once – and barely for a wink – did Jagua manage to catch a glimpse of the human feet beneath the screen. A man's feet – or a woman's? Rhythm. More maddening rhythm. The screen, normally requiring more than one acre of land in which to sweep along and to recreate the wind, the storm, the destruction of crops by the rain.

When this dance was performed in the street, in its natural environment, the hens and the chicks, and the dogs and the children, fled to the nearest shelter, hurrying away from the whirlwind juju. *Brrr-Ga-gaan!* came the drumming. *Brrr-Ga-gaan!* It never varied, except to speed up; and suddenly it had swept out of the stage amidst thunderous applause.

Jagua breathed. She came back to Lagos once more. She had been in Ogabu, Bagana, Krinameh, Onitsha, all homes of traditional dancing. Something of each of those towns had been recaptured by the *Tropicana* dancer. On Uncle Taiwo's face she saw a look of boredom.

'Is all nonsense! We don' come here to see dat. We come to hear *High-life* and jazz, das all! Give us music! Where's Jimo Ladi?'

A man began arguing with him, telling him that jazz had its origins in that kind of fetish dancing, that this was a throwback to the birth-days of jazz. Uncle Taiwo yawned. 'Music! Give us *real* music!'

'You jus' heard real music,' Jagua told him. 'Jus' like in me own country. We get nearly de same kin' of dance.'

'Is bushman dancing!' said Uncle Taiwo.

He roared with laughter, but the tenor saxophone of Jimo Ladi drowned his mirth. Jagua took him by the hand and said, 'I feelin' sleep now. Le's go . . .'

19

Almost six months later Jagua was walking home from the *Tropicana*. She heard a car stop behind her.

'Hello, is that you, Jagua?'

The face was in darkness, but the voice was familiar. It was Freddie. She could never mistake the voice. She went nearer and peered in, remembering one day, almost two years ago when she had been the victim of a dirty trick.

'I see you, an' I not quite sure whedder it be you.' He was holding the door open for her. 'Remember de day when me an' my frien' pick you up here? Dis same street!' He laughed. 'De things we do when we young—'

'So you done become ol' man, in two year?'

'Englan' make me ol' man with experience . . .'

'Which day you return?'

'Today make six days only.'

'Eheh! So I think! We hear rumour 'bout six months ago say you done come back with white woman. Somebody tell we for Club.' She looked closely at him. He was – if anything – younger-looking. The underfed look was gone. 'You very fine now, Freddie.'

'Is because I got woman who look after me.'

'Yes, I hear about de white woman you marry.'

'If you call Nancy, white woman; den is true. She come an' meet me for England, and she studyin' like me, so we plan our life together. She born me two pickin'. De young one is only three month.'

Somehow it did not hurt her. Too much had happened since Freddie had gone away. What she felt now was a mixture of spite and hate, but it was very slow in coming. Depending upon how Freddie conducted himself, it might change.

'Nancy Oll suit you. She young, and her bobby stand straight; not like we ol' women.' She must find a way of humiliating Freddie, but it must come slowly and naturally. Something like poison in a glass of wine. 'But remember, Nancy is Sa Leone gal, from Freetown. She no be your country woman.' Jagua was speaking hardly above a whisper.

'All Africa be same, whedder is Sa Leone or Ghana or Nigeria; even Egypt where de people white.'

'How you talk so? Because you just from England come. You talk like politician.'

'Is true. All black man be same. Nancy be our sister. All dat Sa Leone people, dem come from Calabar, and Onitsha and Lagos. Das de port from which dem put dem into big steamer and take dem to go work for America. Is a long time, in de nineteen century. Long, long time ago. De white traders go and sell dem, and dey live dere and born pickin', till one day when dem get dem freedom, de other white men from England bring dem back. De Government people find a place for dem and dem call de place Freetown – because dem free. And das where dem born Nancy Oll.'

Jagua was not listening to him. She was remembering the day at the British Council when she had walked out and Freddie had run after her in anger. That day – in some way – must have marked the beginning of their separation. Freddie with his pursuit of books and lectures, she with her pursuit of the bright lights, and good time. The gulf had never narrowed since that evening.

'Soon as you lef' for U.K. I touch Bagana.'

'You like de place?' He turned off the engine which had been running rather noisily. 'Uncle Namme and Chief Ofubara write me letter. Dem say you settle de quarrel in de family. I hear also dat Chief Ofubara wan' to marry you.'

'Is true, Freddie, but I don' 'gree. He even give me money. He say de money is bride price. But not so is de fashion. Person who want to marry from my place, he mus' go dere for hisself. He mus' meet de fadder of de gal and talk. After dat, if de gal 'gree and the other people 'gree, den he kin talk about bride price. You see?'

'Das why you don' marry him?'

'Not so.' Jagua toyed with the door of the car. 'I don' marry him because I already promise you.' The tears were running to the tips of her eyes and her nose began to leak. She took out a handkerchief and dabbed it over her eyelashes. She saw now that all her friendships in Freddie's absence were inadequate. Dennis Odoma, though young, was no substitute for Freddie Namme. Freddie had more than youth. He had gentility, royal blood, ambition. She noticed how tastefully he was dressed. He still had on the dark coat and dark bow tie he must have been wearing in a cold climate. London had taught him something, to care a little more for his personal appearance. His profession exalted that trait too. This was the dream she had always wanted. But now here he was and she had become an outsider. 'My England man!' she cried, and began to sob.

Freddie took her into the car.

'Le's reach my place, Freddie. I take God beg you. Le's reach my place! . . .'

'Why you cryin', Jagua?'

'Because I love too much, Freddie. And although ah got sense wit' odder men; with you I just become like fool.' She said no more. He started the car.

'De same place? . . . I drop you dere. I mus' go back to Nancy and de children; dey waitin' in de house for me. Ah love my wife, Jagua.'

She turned her head away from the family picture. 'How you manage when you reach England?'

He told her in a few words how he had 'managed'. The money she had loaned him had helped; but that was only the start. He found that, to get along he had to take a job in London. He got something with London Transport and when he was not working he was trying to read. He was able to live in a two-pounds-a-week room in Paddington, doing his own cooking. The shopping took a lot of time, until Nancy came and they began living together. What really took much of his time was secretarial work for the London branch of the political party O.P. 1.

'Which time you buy car, Freddie?' Jagua ran her fingers over the facia. 'You only jus' return; where you get de money?'

'Is on loan,' Freddie told her. He turned a corner, away from the Main Road. 'Is party car for our people O.P. 1. You know am de candidate for Obanla constituency. Das one reason why I returning at dis time. To contest and to organize.'

'Welcome, Freddie! I glad too much to see you, I nearly die with glad . . . Freddie, I wan' to go sleep wit' you, now, an' see whedder you be same —'

'No more of that nonsense!' A passing car lit up his frowning face. She felt a sudden painful wrench at her heart.

'Freddie, you get de letter I write you?'

'Yes,' he grunted.

'Why you don' reply?'

'Jagua, I reply; sometime you don' get de reply.' They had

entered her street. Jagua recognized the familiar trees. 'Look, Jagua. I will come an' see you nex' time.'

'So what you wan' to do now, as you return? You wan' to forget me, eh? Even as ah help you?' She saw him hesitate, feeling the threat in her voice. Then he stopped the car and held the door open for her to climb out. She got out and the angry words came spitting out her fury. 'You not even goin' to step into harlot woman house? Das what I become in your eye, Freddie! Is good-O! God live above everythin' . . .' She changed the subject. 'Is true you goin' to contest in de election?'

'I goin' to contest in Obanla, sure.'

'Obanla?' Jagua seemed to hear the name for the first time. 'Das where Uncle Taiwo contestin'. And das where Dennis Odoma live.'

'Uncle Taiwo? De same man who bring you to de airport de day I leavin' for U.K.?'

'Yes; is Uncle Taiwo keepin' me and payin' de rent for me. Is a very strong party man and he get plenty money for spend. I don' see how you fit to win from him. I goin' to help him defeat you, Freddie, because me and you not one person any more. Kin you spen' money like him?'

Elections in Lagos, Jagua told him, were not won by wearing smart clothes and appearing distant from the people. You had to show them what you could do for them, before you won. You must associate with everyone, particularly the lowest ones, and regard them as your friends. You must give them the freedom of your time and thought, your car and your room. In such a manner only would you learn how they thought and acted. Uncle Taiwo was working very hard indeed, she told him. Uncle Taiwo was distributing money presents to the people. She told him what happened only last week. She went with him to the court in Obanla and when anyone was fined, Uncle Taiwo promptly paid up the fine. Those men would surely vote for Uncle Taiwo when the time came; and she was sure they would get their friends to vote for this 'good' man. The whole of Obanla was plastered with pictures of Uncle Taiwo and all the women had received matchboxes and cooking stoves with his portrait on them and the schoolchildren exercise books with his portrait. Uncle Taiwo was the man to vote for because he had had a big start already on Freddie whom no one had ever heard about.

Freddie smiled. 'We still got another three month.'

'And anodder thin', Freddie. I goin' to fight you till I die. Me an' Uncle Taiwo. I give you fair warnin'. If you wan' to win, you mus' start now.'

He turned sharply and Jagua saw the expectant spark in his eyes. 'You wan' me to win?'

She turned away. 'No, Freddie. I no wan' you to win.' She saw him sit eagerly forward and frown. She went on. 'Politics not for you, Freddie. You got education. You got culture. You're a gentleman an' proud. Politics be game for dog. And in dis Lagos, is a rough game. De roughest game in de whole worl'. Is smelly an' dirty an' you too clean an' sweet. I speakin' frank to you, Freddie. I don' want you inside at all. I hear rumour dat O.P. 2 wan' to kill one man from your party . . .' She spoke honestly, and hoped Freddie would listen and learn. At some points, Freddie spread his hands and his shoulders tensed as though he meant to interrupt her. But he did not talk. England seemed to have changed him.

Suddenly he said, 'I wan' money quick-quick; an' politics is de only hope.' She saw the flicker in his eye. 'Talkin' about money, Jagua; I aweady write de cheque of all de amount I owe you. Is in de post, registered. You goin' to receive it in a day or two. I thank you for all de help.'

She heard him turn the engine on. The car started to move slowly away. 'So you not comin' into de house?'

'I'll come – nex' time, Jagua.'

And now she saw that England had widened the gulf between them.

20

Jagua sat beside Uncle Taiwo in the Pontiac. On the bonnet the party flag fluttered. On both sides of the street the people interrupted their work to wave at them. *O.P. 2! . . . O.P. 2! . . . Uncle Taiwo on the job!* . . . Jagua felt pleased. They entered the rally ground, fenced high with wire netting. On the rally ground, thousands of people were already massed and above them a man in robes was yelling with the aid of a megaphone. She waited while Uncle Taiwo locked the Pontiac and carried his papers. The O.P. 2 speaker was telling them the issues.

Their rival party O.P. 1 for the Obanla constituency had fielded an Englander, Freddie Namme. He had been studying in England, but did he know the problems of the people of Lagos, after being in residence for a few weeks? In three months' time voters would be called upon to choose a man who would present their views to the Council. It was only in O.P. 2 that such a man was to be found, and his name was Uncle Taiwo! . . . He turned the megaphone towards Jagua and Uncle Taiwo and wild cheering broke out.

When it died down, the speaker promised that if O.P. 2 won there would be bigger markets, education would be free and medical treatment prompt and efficient. There would be wider roads built to all the nooks and corners of the island city so that it would be a real example to the whole world.

Jagua was beginning to like election campaigns. This was one aspect of Lagos life which gave her a chance to exercise her vanity in the sunlight without appearing cheap. When Uncle Taiwo had acknowledged the cheers, he mounted the rostrum. Then he opened his black bag and coming down moved among the people, scattering handfuls of ten shilling notes, like rice grains on a bride. The election ground had become a rugger ground with the printed notes as the ball. Later Jagua asked him where the money came from and he said: 'Is Party money. I give dem de money like dat, so them kin taste what we goin' to do for them, if they vote us into power.' Loyally Jagua followed him, and as they moved on the wild ones closed in behind them, scrambling and fighting.

The campaign continued.

Jagua looked outside her window at the street below. She started back and drew the blinds. Uncle Taiwo watched her with questioning eyes.

'Why you jumpin' about like you seen de devil? Sit down Jagua, le's enjoy our drink!' Slowly he was pouring out her beer. Water had frosted on his drinking glass and was running down the sides in sweat streams. Although the table-fan was turned full on, and directed towards his face, he still mopped his brow with a handkerchief. Jagua could still feel his weight as they had lain together only a moment before. 'You don't fit to talk again, Jagua? I say why you jumpin' from de window like you see de devil?'

'Is Freddie, and—'

Uncle Taiwo dropped his glass. The thin glass broke into fragments and the beer formed little frothy lakes on the carpet. 'My rival! De one who think he kin ruin me. De gentleman of politics!' He roared with laughter. 'What he want here?' His laughter did not impress Jagua who could see that his teeth were clenched.

She picked up the glass pieces and Rosa came in and mopped the floor. Uncle Taiwo rose and went to the window. Both of them looked at the Land Rover, packed full with the wild ones. These youths had the chiselled bodies of fighters. They wore brief shorts and briefer shirts. They were all biceps and calves. They had bull necks. Jagua clutched at Uncle Taiwo's robe. She did not want to think of what would happen the way these two rivals were taking things.

'De boy got some sense, awready!' Uncle Taiwo hissed. 'He got his own bodyguard!'

Jagua knew Uncle Taiwo well enough to detect the unsteadiness in his voice. She saw his eyes darting round the room uneasily as though he wanted to jump into a cupboard. 'You fear dem? You tink dem comin' to beat you up? Uncle, you look like you pissin in your trouser. Well, das how you men do you own politics! You beat your rival with stick. Don' fear. Freddie only making show. He don' get de nerve to beat up anyone. He got too much conscience. Is a gentleman.' Jagua recognized Dennis Odoma among the young toughs. She was glad. It meant the police officer had not yet died. It meant that Dennis was under Freddie's protection. She could sense the mutual advantage to both men. Freddie would gain ground in Obanla, and Dennis would be given expert legal support. She saw Freddie come out of the Land Rover and cross the road. Then she heard a cracking knock on the door. Freddie confronted her in his open neck shirt and thick trousers. He looked handsome and lovable.

'Jagua, I come to salute you an' to keep my promise.'

'Welcome, Freddie.' She knew he must be feeling awkward after their encounter the other night. 'Welcome. You know Uncle Taiwo. He keepin me here. What kin poor woman like me do? I got no work an' you forsake me—'

Freddie extended his hand. 'Jagua said you're my rival for the Obanla seat, aren't you?'

'Definitely! And I'm going to win, hahaha – aaa!' Uncle Taiwo roared out his exaggerated laugh which created the right atmosphere of ease.

They began speaking in what Jagua regarded as 'grammatical English' and she felt immediately excluded. These men: she never could understand them. It was really odd to her, the way they acted. They never seemed to harbour any bitterness about themselves as women did. They called for drinks and Rosa came and brought out two bottles of beer and two clean glasses. She put a bottle and a glass by each man's stool. Deadly rivals, thought Jagua. Look how they drank like two long-lost brothers who had suddenly discovered each other.

When Freddie glanced at her, she thought she could read in his eyes the faintest spark of desire for her. She was wearing her dressing gown, and when she sat down she chose a corner directly in his line of gaze, crossing her legs so that he saw and did not see. Then she went and sat on Uncle Taiwo's knee, asking him irrelevancies.

As soon as Freddie left, Uncle Taiwo swallowed his beer in a quick gulp. He put his hat on his head and without so much as a goodbye, stamped out of the room.

'Where you goin', Uncle T.?' Jagua asked.

He did not reply, but his face was tense.

Next morning Jagua heard that Freddie had been beaten up and was lying in hospital seriously ill. She hurried to the hospital, but was told that Freddie had merely been treated for minor injuries. It was true he had been attacked. He and his group of rascals had been flying the banners of O.P. 1 round the town and shouting their election slogans, when a small bus bearing an equal number of wild ones shouting slogans of O.P. 2 made straight for them and deliberately rammed into them.

A fight ensued, and the man who had engineered the whole thing stood apart, roaring encouraging epithets and bursting into resounding laughs. They heard later that it was none other than Uncle Taiwo. But he kept himself hidden in the background, the engineer who would never expose himself to the flying stones and jagged bottle-ends. All this took place at dusk and before the police could intervene, the streets were clear. Jagua was terrified for these two men. The other candidates for the remaining fifty-nine seats pursued one another in much the same manner, but she did not know them and did not much care.

When Uncle Taiwo came in that evening, she told him to desist. He smiled, called Rosa to give him more beer and said: 'If your man don' fit to fight, den he mus' lef de game of politics.'

'You call 'im my man? Everythin' finish between we two. If I see road for kill Freddie, I kin do dat.'

Uncle Taiwo roared his roar of disbelief. 'You wan' to kill Freddie, an' when you see am, you begin shake your wais' all about de room. You tink I don' see you?'

'Me? Shake my waist? You don' know what you talkin'.' She crossed her legs. 'De man come here, and if to say he wan' to kill you cold, he for kill you, like small rat. He got all de wild ones with him. An' he meet you for woman house, after you done tire!'

His face flushed. 'Why he don' kill me den? If is so easy why he don' kill me?' A smile played on his lips. 'Since he don' wan' to fight, I must fight him firs'. Das politics. Spare no foe!'

Jagua knew it was useless arguing with him. This was the kind of moment when she looked at him and hated him. She looked round the room and saw how cosy he had made it for her. She thought of the generous allowance he made her every month. She decided not to speak.

'Remember de meetin' dis evenin'.'

'Which meetin'?'

'Campaign meetin' of de women. You promise to address dem for me!'

'But I don' know nothing about politics.'

Uncle Taiwo laughed. 'What you wan' to know? You already been to campaign meetin' with me, almos' daily.'

Jagua was terrified. When she made the promise to address the market women on Uncle Taiwo's behalf, she did not know he would take it seriously.

'Dis evening by five,' Uncle Taiwo reminded her.

'So soon?'

'Five is de bes' time; dem will be returning from market den.'

'Ah don' know what ah will tell dem.'

He leaned back and slapped his knee. 'Tell dem to vote for O.P. 2. What? You tellin' me you don' know what you will say?' He began to laugh and to slap his knees, the stool, shaking till the beer glasses bounced off the stool. 'You don't know what you will tell dem? Oh, you jus' too funny. Tell dem to vote for O.P. 2! Tell dem our party is de bes' one. We will give dem free market stall, plenty trade, and commission so dem kin educate de children. Tell dem all de lie. When Uncle Taiwo win, dem will never remember anythin' about all dis promise. Tell dem ah'm against women paying tax. Is wrong, is wicked. Tell dem ah'm fighting for equality of women. Women mus' be equal to all men. You wonderin' what to tell dem? Oh, Lord! Tell dem all women in dis Lagos mus' get good work if dem vote for me. No more unemployment. Women mus' be treated right. Dem mus' have status. Dem mus' have class . . .'

Jagua listened to the male roar of Uncle Taiwo's voice. She admired the big arms that waved in sweeping arcs, encompassing the stature of the man who had grown doubly large in her eyes.

'Is enough!' she said, bright-eyed, feeling herself a little girl beside the Party Agent. 'You not in de market yet!'

Uncle Taiwo roared his roaring laugh. 'God, ah mus' win, I mus' win and become Councillor.' He pulled her to him in a sudden romantic outburst and slapped her jutting buttocks. 'When ah become Councillor, den my woman will be a big woman. Den ah will marry you.'

'What of your odder wives?' Jagua pouted. 'Where you goin' to keep dem when de Council give you big flat?'

'My other wives?' He laughed again. 'You will join dem. I got only three now in de house. You're de only one I got outside. Ha-ha-ha-aa! . . . You worryin' about Freddie Namme. He already marry anodder. He return from U.K. with wife and two pickin'. The man is findin' way to make quick money, but is a pity he got no idea of politics; so he can't win me in de election. People never hear of him.' He slapped her bottom once again and she cried out. 'You mus' forget Freddie at once. Because now I keepin' you for meself. I paying de rent. I furnishing dis room, so you got every comfort to enjoy.'

When Uncle Taiwo talked like this, one part of Jagua always longed for Freddie Namme. Uncle Taiwo, for all his kindness was coarse, believing only in the power of money. In the campaign meetings she had helped him buy loyalty but he forgot that life was far bigger than campaign meetings.

Jagua went down to Obanla to speak with Dennis and to find out what had really happened. It was a bright afternoon, intensely hot. She got down from the bus and walked under the trees. The barber in the corner of the street waved at her but she paid no attention to him.

The house in which Dennis and the gang lived was the third on the right, facing a large piece of farmland where faeces and refuse were dumped. She walked to the door and knocked. The hollow sounds gave her a fright. She pushed the door and walked from one room to the other in a dream. There was not a soul. A dog rushed in from the courtyard and began whining. She caressed the lonely animal, walked along the verandah and shut the door. Dennis and his group had disappeared.

As she walked up the path, she saw a blue Pontiac flash past and remembered Uncle Taiwo. She remembered too that in a matter of hours she would be addressing a campaign meeting of market women.

Jagua stood on a box and looked down on the heads of three thousand market women. Near her was a microphone and above the little square the O.P. 2 flag waved its orange and white stripes. She had been studiously following Uncle Taiwo to all his meetings, but today it was Uncle Taiwo's turn to follow her. She found herself nervously caressing the microphone, but as the first few words shattered the hubbub and the chattering, Jagua experienced a new sense of power. Her voice was new, attractive. The women turned their heads to see who was speaking. They listened. Far away across the bridge, right down to the lagoon-side where the long cars were parked, the people seemed to start and look up at the unusual interruption.

Yes, the women had come to the campaign meeting of Uncle Taiwo. They had come to listen to the man. They had been listening to him now for weeks. Jagua knew these women; astute, sure of themselves and completely independent and powerful. Their votes could easily sway the balance because they voted en bloc. Some of them had children studying in England and most of them had boys in the Secondary Schools. To them education was a real issue. They went to the mosque on Fridays and to market on Sundays, if the market day fell on a Sunday. From dawn to dusk they sat in the squalid market with the drain running through it: a drain that could never drain because the water in it was an arm of the lagoon which was part of the Bight of Benin which was part of the Atlantic and Pacific and Indian Oceans, and these could never be drained. In the middle of the market stood the refuse dump from which the sanitary lorries came to shift the rubbish once a day. Many men in the 'Senior Service' came to this 'cut-price' market to squeeze away a few odd pennies from the grasping hands of the big Department Stores. They bought tea and towels, sugar and coca cola, coffee, milk and peanuts from these women who could undersell anyone else because they bought wholesale from shady sources and were content with little or no profit. In many ways these women reminded Jagua of the Merchant Princesses of Onitsha, but these Lagos women did not seem to have quite the staggering sums of money used by the Princesses. Jagua knew that some of them came because they imagined that an election campaign meeting was a carnival, a meeting place for high fashion and love. So they came in their velvet specials: blues and greens, mauve and gold velvets to delight their men who liked them rounded in the hips. Their blouses were made of the sheerest transparent nylons, so that Jagua was gazing at three thousand brassieres (of those who bothered to wear brassieres). In most cases anyone who had the keen sight could look through and see the dark areolae and the long child-sucked nipples.

'How many of you can remember your own birthdays?' Jagua asked them. She did not need to be subtle for the language she used was not English. A silence fell at once on the multitude. 'Very few of you. But most of you remember the birthdays of your children. Now is it not a wonderful thing to us Lagos people, that in O.P. 1 an official of that party should be given a wedding anniversary present by his wife? Mark you, I do not say it is a bad thing. I say it is a wonderful thing indeed. But you must all bear with me. The woman who gave her husband this present is a woman like yourself. On the wedding anniversary, she called her husband to the seaside. Then this woman of O.P. 1 said to her husband. 'My Lord, may we both live happily for ever. Here are the keys of our new building. I built it to mark our wedding anniversary.' And she gave him a bunch of keys and pointed to a new house standing on the beach, all six floors of it, and magnificent. A woman. Where did she find the money? A trader, like ourselves!'

A hubbub arose. Jagua waited for the din to die down. 'Of course, her husband was very surprised. He took the keys, and sure enough, he was not dreaming. They were the keys of the new building and the building cost – I think, I am not sure, exactly – fifty thousand pounds. I have said the figure in English, so that you can all interpret it to your friends. £50,000. Yes, about that. Every amenity was there. A £50,000 house, built on the beach, by a woman like yourself. So what are you all doing? Go and build one like that for your husbands, or is it that you can't find £50,000?'

'She stole it! . . .' came the throaty accusation.

Some of the women took down their head ties and threw them on the floor and stamped about, slapping their hips in anger. Jagua spoke into the microphone. 'I am still coming to the end of my story.' They listened, and she went on: 'You see the sort of people you will be voting for, if you vote O.P. 1. You will be voting for people who will build their private houses with your own money. But if you vote for O.P. 2, the party that does the job, you will see that you women will never pay tax. Don't forget that. O.P. 2 will educate your children properly. But those rogues in O.P. 1? They will send their children to Oxford and Cambridge, while your children will only go to school in Obanla. No: Obanla is still too good for your children, because – oh! – how can your children find the space to be educated in Lagos schools, if O.P. 1 ever comes into power? No, your children will be sent to the slummy suburbs. These people will open a hundred businesses using the names of their wives. But you? You will continue to sleep on the floor with grass mats while their wives sleep on spring mattresses. You will carry your things to market on your head, and while in the market, you will be bitten by mosquitoes, and your children will be bitten by mosquitoes and develop malaria. And you will console yourselves that you are struggling. Tell me, what are you struggling for? Or are you going to struggle all the time? Now is the time to enjoy! On Saturdays you will kill a small chicken and call your friends. You will shake hips to the *apala* music and deceive yourself that you are happy. But look! The roof of your house leaks when it rains. The pan roofs are cracking with rust. There is no space in the compound where your children can play. The latrine is the open bucket, carried by nightsoil men who are always on strike, so the smell is always there. The bathroom is narrow and slimy and it smells of urine. You call that life!' Jagua was tempted to roar with laughter in the best Uncle Taiwo manner. 'You call that life? Yes, that is the life they have given you and will continue to give you if you return an O.P. 1 government to power. See now, see what they've done? They've gone and brought an Englander, to contest against Uncle Taiwo.' She turned and looked at him. He was shaking his head sadly, and presently he rose and the crowd cheered him. 'His name is Freddie Namme, this Englander. And do you know where he went to marry his wife? From Sa Leone. It is one thousand miles from Lagos. The people do not speak Yoruba there, neither do they speak Ibo or Hausa. It is a different part of Africa. Now tell me: if you vote for a man marrying such a foreign woman, do you think he will understand what you want, you Nigerian women?'

'No!' came the angry reply.

Jagua paused and drew in some breath, looking aggressively round at the three thousand head-ties. They were all still, but in the distance she saw a small boy in white, throwing a football at his mother who wore a red scarf.

'Uncle Taiwo is your man, my sisters! He is a businessman, so he understands business – like yourselves. He knows your problems, even before you bring them to him. He will press your case in the Council, give you a decent market, block off that stinking drain, a shameful smelly thing. Go to Onitsha and see what a market should be like. I've been there myself, and I can tell you this: Uncle Taiwo will plan for you a bigger and cleaner market where you can sleep, if you like. Vote for him! Vote for Long Life and Happiness. And Freedom. F r e e d o m ! . . .'

The drums began to beat and the specially hired orchestra sang with rhythm. Jagua slipped back and left the microphone to Uncle Taiwo. She was exhausted and thirsty. The orchestra had crowded round the microphone, twelve men in a uniform robe. One man at the microphone rapidly improvised a new song based on the goodness of Uncle Taiwo and the honesty of O.P. 2. The others handled a variety of percussion instruments and chanted the rhythmic *apala* music that transformed the women into wiggling maniacs. They jutted out their buttocks and leaned low, wiggling from side to side and hissing for man-contact. The men held on to those hips and shook in rhythm with them. The campaign had become a carnival, but Jagua felt they had listened.

Vote for Uncle Taiwo!

'Jagua – who teach you politics?' Uncle Taiwo asked, when he had finished making his own speech (to which no one had listened).

'Is you,' said Jagua. 'An' again – everythin' I say is how I feel. Oh, I tire. Make we go home – or *Tropicana*, any one.'

Uncle Taiwo led the way. 'Now I sure I goin' to win. Le's go celebrate in de *Tropicana*!'

They pressed in on Jagua from all sides, wanting to shake her hand, to detain her, to chair her. She felt truly proud. She had struck the first nail. Freddie would soon be buried.

21

When Nancy stepped across the *Tropicana* floor, all the men fixed their eyes on her for she did not look the *Tropicana* type. Jagua swivelled round. She saw not the Nancy Oll of old, young and lithe, but an even more superb Nancy with a brilliant touch of sophistication to her. She had learnt in England how to use make-up that heightened her personal charm. Lipstick that blended with her natural complexion, nail varnish that did not convert the nails into bloodstained claws, foundation garments that yet left the body free. Jagua had to admit that Nancy was stunning.

'You seen Freddie?' she was looking steadily at Jagua.

'Why you ask me, Nancy? First of all, welcome from Englan'! Since I lef' you for Bagana we never seen. I don' know say you and Freddie done return from England.'

'You tellin' lie, Jagua! I awready hear everythin' about you and him.'

Jagua was startled by Nancy's manner. She tried to keep her voice down. 'Ah swear to God. Why I will tell you lie?'

'Don' call God in this matter, you devil-woman!'

'I swear to God! I got nothin' to do with your man since he return. I wantin' nothin' from 'im. And he awready pos' de money he owe me. What more?'

'I say you lyin', Jagua!' The words were slapped out in anger. 'Since we return, Freddie's been strayin' from de home; and he strayin' to your place!'

Jagua could endure the taunting no longer. 'Excuse me, Nancy! Who you callin' liar? Me? I beg you not to call me liar again. Or you done forget your experience in Bagana Creek, how I save your life? I'm not your rank. I don' care whedder you from England come. You be only small pickin' to me. I fit born you from my belly. I got nothin' to do with small pickin' like you who don' respect her senior. Go call you Mama an' I kin talk wit' her, not you. You're only small pickin' to me. I awready dismiss Freddie from me mind because I don' love him no more. If he runnin' after some woman, is your own fault, das all! You don' fit to hold you man!'

The man seated beside Jagua folded his robes and glared at Nancy Oll. 'Who's this lady?'

'She's de wife of dat man, Freddie Namme who jus' return –'

'Jagua, but I warn you already about . . . not to—'

'Shut up, Uncle Taiwo. I don' know anythin' about Freddie, das all I say!'

Men began to crowd round Jagua and Nancy. They formed a ring and their girls enlarged the ring. Jagua turned to them. 'I jus' sitting here, drinking with me Master.' She nodded at Uncle Taiwo. 'All 'pon sudden, dis small pickin' of yesterday come to see me to accuse me, where's her man? I tell her I don' know who's Freddie. And she begin curse me—'

'You're a liar,' Nancy insisted. 'You know Freddie – too much! I come here to warn you! Leave my man for me? He see you harlot woman before he marry me. You miss your chance.'

'You bastard!'

'Harlot, you got no shame! So you use to run after man who you can born. I don' blame you, your womb done dried up. You old hag! You kin never born any more.'

The words slashed deep into Jagua's pride. She could forgive anything but that taunt about childlessness. She leapt at Nancy, straight from the stool. Nancy clenched her fist to strike a blow, but it never landed. Someone seized her from behind. Jagua found herself entangled in Uncle Taiwo's robes and he was taking her forcibly out of the *Tropicana*.

Uncle Taiwo was shaking his fist at Nancy. 'You call yourself a lady who been to England. What d'you learn dere, I wonder? You call my missis harlot woman! Wait till I face your man. He goin' to run out of dis Lagos.'

Jagua felt his protective hands on her as he took her towards the Pontiac. It was a new feeling to her.

Jagua knew when to expect Freddie. He always came when Uncle Taiwo was away. She took off all her clothes and scented her ear lobes, the pits of her arms. She rubbed scent on her breasts before encasing them in cotton cups. She darkened the lights of the room, then went back into bed. Now she was determined to turn Freddie against his wife, to make him loathe the very sight of her, to break up his home if only to repay Nancy's humiliation of her. She would show Nancy that a harlot can wield great power over men's homes. Uncle Taiwo she had already worked up into such a state of anger against Freddie that he could easily waylay and fight him. She had told him that Freddie was pestering her life, that she had warned him often never to come to her but obstinately he still came to worry her in her home. Also that Freddie was resorting to subterfuge to snatch Obanla constituency from him. All this made Uncle Taiwo determined to get even with Freddie.

Jagua rolled over in the soft bed. She thought of Dennis Odoma. It was now known that the Police Officer had died in hospital. When Freddie Namme came she would appeal to him to help defend Dennis. She was sure Freddie could do a lot for Dennis, if only she could convince him to undertake the defence.

She heard voices outside. Rosa was speaking to someone. She listened. 'Sleepin'?' she heard Freddie say. 'At this time of de night?'

'She jus' return from outside.'

'Go an' wake her! No – never min'.'

Then she heard the door being softly knocked and she turned and hid her face against the wall and started snoring. She threw her limbs carelessly about the bed, half covering her thighs. Freddie would come in and see her lying seductively. Then he would touch her, and she would sigh and open her eyes and roll away from him.

But it was Rosa who came into the room. 'Who dat?' asked Jagua.

'Is Freddie, an' one man. I tink is dese election people, I tell dem you sleepin' . . .'

'Fool! I don' tell you say whenever Freddie come here, you mus' let him enter de house.'

'So you tell me, Ma; but—'

'Outside now. Let me res'.'

Later that night, Jagua dressed with great care. She went to the *Tropicana* and sat in a corner. They brought her beer. Not long afterwards she saw Freddie come in. He was surrounded by a number of youngsters, bearded, in bright shirts and boots. He looked

worn out. He came and sat by her. The five stalwart ones formed a
ring round their table.

'Freddie, who all dese men?'

'My bodyguard.' He laughed his harsh laugh. 'You don' know
say every candidate mus' have bodyguard nowadays?'

Jagua fidgeted with her glass. 'As you come sit near me with all
dese men; suppose Uncle Taiwo come here into de *Tropicana* and
fin' you with me?'

'Uncle Taiwo and him people done go to de village to campaign.
We lef' dem dere. He won' come here now.'

'Freddie, I tink ah already beg you to lef' politics. Is too dangerous a game now. Fancy, you goin' around with a bodyguard. You
givin' employment to wild boys who care nothin' about person life.
You ready to take responsible when dem kill some man? Or you
think all dis be play?'

'I don't care now. Is too late to go back. I want money.'

He told her how he had been campaigning one afternoon when
Uncle Taiwo let loose his boys and they ran into his own men,
injuring more than a dozen people. He himself was cut in the face.
Since then he never went outside without these five boys who had
all been in the Burma Campaign. He protected himself because he
had been told that Uncle Taiwo was planning to kill him.

'Nonsense!' Jagua said. 'Is your political rival, but Uncle T. is not
person who will kill somebody. You jokin', Freddie! Das de change
I seen in you. Since you return from Englan', you want money, and
because of dat you trustin' nobody.'

He smiled. 'Is true, but de man hate me for nothin' sake. I done
nothin' to him.' His hands did not even shake as he poured the beer
from the bottle.

'By the way,' Jagua said. 'You hear about Dennis Odoma? De
man I seen among your bodyguard sometime? Dem say de police
arrest 'im.'

'So I hear. I sorry for Dennis. He done a foolish thing. No way
out for him. He done a very serious thing against de law. Dem goin'
to hang de poor boy, for murder of a police officer. Is a very serious
offence.'

There was something final in Freddie's voice. Jagua felt the tears coming to her eyes. 'Freddie, I beg you; go and defend de boy.'

'No, Jagua. I got no time. I got to concentrate on de election. De Government will give him their own lawyer.'

Jagua sighed. She could not help liking Dennis. Desperately she prayed the law would overlook his mistake and spare his life.

Jagua did not miss a single dance. It must have been the exhilaration of her election speech, but she found she could not sit still. She tapped her foot and shook her shoulders. The rhythm seemed to filter through her pores into her skin which was now afire under it. Finding no partner she wiggled away alone leaving Freddie at the table.

She had been dancing alone for some time, when other women joined her, also unpartnered. *Tropicana* girls sometimes revelled in this kind of exclusive 'all-ladies' dance, a fashion parade in Accra wax prints and colourful velvets. Men, take your choice, they seemed to say. Encouraged, Jimo Ladi and his Leopards played even louder, and the *high-life* spun along for a quarter hour, half-an-hour, one hour non-stop. The tune changed, the rhythm remained solid. The dancers sweated under the heat.

When the music stopped, they yelled 'More, more! . . .' but it was one hour and Jimo Ladi and his Leopards sat back exhausted. Jagua held her aching hips and went back to the table. She glanced round, but Freddie was not in sight, She sat down with a vague unease. He should have told her before he left; or perhaps he did not want to disturb her dancing. But a wave would have been sufficient. She did not sit long before Number Seven, one of the stewards, came and told her that a man wearing the badge of Freddie's party, had come in and had called him out 'urgent', with some strange message. Freddie had gone alone. Soon after, the five wild ones had rushed out, and 'I tink he got accident, but I don' know,' Number Seven concluded.

Jagua got up. Instinct told her that something suspicious was going on. Many years later when she remembered that night she never could tell just why she felt so very uneasy. She passed the man at the gate, looked outside the club. Over to her left, near the gutter, a crowd gathered, watching something which looked to her like an accident.

Jagua pushed through, forcing her way to the front. A man was lying in the gutter with the blood gurgling from his mouth. His head seemed to have been broken into two halves. At first she thought he was quite dead, but looking closely, she saw that he moved his hands. It was Freddie Namme. And nobody could say who had done this to him or what it was all about.

'What you all standin' there for!' cried Jagua. 'Ring for ambulance. Go into de Club and ring for an ambulance!' But as nobody moved, she began running back to the *Tropicana*, murmuring, 'I know who do this! Dem done kill my poor Freddie!'

For three successive days now Jagua had been trying to see Freddie in hospital. Always it was the same orderly who barred her way. 'Is better you go back, Madam. Dem say he critical now. Too critical!' He lingered on the word he had obviously been taught to recite.

As she went back, she saw Nancy in a neat blue frock and white shoes pass her. Nancy did not so much as glance at her. Nancy received a courteous bow from the orderly who opened the door wide for her. Jagua squirmed. Whatever she had been to Freddie, Nancy was the woman they recognized as his wife.

Freddie was lying in a private hospital. Jagua remembered now that it was their ambulance which had arrived when she telephoned and took Freddie away. The story came out in the O.P. 1 paper that the man who had called Freddie out of the *Tropicana* was an O.P. 2 man dressed as an O.P. 1. When Freddie came out he was set upon and beaten up. The paper called on the leader of O.P. 2 to account for Freddie's injuries and critical condition. But she heard that the O.P. 2 people denied knowing anything about Freddie's beating-up. They called everything connected with it a 'frame-up' – down to the doctor who owned the hospital in which Freddie lay. They said this doctor was known to have O.P. 1 sympathies and therefore any report he might give for the court hearing must be discredited as he was a biased witness. All this Jagua heard as a kind of rumour and she knew now that it was all the kind of complex situation she disliked.

On this particular afternoon Jagua dug in outside the hospital, hoping that when Nancy left, she could bribe the orderly into letting her in – just for one moment. She could not bear the thought of Freddie so critically ill without some comfort from her. She kept pacing up and down in front of the gate and when one Land Rover drew up she saw it but it did not at first strike her as unusual. Close behind the first Land Rover came an ambulance which parked aggressively into the gate; but the sign she noticed on the ambulance did not belong to this private hospital. From the ambulance emerged two policemen, one of them, the driver. Jagua sensed something unusual. She was now all eyes. Soon afterwards she saw a third Land Rover, slightly shorter than the first and bearing the sign POLICE just beneath the aerial. One of the Officers was holding a mike in front of him and shouting, 'Calling Robot Two . . . Calling Robot Two . . . Over! . . .'

Jagua saw the crowd beginning to press against the door of the police ambulance. In a few moments, market women, clerks, cars, lorries, taxis, they all took up position and they were an angry crowd. 'Stop dem! . . . Dem want to remove Freddie from de hospital. Is all engineered by O.P. 2! . . .'

'Suppose he die? Jus' let dem try. Dem responsible for Freddie's life!'

'Them can't remove him. The doctor won' agree . . .'

The police cars had blocked up the road. Horns blared impatiently from the far end of the street. But the drivers, getting no attention, reversed their cars and branched out on a side street. It seemed to Jagua that this went on for hours, and that some deadlock had been reached within the hospital. The passers-by kept swelling the crowd and shouting angry words at the police. Among them Jagua could see the Volkswagens of O.P. 1 supporters and some newspapermen she had often seen at the *Tropicana*. They stood in a corner, writing furiously in their slim notebooks. The police would not budge. The crowd surged away from the hospital gates. Jagua saw the stretcher bearing Freddie come down the steps into the ambulance. She caught one glimpse of Nancy's face, red with weeping. She was crying quite shamelessly. She tried to see

Freddie's face, but it was all wrapped up in bandages. She watched the ambulance drive off, carrying Freddie on the stretcher and guarded front and back by the Land Rovers. The police had won.

Jagua walked home in fear. She was thinking how very stupid the police can be, how ordinary people she knew became transformed by this strange devil they called politics. When so transformed a man placed no value on human life. All that mattered was power, the winning of seats, the front-page appearance in the daily papers, the name read in the news bulletins of the Nigerian Broadcasting Corporation. When they asked her, she never could tell whether Freddie was alive or dead. But she knew this strange fear and it was something she could not dismiss lightly.

Jagua mingled with the crowd and slipped into the Namme household, the house of death and mourning. Nancy was sitting on the bare cement floor surrounded by weeping women. Her eyes were red, and there was still a look of doubt, of hopeful disbelief on her face. She turned these yellowish-red eyes here and there as more and more men and women flooded the sitting room, her small lips parted, the breath coming in short puffs like the panting of a small engine.

With all, Jagua found her attractive in her raggedness and misery. When she saw Freddie's friends, all dressed in black, she seemed to crumple up, and a loud moan escaped her. One man dressed as a lawyer went up to her and said: 'On behalf of all of us at the bar, we come to express our heartfelt sympathy . . .' He stopped short because a chorus of wails answered him. He turned to his friends: 'Let's go outside, friends. She can't take it.'

The body of Freddie Namme lay on the bed, behind the mosquito netting. They said he had died in that long drive to the hospital. They had dressed it up in black with white socks and white gloves. The head was bandaged in white and the nostrils had been plugged with cotton wool. Jagua looked at it and began to sob quietly. It could not be true, she kept telling herself. Freddie dead! The shuffling feet of strangers, the thudding, scraping feet of curious men who had come because of the big incident outside the hospital, the sighs, the groans, the moans and expressions of sympathy, all seemed to her like something happening in a film she was watching. She sat completely mesmerized and surrendered herself to the atmosphere of gloom. She saw old women in white, attractive young girls pulsating with life, one of them especially caught her eye: a light-brown-skin girl in a fanciful headtie and blue velvet wrapper. So alive, and so incongruous in the room of death. Who was she? And did Freddie, alive, know all these people?

Turning her eyes towards the bereaved Nancy, Jagua came face to face with the two wet red eyes and their look of hostility. At that moment she could see that grief was a private thing, to be shared only by friends; and she was an enemy. As soon as Nancy saw Jagua she sprang to her feet.

'What you want here? Leave de house, at once!'

'Nancy, no talk like dat, I beg. We all feel de sorrow for your husban' death; especially as de police handle de sick man. I beg you, let me stay an' cry with you; I do a lot for Freddie, you know. And he love me in him own way, though is you he marry after all!'

'You love him, and you kill him! You an' your Uncle Taiwo. You kin have de seat in Obanla now. But jus' leave me with me own sufferin', and de children too. Leave one time, or I will call police for you, quick-quick!'

Jagua began to mutter in protest, but she felt the imperativeness of the cold silence. She was not wanted.

'Awright, Nancy; I goin' to leave! But look all de people who love your Freddie! You know all of dem? Or you goin' to drive de ones you don' know? Your Freddie was a famous man who people love. If to say he livin' he for no drive me from his house.'

Slowly Nancy sat down as Jagua slipped out. But Jagua was unable to leave. She heard the elderly people suggesting that because of the manner of his death, Freddie must be buried quickly. Normally they would have kept his body two or three nights. But he had been badly beaten up and the very next afternoon the hearse was waiting outside the church, bundled with wreaths and flowers. The legal practitioners were all dressed in black and stood nearest it, and then the women of O.P. 1 had all come in one uniform dress:

blue headtie, thin nylon blouses, blue wrappers. They formed a very striking block. Freddie's former students at the National College came too, carrying a flag. They all wore white and looked sweet with their wreaths.

Inside the church, Jagua listened to the parson when he began to speak about Freddie's illustrious career as a teacher. Then he went on to the years of struggle in England when Freddie 'unknowingly was sowing the seeds of his own destruction by joining a political party, but he could not help it; he had a deep feeling for his people and thought he could speak their case in that manner'. He talked about the wonderful bereaved widow who had been his wife. Nancy came to Nigeria, became a Nigerian, though her parents were Sa Leonean. Her parents had been in the civil service, helping Nigeria at a time when the country did not have its own trained men. 'God bless her and the children.'

They were opening hymn books all about her, but as Jagua had none, she peeped over a woman's shoulder. The pipe organ moaned out a painful tune, and as soon as the tune came to an end another voice, more solemn, began to preach in *Yoruba*. The congregation said, 'Amin!' to almost every phrase he uttered, and Jagua joined them too, saying 'Amin! . . . Amin! . . . ' a split-second after the others. She stole a glance at Nancy. Her eyes were blurred with tears. A man beside Jagua began weeping openly.

'Let us pray!' said the parson.

Jagua had a confused impression of deep throaty voices, of rhythmic 'Amin!' and of the pipe organ stealthily swelling with soft sweet music. The music became infinitely finer as the coffin began to come out, born on the shoulders of the Law Society. Suddenly, Nancy broke away from the crowd. She ran after the coffin but hands grabbed her, pinned her back.

'Freddie! . . . Come back to me and de children! . . .'

Jagua wept too.

All along the way, crowds came out on the pavement to watch the already famous man, to join in the singing. Nancy was surrounded by a number of men who watched her with keen eyes. They passed over the last bridge before the cemetery. Men in canoes sat still and seeing the funeral train bowed their heads. Some took off their caps.

'Jesus is God!' sang the choir.

All about Jagua people were talking in undertones. Some of it she heard, some floated away and mingled with the singing.

'You'll see how they're going to vote now . . .'

'I think O.P. 2 made a mistake to beat up Freddie . . . Now the public is against them, especially the women voters, Jus' see the number of women at the funeral . . .'

'Jesus is God! . . .' sang the choir. Jagua looked and saw that it was really true. There were ten women to every man, especially the kind of market women she had spoken to, not long ago.

'May his soul rest in peace . . .'

'Freddie was a fine man . . .'

'At least we're giving him a decent Christian burial, though he died at the hands of the devil.'

Jagua heard it all with a feeling of pride. The hearse turned under the mango trees into the burial ground.

22

Jagua followed Uncle Taiwo out early on Polling Day. Freddie's death had not disturbed the polling or altered the fact that the election was a straight fight between Other Party Two and Other Party One. Of the sixty constituencies, she was most interested in one – Obanla – where Uncle Taiwo was representing O.P. 2 and a new candidate, a nonentity, had been chosen overnight in place of Freddie Namme. Jagua's one fear was that the women might react against the killing of Freddie Namme outside the *Tropicana*. Nigerian women, she knew, do not listen to election promises. Their minds are often made up in advance and it takes a little thing to swing it the other way. She knew they voted for party symbols, not for people. Thus, the death of Freddie Namme would not alter the sum total of the votes for O.P. 1 by a single vote. When she thought of Nancy's face at the funeral, and again heard the words: 'You can have the seat in Obanla now,' the way Nancy said them, she felt even more terrified. It seemed as if a curse would go with the seat. But suppose they lost? The shame would be quite unbearable.

Early in the morning she and Uncle Taiwo drove around the town, watching the women who had already begun trooping to the little grey sheds marked POLLING STATION. But the electoral officers did not turn up until nearing eight o'clock when the women, grimly, checked their registration numbers against a long roll, some distance from the box. They went in, one by one, dipped their fingers in ink, and vanished into the loneliness of the polling booth.

When they came out, Jagua could not guess where the vote had gone – whether to Freddie Namme's O.P. 1 or Uncle Taiwo's O.P. 2; but she thought that most of the women who came to that particular station looked like the market women she had addressed that evening. She stole a glance at Uncle Taiwo's face. It was tense and aggressive. For him, so much depended on this election. If he won, he would become a Councillor, able to use his influence the way others had done before him. His position would be very much higher in the City. She too, would benefit as a result. She would be the mistress of a Councillor. He would use his influence to establish her as a Merchant Princess. She would have to give up her present style of living, and be loyal to him alone.

She watched them quietly checking the names in Obanla Polling Station. The Electoral Officer for this constituency had been specially chosen because Obanla was the hottest spot of all. He was a white man, a Broadcasting Officer, from an organisation noted for its fair play. He smiled and looked round benignly at the other representatives of political parties. Jagua saw Uncle Taiwo fidgeting nervously around. He could not keep still for more than a few seconds. He was like a sentry who has been warned of housebreakers in the neighbourhood. jumping up at the slightest provocation. Suddenly he shouted: 'I object!' and pointed at a voter. There followed a hum of voices, then the voter was allowed to cast his vote. Uncle Taiwo said he had observed this man vote twice, but the man explained that he had returned to vote for a friend who was ill. The law did not disallow that, so the Electoral Officer had to allow him to vote. Jagua watched the man come out of the booth, but that was not the last time. Each time he voted a new finger was dipped in indelible ink. A few moments later, he was back again, till all his fingers had been inked. He had voted for all his nine friends. Jagua heard Uncle Taiwo cursing him under his breath.

She had brought along sandwiches which she passed round and also two flasks of coffee. Uncle Taiwo would neither eat nor drink. By afternoon the voting had slackened, but towards evening the men began to return, and they continued to flow into the booth until sundown when the Electoral Officer went in and – before their eyes – sealed off all the boxes.

Jagua, Uncle Taiwo and all the others followed him to the counting hall where dozens of polling boxes had already been assembled. Uncle Taiwo sweated and wiped his face and paced about. Jagua felt sorry for him. He would not let her speak with him; he snapped out angry words if anyone approached him. She had never known how much the election meant to him. Suppose the ghost of Freddie Namme should suddenly appear in that counting hall, the ghost of Freddie, laughing at Uncle Taiwo: a remote ghost, all powerful, multiplying the O.P. 1 votes so that Uncle Taiwo not only lost the election, but also lost his deposit. And suppose all the people who had received money from him came out now into this hall and laughed and said: 'Uncle Taiwo! . . . we done chop all you money, but we don' vote for you. You can't buy our vote, which is a secret thing. De greates' power dat democracy give we poor people! After all your talk we kin enter de secret box an' use our vote to cut your neck . . .' Foolish imaginings, Jagua told herself. But it was possible that all these things would be haunting Uncle Taiwo now.

The counting officers were breaking the seals now. Jagua saw them tying the votes in bundles of fifty. Long before the last bundle had been tied, she felt a tap on her shoulder. It was Uncle Taiwo.

'Le's go.'

'You no go wait till dem finish? Or you wan' lissen from de radio? I wan' to see how dem will count de vote . . .'

'Le's go, Jagua.' There was something brutal in his gruffness. She felt a deeper fear then.

She followed him into the streets, crowded with traffic police in grey shirts and white shorts, waving their arms to divert the traffic from the counting hall. Some of them were holding truncheons and shields and wearing steel helmets. Jagua heard them call silently, 'Uncle Taiwo', as they passed. 'The man for the job.' He waved at them, and walked more briskly. While he fidgeted with his keys, Jagua asked him something which had been worrying her.

'Uncle T., I been wantin' to ask you somethin'. Who kill Freddie Namme?'

The keys dropped from his hands, but he picked them up and for one nervous moment could not find the right one for the car. 'Why you ask me? Is dose wild boys. Dem always beat de opponent.'

'Why dem beat de opponent?'

He laughed. 'Is de instruction. When de wild ones of O.P. 1 see *any* O.P. 2 man dem will beat him, and vice versa. De V.I.P. in any party pay de wild ones £1 a day to start fight. Is what dem get paid for. And if dem beat any important candidate, dem get bonus.' He laughed. 'You still thinkin' about dat Freddie? I tol' him politics not game for gentlemen . . .' He found the right key at last and held the door open for her.

She slipped into the car. 'So as you goin' now, your life is in danger? De O.P. 1 ruffians dem lookin' for you?'

'Jus' so; but I don' fool so much, you know. See dis!' From under the seat of the car, he drew out a cutlass. The blade was so sharp that it could have cut off a person's ear with the painlessness of an anaesthetic.

'I beg,' said Jagua, as he started the car. 'Hide am! Don' let de police see am!'

He pulled away, and she looked at his face. She knew the truth now. He did not want to remain there in the counting hall because he had lost. And because he had lost he was grey with terror. All that money, all those promises, all the energy lavished on campaigning and paying hired thugs one pound per day, and driving along every road with a blaring loudspeaker, and haranguing the people, all that had been wasted. But most terrifying of all, she knew that Uncle Taiwo was terrified of the retribution. His party did not stand for failures. And as Secretary of O.P. 2 he must carry full blame. That fatal beating-up of Freddie may have done something. She suspected that the ruffians had not been sent to *kill* Freddie, but the result of the beating-up had been death, and now the case was in court and O.P. 2 would answer for it. Freddie had been a lawyer and the Law Association was standing behind him with all their brains massed against the party.

Jagua hung her head. Although she did not know it yet, her own loss was much the greatest.

She heard him muttering, swearing and cursing as he drove like a dervish through the town. What he said made no sense to her and she was quite certain the shock had shattered his mental balance. He dropped her somewhere at the junction of Skylark Avenue and Odoba Street, waved, and still muttering, fired off.

She was walking away when she heard the insistent blaring of horns behind her. It was Uncle Taiwo. He was holding a bag aloft, and calling out to her.

'Jagua, keep dis bag for me,' he said when she walked over. 'In de house, till I come. Don' give de bag to anybody. Even if de man say he's de president of O.P. 2. You hear dat?'

The bag appeared to be full of documents and party papers. Jagua asked, 'Is not dangerous? I don' want to keep somethin' dat de police will come an' search my house!'

'No, is not dangerous.'

'What time you will come?'

'I don' know. I got to go to Headquarters firs'. Keep de bag till you see me.'

'Don' be long; I waitin' you.'

She never set eyes on Uncle Taiwo again. Looking back on that typical Lagos night, with the lights from the petrol station shining into her eyes and the girls in red feeding the cars from long silvery hoses, she never could tell what devil possessed Uncle Taiwo. As he shot the car forward, he very nearly crushed a woman and child who were trailing across the road, trying to catch a bus which was being delayed for their sakes.

Jagua got back to her room and looked at the furniture. She saw one of the old pictures of Freddie Namme, taken when he was yet a teacher at the National College. She took it down and slipped it under a paper. The eyes were too unbearably accusing. She waited for Uncle Taiwo to come in at midnight as he usually did. He never came; he never sent a message.

Instead, a lot of strange men began from that night to miss their way to Jagua's door. They came knocking and asking for Uncle Taiwo. One strange man carrying a blue despatch case would not believe Jagua. He stood obstinately at the door.

'He don' live here,' Jagua told him and she gave him the address at which his wives lived.

'Ah been there and his wives tell me to come here.' He pulled out a notebook and checked the address and still stood there irresolute.

Jagua – who had only one print cloth draped over her naked breasts and her hair in curlers – slowly shut the door and went back to bed. But in another few moments two other men came. They did not mince matters.

'He borrow money from us!'

'He don' live here. Go to de house.'

'We been dere, his wives direct us here!'

They stamped out, muttering angrily, and threatening to bring the police to search the house and to nail up the doors and put up Jagua's things for sale. By evening their threat seemed to be more than a mere joke. Two men came and looked round the house, and asked questions. They did not mention anything about debts. They went away. Jagua was restless. Where was Uncle Taiwo? She was smoking cigarette after cigarette and draining the last few drops of whisky from a bottle which Uncle Taiwo reserved for himself.

Without knocking, Rosa came into the room. Jagua had not seen her for a long time. Rosa had gone away one afternoon with the young man in the blazer, saying she would return that evening. She did not return, not even to collect her things. Jagua concluded that Rosa had found a new love nest.

'Jagua, I come to warn you! Trouble dey come! De O.P. 1 people . . . dem done seize Uncle Taiwo house, lock up every place. I come to warn you to run, before is too late because dem comin' here next! Let me take me own thin' before is late.' She was casting round the room, quickly bundling her things into her suitcase.

Jagua tried to lift the radiogram. She gazed fondly at the studio couch on which she was so fond of curling up. She pushed the wardrobe, rolled the unrollable interior spring mattress. She was in a quandary. What could she take away? So all this had been bought with borrowed money and had not yet been paid for? She lifted the carpet and leaned it against the wall. Then she remembered that she had to put on her clothes. It was the usual time to go to the *Tropicana*. She heard a conversation going on downstairs.

'Yes, he use all our money to furnish de bloody harlot house!' The strange voices were talking about her.

'Jagua, pick up de dress quick,' Rosa urged. 'I hear dem comin' up to dis room.'

'Boy, which room she livin?' roared a voice.

Michael answered: 'Who? Ah don' know who you talkin' about?' And Jagua thanked God for Mike's stupidity.

Rosa kept saying: 'Quick, quick! . . . We got no time! . . .'

Jagua crammed what she could into a small suitcase, threw a last look at the room where she had lived for so long: at the wardrobe, hanging with her silks and velvets, her *Jagwa* fashions. At the door she remembered something, and went back into the room. From under the bed, she pulled out the bag which Uncle Taiwo had trusted to her care. She was just in time.

'Dis way,' said Rosa. 'Come de back way, quick!'

Even as they were descending the steps, Jagua heard the loud crash. She knew her door was being bashed in. She stopped and clenched her fists. She started back for her room.

'I goin' back!' she cried, suddenly bursting into tears. 'I goin' to fight dem. Dey got no right!'

Rosa seized her. 'You done gone crase? Dem will jus' kill you for nothin'.'

Jagua rolled on the floor, crying aloud: 'I done die! . . . I done die, finish! . . .' And it was Rosa who hailed the taxi that took them to safety. 'Don' cry,' Rosa said, placing an arm round her.

*

Jagua followed Rosa to the outskirts of Lagos, to the slum of slums, a part of the city which she had often heard of, but had never visited. They changed direction at least three times and passed by an open expanse of ground where cattle were being bought and sold by men in white gowns and white caps. Then the taxi took them over a wooden bridge and after it had put them down they walked along a sandy road for ten minutes, carrying their suitcases on their heads.

As soon as they entered the house painted grey and red on the outside, Jagua took off her shoes and held her burning feet. Rosa lived in a room of her own where she said she paid two pounds a month rent. Filth was scattered everywhere in the surroundings. They could still hear the buzzing and the humming of the market which they had just passed.

'You kin stay with me till everythin' die down,' Rosa said.

Jagua looked at the degradation. Bare floor which came off in powdery puffs if you rubbed your foot too hard. The bed was in the same room, wooden, with a mattress stuffed with the kind of grass cut by prisoners at the racecourse. Rosa had become – like many women who came to Lagos, like Jagua herself – imprisoned, entangled in the city, unable to extricate herself from its clutches. The lowest and the most degraded standards of living were to her preferable to a quiet and dignified life in her own home where she would not be 'free'.

How am I better? Jagua thought. She ought to have remained in Onitsha with Brother Fonso and tried to become a Merchant Princess. Or better still, she ought to have married Chief Ofubara. Even before that, before she came to Lagos, she had a real husband. She thought of him now. She thought of her whole past life, sitting there while Rosa went into the back of the house and came in and asked her if she would like bitter-leaf stew with pounded yam or rice with pork.

'We got plenty pork here,' Rosa boasted.

'So ah see,' Jagua said absently.

'Gunle is a fine place.' Rosa was making lame excuses for her depraved surroundings. 'No one kin disturb you. My man use to come here an' spen' time. He done go back to de College. He's passin' out dis year . . . Dis place is not like Central Lagos where everybody poke nose in your business. I go an' come as I like.'

She bustled back to the kitchen. Jagua could see her putting a pot on the wood fire. The pot was propped on three stones and Rosa shot back her big buttocks and drew up the cloth between her knees and fanned the fire. Her shoulders had become bigger and smoother since she left Jagua and Jagua wished she were as carefree as Rosa. Youth was on her side.

'Too much bad luck in me life,' Jagua mumbled.

She thought of the time when she was living in Eastern Nigeria, long before she went to Ghana, before she thought of coming to Lagos to live, before she met the late Freddie Namme. She was Jagwa then. In her early thirties.

She was an only daughter. Her father doted on her. In his Godly way he wanted her to marry a serious man from the village. Poor Dad. He was only a catechist at the time, although he struggled hard and later became a pastor. The husband he approved of said he worked in the Coal City. He had come to Ogabu on leave and he noticed her and wanted to take her back with him as wife.

Jagua was fond of changing her clothes often, and – in those early days of make-up – of painting her face. Every few hours she went down to the waterside and took off her clothes and swam in the clean cool water. The boys used to hide and peep at her breasts and hips. She knew it and always teased them. All the girls in her age-group had married and had children but she had resisted to the last, hoping ever, for some eminent man to come along to Ogabu to marry her. To the shock of the villagers she wore jeans and rode her bicycle through the narrow alleys of Ogabu and talked loudly and her laughter was throaty so that the men drew to her side and wanted her. She considered herself above the local boys, most of whom she had bedded and despised as poor experience.

The Coal City man pressed home his claim, and he paid the bride price of one hundred and twenty pounds; so the marriage was concluded and later on they went to the church and her father gave her away with his blessing to the Coal City man. God knows, she wanted to settle down and become the good wife. But she was bored. She was *Jagwa*, and the man was not *Jagwa*-ful. His main interest was his petrol-filling station and garage. He was up early and he went there to supervise the selling of his petrol and to make entries in his books. Often when she got there, she found him sleeping on the bare office table. He soon had a chain of filling stations all over the city and was able to buy a small car. But he never took her to parties, and would not dress well, for fear the money would leak away. In no way did his ideas of living attract her. She found that she had obeyed her parents but now they were not there to see her misery and they would never understand her longing, the hot thirst for adventure in her blood. She refused to adapt herself to his humdrum life and she wondered how she had been able to remain with him as she did for over three years. What grieved her most was that no child came. His mother and father and brothers and sisters came and made a fuss about it, and told him to take a younger wife as Jagua was too old. At first he did not listen to them, but after a time he began to weaken. Jagua knew that he took periodical leaves to his hometown to look at some maiden who had been procured for him; she heard also that they brought him brides to the petrol-filling station. She took the blame for sterility, and it was becoming a thing between them.

One day when he went to his filling station, leaving the house to her, she dressed up and walked into the streets. She was passing by the Railway Station and on a sudden impulse she went in and asked for the timetable. A young man smilingly told her when the next train would be leaving for L-A-G-O-S. Lagos! The magic name. She had heard of Lagos where the girls were glossy, worked in offices like the men, danced, smoked, wore high-heeled shoes and narrow slacks, and were 'free' and 'fast' with their favours. She heard that the people in Lagos did not have to go to bed at eight o'clock. Anyone who cared could go roaming the streets or wandering from one night spot to the other right up till morning. The night spots never shut, and they were open all night and every night; not like 'here' where at 8 p.m. (latest) everywhere was shut down and the streets deserted, so that it looked odd to be wandering about.

When she came away from the railway counter, Jagua felt a sudden uneasiness. There was something sinful in her act, and from that moment on, she began to look at her man with a detached air. To her, he was good as dead. Dead and buried in her heart though he did not know it. She gave him her body, and thought instead of the slim young men in the dark bow ties and elegantly cut lounge suits.

She cooked for him, but longed for quiet restaurants where the lining was velvet and the music was soft and wine glasses clinked and men spoke in whispers to girls who burst suddenly into outraged laughter but were devils in nylon skins. She stopped taking treatment from the doctor who was giving her something to make her pregnant. Her husband found out and when they quarrelled she was glad. She waited for him to leave for the filling station. They had not been on speaking terms for two whole days. She caught the train and it was too slow for her mood, taking three days to drop her into Lagos.

She knew no one and was glad when a young bandleader picked her up and housed her for a time. His friends called him Hot Lips because of his manner of playing the trumpet and the scars on his lips. He had no money but he had style in all he did. When he introduced her to girls who came to see him, she saw that her ideas were out of date. Her manner stamped her as 'Provincial' and this bandleader must be keeping her for some reason, but not for her smartness.

Standing in Tinubu Square, she would see the elegant Lagos products step smartly by, hanging on the laughing hands of their young men, and she would want to be like them. She remembered the morning when she was walking down the street, going from shop to shop. Being followed was something new for her then. She did not know why they did it in Lagos. As she turned the corner into William Street, they came quickly to her.

'We live for Ikoyi,' they said, after greeting her. 'Our master – a white man, jus' come out from England. He lef' him wife for dem country. 'Es lookin' for some fine lady, special.' They looked at her with approval. She was *Jagwa*: nothing exaggerated, the earrings, painted cheeks and lips, the cut of the Accra-style printed blouse and sarong-type wrapper, the smooth shoulders elastic and supple in the sun; the toes, waxed and peeping through high-heeled shoes. And when she walked, they whistled. 'He will treat you fine, is a very kind man,' said the second one.

She observed that they were both dressed in white shirts and white trousers, starched and dazzling. She concluded that they must be servants of some highly-placed official. She weighed the situation. If she could break away from Hot Lips and live all by herself in a room of her own, she would be able to buy many of the fine things in the shops and make herself even more Ja-gwa.

'What time he want me?' she asked.

'Is better for night time. If you tell me where you live—'

'No, no! Ah live wit' some man. But I kin meet you somewhere, some place . . .'

Could it be true? Suppose there was some big practical joke in it somewhere? But Jagua believed in daring. If the worst happened, at least she could still find her way back to Tinubu Square. They later picked her up by the taxi park and sped to Ikoyi. When she stepped out of the taxi she glanced round her with breath suspended. She had never in her life dreamt of being in such dazzling surroundings. The deep soft carpets and well-padded chairs were things she saw in films. As she sat down the boys brought her something to drink and with trembling fingers she took the glass from the tray and sipped at the red liquid. Her head seemed to spin round. She lit a cigarette and the white man leaned over the enormous radiogram and put on a long-play record of some Nigerian music. His name was John Martell and he told her that his wife was in England. He had come out to work with a firm of builders. If she pleased him, he would treat her well.

She must have satisfied him for he took a room for her and furnished it, maintaining it till he went on leave. He told her he would be returning with his wife and two children. He would write to her. She never heard from him, nor did she ever see him again.

With the allowance he gave her she travelled by Mammy Wagon to Accra. She had heard that the women of Accra were Jagwa-ful. They were the real black mermaids from the Guinea Gulf and their ideas came from Paris. When she got to Accra she was breathless with wonder. She returned to Lagos loaded with a pile of wax prints and kente cloth which she sold at a profit. She lowered the neckline of her sleeveless blouses and raised the heels of her shoes. She did her hair in the Jagua mop, wore earrings that really rang bells, as she walked with deliberately swinging hips. She was out-Jagwaring the real Jagwas. She found it thrilling to combine the retail of cloth with the dissemination of Accra fashion. In Lagos they called her Jagwa. This must have been her happiest time in the city. Going to Accra was always an adventure and she managed to keep her head high. She made and broke a number of lovers in Lagos and Accra. One whom she remembered well owned the old *Lou-Lou* Club in Accra and the money he made over to her and the contacts he made for her, helped her to establish a name in the wax-prints trade.

But things became different when she found a front room in a street in Lagos just off Skylark Avenue. In the same house there lived a young teacher named Freddie Namme. He lived on the ground floor and he was a bachelor and good-looking. She saw him just once and decided it was time she settled down – with him. She would spare no effort to win him. Imperceptibly her interest in the cloth trade began to dwindle. She thought mainly of Freddie. She passed often by his door and greeted him loudly and clearly. Then she began cooking for him, home dishes that made him talk about his mother.

She discovered that he was not engaged to anyone, but even so she found it difficult to reach his ears with her talk about love. She was afraid of the differences in their ages, but she made him talk of his ambition to become a lawyer. If he would give her the security she craved, if he would give her a child of her own, she would help him . . .

Jagua heaved a sigh. She looked up now at the darkness that had crept slowly into the room. Outside she could see figures, mere shapes, moving along the dark streets, their lanterns shining on their faces. She could hardly believe that any part of Lagos was without electric light and pump water, but Gunle was. Rosa was back in the room, rummaging in a shelf.

'You go bath firs' before you eat, or eat firs' before you bath?'

'No,' Jagua said absently.

'You will eat firs'?'

'I no want anythin'. My mind no good. I jus' wan' to think serious about life.'

Rosa came and put an arm round her. 'What you worry yourself for? You no fit to change nothin'. Whedder you laughin' or you cryin', what happen, happen. De man done run away. De people he owe done lock up you house. Thenk God, dem don' meet you and wound you. Is better you hide here small, till everythin' col'.'

Jagua rose and began to take off her clothes. She wanted to go home now, back to Ogabu. She wanted to go to Krinameh to see if Chief Ofubara would still take her. She felt a deep hungry longing for her mother. Lagos for her, had become a complete failure. She must try and start life all over again, but not in Lagos. If Brother Fonso could help her, she wanted nothing better than to be a real Merchant Princess at Onitsha.

'Put water for me, Rosa. I wan' to bath firs'. But I don' think say I kin chop. I got no appetite.'

Rosa in her bare feet swung out of the room, and Jagua found the sight of her really comforting.

23

Jagua found the new life degrading. At night she and Rosa would leave their home and travel to the *Tropicana*. They never got back before three in the morning and sometimes when they returned they would tell the men who brought them back to park outside. The men, horrified, would hesitate. Two strange men – in one room. But Jagua would speak nonchalantly to them, and they would overcome their shyness and come in. Sometimes Rosa and her man would take the bed because it was her room. Sometimes it was Jagua who took the bed with her man while Rosa and her man would lie on the mat. Before dawn the men had started up their cars and disappeared. Rosa and Jagua would then compare their takings: red for pounds, green for tens, and violet for fives.

One evening, just as they watched the men secure their cars, a third car drew up behind them. It was a taxi. Jagua and Rosa ignored the taxi and went inside the room. They had scarcely closed the door when they heard violent knocking outside.

'Excuse! . . . Excuse me! . . .' A persistent hammering.

Rosa was still fidgeting with the hurricane lamp. Jagua glanced at her, and said: 'I goin' to see . . .' But Rosa had already dashed angrily past her and was at the door. Jagua listened with half an ear and thought she could hear her name mentioned. Another suitor, she thought. Too late for this night. When Rosa came in, she said: 'De man say he want you, Jagua. I wonder who he kin be.' She tried to describe him, but Jagua could make nothing of it. She handed over the lantern to Rosa and went outside.

The door was only half-shut, with a beam of light cracking through it. The light fell on the face of the man who stood on the other side of it. Jagua looked at the face, and stepped back. 'Brother Fonso!'

'Sister I've looked for you – the whole Lagos!'

'You can't come inside, Brother Fonso.'

'I know,' he said.

She slipped out into the darkness and at once Brother Fonso began to tell her how he had been told to seek her at the *Tropicana*. He had actually seen her and the other woman enter two separate cars. He had hired a taxi immediately but they seemed to be going very far and fast. He was lucky to catch up with them. Then he talked about his journey to Lagos, why he had come and why it was urgent that he saw her.

'Home is bad, that's why am here.'

Jagua's heart leapt. 'Money?'

'No, more serious than that. What I tell you in Onitsha?'

'Brother, you say – you say dat de day you'll come Lagos . . .'

She felt a sudden panic mixed with irritation. Something she could not imagine had happened. She felt it in his manner.

'Yes, I've come . . . Is about Papa. He's dying . . . Dying. And de only name he calls is your name, *all the time*. If he don' see you, he won't die, so we mus' go find you anywhere you are . . .'

Jagua sucked in her breath. She looked at Brother Fonso, and Fonso was not there, only the darkness. She listened but heard nothing; she looked and the accusation of her own conscience reared itself obscuring her vision. All the sins of her past and future life were crowded in that one moment when Fonso stood before her, the archangel of misfortune and death and condemnation. She was the only daughter whom her father loved and doted upon. Her father had never denied her anything. He had seen her married off and she had been wayward and had come to Lagos to pursue the *Tropicana* lights and the glittering laughter of seductive men, the sequin sheen of the fickle fashions. She had forgotten that she had a father and mother who needed her love. Husbandless, parentless, she had roamed the Nigerian world, a woman among the sophisticates with hollowness for a background. And out of that hollowness this had come.

'So will you get ready and come *now*,' Fonso said with finality.

'Now? Leave Lagos . . . now?'

'Yes, now. There is no time, sister.' She could feel the intense fire in his glance. 'If you like, you stay. Papa will die. Is an ol' man, awright; but he jus' wan' to see you before. Doesn't matter to you. Awright! . . . I've done my own part. Left my business to come to Lagos and look for you the whole town. Lagos which I've never been to before. Just to please Papa before he goes.'

Jagua began to cry. 'But I have nothin'. Them seize all my thin'. How can I come now? Funeral is not a small thin'. How I can come without money! Is a shame! And I never been home for over ten year! No, is too much shame!'

'No money – all these years?' His voice was biting. 'Not you tell me when you come Onitsha that you got cloth business?' He laughed. 'And I tol' you, stop in Onitsha and trade with the Princess! By now, you should have known where you reach.'

Jagua began to sob quietly. She knew Brother Fonso was being cruel to her. She moaned and hung her head, and then she half heard him still talking.

'Did you hear that Papa wants your money? He never had much money in life. He doesn't want your money now, in death. He jus' wants you – Jagua, his daughter who he love. I use to jealous you because of how Papa gone foolish with love for you, Jagua. You, the wayward one; we all try, try, but no: is only you. Now, he's dyin', and he forget all you done him—'

'I don' fit to go now, Brother Fonso. What I will say dat I bring with me? No, is a very bad time for me. I got nothin'. Funeral ceremony in Ogabu is no small thin'.' She saw the cynical flash of teeth as Fonso mocked her.

'Is it because of the men in the room? They're more important to you than Papa? The money they will give you this night, in this place—' and he glanced up and down the street, 'that money will surpass all the money you have seen since dem born you . . .'

Every word Brother Fonso said gored her consciousness and fermented her spirit till it fizzled out in a cloud of shame. 'Brother Fonso, is a shame you come meet me like dis. But – to talk true – not because of those people I say I cannot go. Is jus' – I mean to say, I already shame too much. I don' fit to reach home now and show my face.'

Imperceptibly Fonso was straightening himself as she talked. By the time she had finished she saw that he was as straight as a palm tree. He had become to her the Day of Judgement, the silent symbol of torture. She pleaded with him, she cried, she struggled to make him see the logic of her decision. He stood there, silent as the dead weight of her past misdeeds, shattering all her coherent thinking and speaking.

'So you will not go?' Brother Fonso's frozen voice chilled her spirit. 'You leave our Papa to die, to *die*. He will not come back, you know! You saw him last over ten years ago, and –'

'Not so, Brother Fonso. I will come, but – give me time.'

He laughed. 'Till when? When he's already buried? But, what does the dying man care? Go on! Take the time you want! Death give you de time. He will wait, till you ready for come.'

Brother Fonso turned and walked slowly towards the taxi. She heard him swearing at her. She would have called out to him but her tongue was swollen in her mouth and her voice was dry in her throat. Even her eyes had failed to see the tall form melting quickly and angrily away from her. She heard the taxi reverse, wheel round, move away.

She was standing there and Rosa came and touched her and said: 'Who dat?' And Jagua merely looked but could not talk because her throat was parched.

She went at last. In three days she had been able to go round her former friends and to borrow some money. She knew she could never repay the money but she had to obtain it somehow. Something told her that all the money she could find would be valuable. It might even be necessary to pay some very exorbitant medical fees.

Rosa saw her off at the motor station. In her maroon and yellow wax-print dress with the sun on her, she looked fetching. The young man in the blazer came too. Rosa said he was in Lagos for the weekend.

'What time we expect you, Jagua?'

'I don' know, Rosa.'

'But you goin' to write we letter, so we know how everythin' be, not so?' Rosa smiled. 'By de way. Jagua. Hope you remember to take de bag dat Uncle Taiwo lef' with you! I don' want de politician people to come search me house an' kill me!'

'I got it here. Don' fear, Rosa.' Jagua glanced by the side of the seat to make sure.

She could not even remember how she performed that journey, but when the lorry turned into the familiar jungle drive, she knew she was home. Home was silent, but it was a silence she could read. Papa was already dead. She knew that now, as the tears came unbidden. No one told her. She could see for herself the cold look in the eyes of all, even the children. The forest road was deserted, and as she trudged along a twig snapped under her foot and the sound reverberated through the jungle. No wine tappers looked down on her from the tree tops, no squirrels chirped as they ate the palm kernels. She saw the dogs, black and dirty, lying dejectedly under the trees. The signboard, DAVID OBI, PASTOR, was covered over with black cloth. Her mother was standing in the middle of a group, head bowed, the women silent and drifting about like smoked ghosts.

'Mama!'

Her mother's eyes were yellow. She had shaved off the hair on her head and the clothes she wore, ragged and dull, were in keeping with custom. She saw something else. In the very heaviness of the atmosphere, she felt her mother's complete loss of hope.

'You have come at last.'

'Where's Papa?' Jagua asked. She saw the tears. She heard the long howl, from somewhere in the rooms beyond. She had mentioned the unmentionable.

'Today makes four days,' said her mother. 'And you did not come!'

'Buried . . . long ago,' murmured the other women. 'You did not see Brother Fonso? We sent him to call you. Your father was calling you. Before Fonso reached twenty miles, it happened.'

She watched her mother where she sat, rocking from side to side. 'Go put down your box, Jagua. And that bag – like that of medicine man.'

Mother. Sweet and trusting and so kind. She had aged terribly, suddenly. Mother was speaking to her as if she had always been there; as if she had *known* that Jagua would return one day, and for good. Jagua's other brothers had come down for the burial. Fonso was there, so was Matthew Obi and John. This year was to have been her father's jubilee at the Mission. Jagua heard the story of his death. He had died of stroke. He was taken ill after his long tour and before they could rush him to the hospital, he had died.

Jagua's mother said: 'Only one name he was calling till he died. Jagwa . . . Jagwa . . . like that. He did not eat, he did not drink. Jus' callin' your name. Oh, if he had seen you!'

'God forgive me,' said Jagua.

Drums began to sound from a corner of the room. The room was thick with the smell of palm wine and home-distilled gin. When the moon came out the girls formed a ring and began to dance and sing and Jagua went among them and danced and cried too. While they were dancing Fonso came to her.

'Jagua, you mus' look after Mama, or she will jus' follow Papa. You know de ol' people, how they love themselves.'

Jagua looked at him, her heart pounding. 'How?'

'You stay with her and help her; at least for some months.'

'Here or in Lagos?'

'Leave Lagos out of this! You got to stay in this place. That's the custom. You know Mama mus' not leave Ogabu, she mus' not dress her hair or wear any fine cloth for at leas' six months. And there's nobody left at home . . .'

Someone came and drew Fonso away and Jagua went back and joined the dancers. No, it would be too much of a sacrifice to remain chained to Ogabu.

Later she went to the churchyard where he had been buried. Was this really him, this mound of earth, red, hiding the man? His soul had fled, or so they said. She used to be in the choir once. She had a good voice. She knelt down now. Oh, God! She had not prayed for years. She had not been to church, and yet her father was a pastor; born in the church, died in the service of the church. And she had renounced God and chosen Mammon. 'Look him well. Keep him safe, till I come, O God! I not got long to stay now, me an' Mama.' The earth was biting her knees. She rose. She breathed a deep sigh. She felt better. She walked away, glancing over her shoulder. A woman carrying a basket on her head met her on the path.

'Jagua?' she smiled. 'So you come, after all?'

'I come.'

Jagua could not remember where or when she had known the woman, or whether she was really a woman. Her teeth were stained a dirty brown and burnt to blackness. Her skin was harsh and full of suffering. 'I don' think you remember me,' she said. 'When you were small, like this . . .'

Jagua started to cry. When she was 'small like this . . .' how could she know her life would run into these cross-currents of shame, bitterness and degradation? 'When she was small like this . . .' she had lived free and simple in Ogabu. But now, she was chained down. She let the woman speak, nodding grimly, biting her lips, pointing with her gnarled fingers. Then she walked home to her mother, crying.

24

All the mourners had gone. The dew came down in the morning and settled on the cold trees and shrubs. The sun would not show its face. The girls going single-file to the waterside shuffled along without their usual chatter, keeping together as if their very company gave them protection against some vague external fear. The house in which Jagua's father had lived had become a coffin and inside this coffin Jagua Nana sat on the deckchair and her mother lay on a grass mat on the floor with eyes closed but not asleep.

There was no choice now for Jagua but to cast aside her city ways and settle down to living in Ogabu. For her it was no easy task. The people still looked on her as a kind of curiosity. The way she talked and dressed, her moods and manner of eating, these were out of keeping with Ogabu ideas. She had overheard them whispering about her, that she was in mourning not for her father, but for some man who had died in Lagos. Some said she was a 'Miss' who taught in a school in Port Harcourt and had been recently transferred to Ogabu. But all of them knew that there was about her an aura of tragedy. And so the young men were too young and frightened to make passes at her. She remained isolated from the very surroundings from which she sought acceptance. She soon found that if she wanted company it was not to be found in Ogabu, but in Onitsha or Port Harcourt where she would embarrass no one. She knew her mother would never think of leaving Ogabu: it would not even be right to talk her into leaving Ogabu, her only home.

When the first rains came she and her mother went to the barn and examined the yam seedlings. They took the labourers out into the farm and tilled the soil and planted the corn and the yam, the cocoyam and the okro. This was earth, this was life. Once in four days she accompanied her mother to the market, or went alone. Sometimes a letter would come from one of her brothers working up country beyond the great River Niger. There the trade was brisk and money passed from hand to hand more briskly. Ogabu had a postal agency over the waterside; although it was six miles off, it took more than three days for a letter to be delivered to their owners across the water. During the rains when the bridge was dangerous no letters came and no one worried. Ogabu went on in its own isolated way.

A few weeks after Jagua left Lagos she received a letter from Rosa to say that she would like to come to Ogabu as she was very lonely and things were bad in Lagos. Jagua dismissed it as idle talk. She did not want to hear from Lagos, as it might reawaken her desires to go back there. To avoid boredom Jagua obtained permission from her mother and went to Onitsha. She sought out Brother Fonso who helped her choose a sewing machine. Every morning she had it taken out to the main Port Harcourt road by the market and in a shed which had been built for her, she would sit sewing. There were four other sheds like hers, side by side. Soon she grew to know its owners, and because she was Jagua, from Lagos, the girls in the village came to her bringing her work and wanting to learn the craft of fashion from her. The village women in the nearby sheds did not like that, but Jagua paid no attention to them. She started by sewing odds and ends for the convent girls, and then some of the more daring women brought her material for blouses. The occupation gave her a direct contact with the world she knew and loved. She found herself sitting – as it were – on the edge of her old world, daring to watch it with an amused smile. When the cars and trucks and buses and lorries whizzed past, speeding towards Port Harcourt, she sometimes wished she would go with them and from there by outboard-engined canoe to Bagana and Krinameh. But if she went now, she would never return and her mother would be left unattended. Besides, what was there to find in Port Harcourt which she had not already seen in Lagos? It was true Port Harcourt was to the eastern part of Nigeria what Lagos was to the western part: a port, a conglomerate of peoples drawn from all over the world, fleeting, hungering for sensation and diversion, hands in their pockets fingering the all-powerful sterling and dollars, a polyglot world with quite different ideas of conduct from Ogabu. If ever she went to Port Harcourt it would not be to pick up the threads of her Lagos life. There must be some definite reason: to buy dress materials, to steal to Krinameh, for instance . . .

In the evenings, she would walk home, balancing the sewing machine on her head. When she got home she would be pleasantly tired, but would still help her mother until late when she would be told like a child to go to sleep. Soon she was able to buy a bicycle of her own and while she rode to the shed, a boy would take the machine out on the road for her. She had become housekeeper to the family, and more important still, custodian of her mother's will to go on living. Her duty was to look after the property, to avoid marriage, for that would take her away from home and mother. If any children came to her through casual love affairs she must bear them and they would simply become part of the household. She was still free, but in a new and penitent way. So her brothers had decided at the family meeting before they all dispersed and so it must be. She must suffer in silence.

Jagua never thought she would be able to adapt herself to the new life. She found, after a few months of it that the atmosphere in Ogabu had a quality about it totally different from the Lagos atmosphere. That driving, voluptuous and lustful element which existed in the very air of Lagos, that something which awakened the sleeping sexual instincts in all men and women and turned them into animals always on heat, it was not present here. Here in Ogabu, men dressed well but sanely. Women were beautiful but not brazen. They had become complementary to the palm trees and the Iroko, the rivulets and the fertile earth. They were part of their surroundings as natural as the wind. Whereas in Lagos MAN was always grappling to master an ENVIRONMENT he had created. It was money, money, yet more money. She did not find the same rush here, the desire to outstrip the other fellow. No time, sorry, too busy, time is short. Time, time. I must go now! . . . None of that here. She was resting.

Not that she preferred the quiet life, but she had gradually ceased to picture the riotous life. It had become an echo too distant to touch her. Once a man came down on leave from Lagos. He was not an Ogabu man, but happened to be passing by their stalls. There must have been something about Jagua which made him stop his car and come along the road to her shed. A young man, neat and smiling. He was sharply dressed in the manner that made her heart leap. He talked trifles with her for a long time, flashing his teeth and fingering his silk tie. She liked his silver cigarette case, the way he flicked it open, offering her a cigarette and taking one himself. As she drew in the soothing smoke it occurred to her that she had not smoked for almost six months. This was a polished young man, sophisticated too. She liked him recklessly. He took to coming to her shed, not saying why he came; and every day her eyes wandered up the road, resting only when they lighted on the familiar grille of his car. She began to brush her hair and to dip into her suitcase for clothes she had not worn for months. And one evening she closed early and followed him out in his car. They drove about until evening turned to dusk and he took her to a shed by the river, a stone's throw from the shrine. Here in the silence of the trees he took her and had her, and the fragrance of the forest gave it a romantic tang that remained with her.

He visited her again and took her to the shed but soon his leave was over and he went back, romantically promising to write to her, to send her presents. When the month came round, she did not see her period. Thrilling, but a secret she must nurse within herself. She would not tell her mother, yet. If it was true, it would be quite impossible to believe, she told herself. But the second month passed and the third. In a trembling fit of joy she took her bicycle and rode thirty miles to the nearest hospital. She told the doctor, 'I am the daughter of the late David Obi.' She spoke in Ibo, and the name sent the doctor bustling about the clinic. Oh. He took her into a little alcove. It was only a wooden hospital built among the palm trees, but it served the people and they came to it from eighty miles around. It had been a 'temporary' hospital for thirty years now. The Government kept on promising to build a bigger one. The doctor talked about the hospital while the nurse stood by, watching the examination.

'Yes,' he smiled, rubbing his hands. 'God is wonderful. Your husband will be a happy man.'

One afternon Jagua was seated in her roadside shed showing one of her girls how to embroider the neckline of a child's dress. A lorry stopped across the road. A woman came out of it and crossing the road began asking an old woman questions. The old woman eased her basket from one shoulder to the next and pointed. Jagua saw the stranger turn. A vague resemblance stirred somewhere. When she looked again, she recognized Rosa.

She dropped the dress and ran across the street. 'Rosa! . . .'

'Jagua, mother mine!' Rosa threw herself at Jagua, clinging to her, moaning with delight. 'I was jus' askin' de woman de way to Ogabu . . . I follow de address you give me till I reach here, den I loss . . .' She spoke rapidly in Ibo now that they were in Iboland.

Rosa seemed pale, wide-eyed and nervy. It could be the long journey by lorry but there was that sleepless glint in her eye, a kind of permanent frown not based on anger, which worried Jagua and made Rosa's appearance in the forests seem imaginary. Jagua touched the bright youthful skin, and the scarlet and yellow cotton-print blouse. They felt real and she was reassured.

'I come home with my man, so I remember you.' Her man's home, she explained, was not very far from Ogabu. She told Jagua that the young man in a blazer was on holiday and was taking the opportunity to come and speak to Rosa's people.

'You get good luck,' Jagua said. 'I don' know say he serious with you.' She immediately told her girls to pack up, hailed a porter to take Rosa's suitcase. Together they walked through the woods. The six miles seemed like six yards, so exuberant were they with reminiscences.

'You hear anythin' about Dennis Odoma?' Rosa asked at one point.

Jagua's heart began thumping hard. 'No! what happen?'

'You don' hear say dem hang him?' Rosa asked.

'No,' Jagua said, and began to cry.

'I goin' to tell you de full story sometime,' Rosa promised.

With her usual energy Rosa peeled the yam and ground the pepper. She made the stew and pounded the yam. She had stripped her print dress and had only a sleeveless singlet and bright green wrapper tied sarong-wise round her hips. Her small breasts danced, her rounded hips rolled as she descended the steps of the courtyard at the back of the house. Jagua admired her complete 'at-homeness'.

'Mama, we have one who has come.' Jagua said when her mother came in. 'Her name is Rosa. In Lagos I knew her.'

'Welcome, Rosa. You come well?' She turned to Jagua. 'She has eaten? Quick now. Give her food.'

Jagua smiled and pinched Rosa. 'My mother likes you,' she whispered.

When they had bathed and eaten, Jagua and Rosa sat on the piazza and five hundred miles from Lagos Rosa told Jagua what happened to Dennis Odoma and Uncle Taiwo. After endless minute questions, Jagua knew the story of Dennis as if she had been at the trial herself. According to Rosa, the magistrate had tried to save him. But his case was hopeless. Rosa told how the magistrate's face clouded as he added up the pros and cons, how Dennis stood in the dock, trembling. He had grown extremely pale and unkempt, his beard was unshaven and his clothes looked as if he had slept in them. It had been raining for ten days in Lagos, without stopping. Grey bleak rain, slamming down, eating into the tarmac and unearthing the stones, running into rivulets, rushing into streams that clogged the gutters and floated the wood and silt, the carcasses of sheep and dogs. At night when the moon struggled out, the rain stopped and then you could hear again the city sounds – horns bleating in the distance, trains jangling over the rails. She was miserable and so was everyone, particularly the prosecution police who put their heads together, conspiring, while the press boys scribbled away and everyone waited. At this time those who came to court talked, but only in whispers.

This was the time when Rosa hoped that Dennis would be freed or given a light sentence, because everyone was getting tired of the case and the public were all for Dennis. But the police went on to prove that he was a thoroughly bad character. He was an 'habitual'. He had attacked a police officer before, about four years ago. They proved also that in the last four years, Dennis was in and out of prison five times. Rosa was amazed. She said she could never have guessed it from the way Dennis behaved when he came to visit Jagua. The police prosecutor read out: 'House-breaking and stealing – 15 months . . . Counterfeit coins – 9 months. Under the name Matthias Oemji, 9 months for stealing . . . Again, 4 months for stealing . . . And again, 4 months for stealing . . .' Rosa dramatized how the police officer was shuffling the cards as he spoke and how Dennis in the dock, bowed his head and said nothing. When they began to speak of how this merciless and wicked boy had planned to kill the policeman, had lured him into a side street 'with intent', Rosa knew there was no way out then. And when later on, she saw his picture in the paper, saying he was to hang, she was shocked but no longer surprised. She heard that Dennis appealed, but nothing ever came out of it.

Jagua said not a word. All she could murmur to herself was: 'An' de boy love me so much. He use to call me Ma. I try to teach 'im to be gentleman, but is a different kind from Freddie Namme. Differen' kin'.' She spoke up now. 'You know, is like say his body on fire all de time. When his body wake, he got enough power to kill

179

man with one blow. But he gentle when he love, though he kin hardly control hisself whenever he see me naked.'

'I jus' remember somethin', Jagua!' Rosa came running up from the forest. Jagua was sitting on the verandah in front of her father's house.

'What thin', Rosa?'

She came up the steps and said, 'You know any man dem call Ofubara . . . Chief Ofubara? From Krinameh?'

'Chief Ofubara,' Jagua whispered, holding her breast. 'Yes, is de time I go Bagana. From dere I reach Krinameh and . . .' She checked herself, unable to tell Rosa about the jealous incident when she had pursued Nancy Namme into the waters of Krinameh. But she talked of how she had been really Jagwa, the day Chief Ofubara first set eyes on her.

'Soon after you lef', de man come to Lagos. He worryin' about you till he nearly crase. He say you promise to marry am. He come till he tire, worryin' 'bout you. So he don' come here to find you? Sometime dem take de steamer go home . . .'

Rosa told how Chief Ofubara had come with some others for a conference in Lagos, something to do with chieftaincy.

Jagua sighed. 'Dat man you see, is a very kin' man.' She knew now that she would like to see him again, but not now, when she was carrying another man's baby. In a way, she regarded herself as his wife. Though he had not gone to speak to her parents in the traditional manner, he had paid the price on her head, but got no bride. But no, she could not marry him now. She might go to the Port Harcourt wharf, or even as far as Bagana, for news of him. Krinameh was not so far away now, on this side of the Niger.

Night after night, they sat and talked. And on the second night, Rosa told the story of Uncle Taiwo: a terrifying one indeed, and one that taught Jagua that politics was dirtiest to them that played it dirty. Rosa told how she was going to market and she heard that a dead man was lying at the roundabout in the centre of the city. She was terrified. It was said to be lying near the marketplace, in front of the Hotel Liverpool. People going to work saw it from their cars in the early morning as they came up the hill. The policeman at the control point had the cape of his raincoat up and his white cap was sodden with the endless rain. The roads were all muddy and pitted; the gutters were full, the farms in the suburbs were overgrown with weeds. Lagos was in a state of chaos that day. It seemed as if the ghost of that corpse had gone abroad among them. The body was lying there twisted and swollen; one knee was drawn up against the chest, the arms were clutching at the breast, rigid like a statue. Rosa tried to imitate the position of the body on the floor, and Jagua, horrified, hastily begged her to get up. She was shaking with fright.

In Africa you see these things, Rosa reminded her. Rosa said she circled round the body three times. She saw some dogs circling too. Perhaps they were waiting for nightfall to feast on the body of the famous man. This was in Lagos, nowhere else. Then she went up into the Hotel Liverpool and stood looking down from five floors at the chain of red, blue, green, scarlet, yellow and cream cars; at the slow jerk and stop of the traffic flowing into the island. But it was the body of Uncle Taiwo, lying in the rain that seemed to rivet all the attention and to spread terror among the drivers . . . She ordered brandy and sipped it slowly because she was feeling sick. The waiters in the white uniforms chattered but none of them knew Rosa and none of them said anything she did not really know. They said, however, that he had been murdered by his party and abandoned at the roundabout. He had broken faith with them and they blamed him for losing the elections.

It kept on drizzling, rattling on the roof. A bleak day on which Uncle Taiwo died. Rosa said she came down from the hotel and went home in the rain without entering the market.

Jagua was horrified by the story. She had never loved Uncle Taiwo. She had been a mere tool in his hands, an elderly man who knew what he wanted and did not complain when asked to pay for it. She had never realized that he was so deeply enmeshed in political ties and societies he would never mention in public. How different he was from Dennis, with his pulse-beat of life and his daring disregard of convention, his youthful urgency, a young man who had stirred her deep down and made her restless and inadequate.

When Rosa had gone to bed Jagua thought over the story of Uncle Taiwo. There was now no point in keeping the bag any longer. She would go now to the backyard and destroy all the papers. She lit a hurricane lamp and went to the cupboard in her mother's room where the bag was. She took it down and tried to open it but it was locked. With a knife she cut open the leather flap and the contents poured out at her feet. She stood back aghast. The bag was full of notes, stacked in bundles of £50. She counted twenty such bundles before going over and shaking her mother by the shoulder.

'Mama, Mama, get up! . . . Come an' see what I see!'

Her mother rubbed her eyes and stared. 'I'll not touch it,' she said, when she had heard the story of the bag. 'It's blood money.'

'Is not blood money,' Jagua explained. 'Is party money.' She was sure it was O.P. 2 money given to Uncle Taiwo to spend for the elections. The elections were over, Uncle Taiwo had been killed. This portion he must have kept back for himself, hoping to come back later and use it for his own ends.

While her mother stood aghast, Jagua knelt down and counted one hundred bundles of £50.

'Do as you like with am, I got no hand in it.'

Jagua threw her hands upwards in an attitude of prayer.'God know, if I do wrong to take dis money 'pon all my suffer dat I suffer.'

In the morning, she was a different person. She talked with a new air of authority. 'Mama, when de time come, I know what I goin' to do widde money. I will give some to de Mission in Ogabu for take finish de church buildin'. De res' I goin' to put in business. Las' time when I was in Onitsha I see some shop in Odoziaku Street, very near de Company. I goin' to buy dat business and God will help me for become real Merchant Princess. But de first thing I wan' to go Port Harcourt firs'.' She raised her hands, and threw her face at the skies. 'Dis one be God work! . . .'

★

Rosa accompanied her to Port Harcourt to buy dress materials. As they walked along the street, their eyes darted from window to window. It was raining here too and they had to take refuge now and again in the shops. In one of the shops Jagua saw a lawyer whom she had observed at Freddie's funeral. From him she inquired about Nancy.

'Nancy? . . .' He pondered it over, his eyes on the rain outside. 'You mean Nancy Namme . . . Oh yes! . . .'

That had been a real fight, the man told her. Yes. The Bar Association had taken up the case seriously on behalf of the doctor who ran the private hospital from which Freddie had been forcibly removed in his critical illness. Removing a man in that manner amounted to a felony. They had asked for a compensation of £20,000 to be paid by the police to Nancy, the widow of Freddie. After all, if they had not moved him the chances were that he might have recovered. But all they got was £2000. 'We should have asked for £200,000,' the lawyer grinned. 'Always ask for ten times what you want.' But it was not the money they were fighting for so much as the protection of the dignity of professional men like the doctor from political nonsense; and also to bring the misguided police officials to book.

They talked at length about Freddie and how rash he had been to get himself involved in the rough and tumble of politics. Jagua was glad Nancy would not suffer. But she did not tell the lawyer how she had loved Freddie, pinning all her hopes for the future on him, and how she had lost.

While still in Port Harcourt they took a taxi and went down to the waterfront to see if they would meet anyone Jagua knew coming from Bagana, so that they might ask about Chief Ofubara. Jagua sat on a cement banking for a long time, watching the canoes land and the women board them, carrying their oranges, yams, vegetables. It did not appear that anyone she knew would be coming to Port Harcourt from either Bagana or Krinameh that day. Rosa walked up to her, a sling bag over her shoulder.

'What we goin' to do now?' she asked. 'You wan' make we go Bagana an' Krinameh? Is only two hour from 'ere, so de canoemen say.'

Jagua glanced at the mourning dress she was wearing. 'I wan'

go, because I promise Chief Ofubara I mus' come back to Krinameh. But dis dress!' It was a far cry from the *Jagwa*-ful outfit in
which she had first appeared before the chief.

'What you goin' to do?' Rosa said. 'Is only to salute de man, das
all! If he ask why you wear black, you kin tell 'im you loss your
fadder.' She pointed at the beach. 'Look! De canoe dere almos'
ready. Make we go join am.'

They raced towards the canoe and were the last two passengers
in. The engine of *Ever Jolly Time* was already running. It began to
rain, gently. A mistiness shrouded the mangrove trees. Out of the
mistiness, Jagua saw the Church steeple of Bagana, pale and ghostly
against the black sky. Her eyes filled nostalgically with tears when
she sighted it.

At Bagana beach, no one came to meet them. They walked up to
the Palace in the rain. The maid recognized Jagua. She smiled and
offered them seats in the lounge. Jagua looked up at the walls,
showing Rosa the photographs of Uncle Namme, David Namme
and Chief Ofubara. The maid beamed a welcome and told them
that the three men left for Lagos two days previously. They had
gone to see the Governor-General over some matter. Jagua and
Rosa consulted and agreed they would not stop in Bagana, but
would go on to Krinameh, just to see it. They walked down to the
beach-side and Jagua saw the bathing place where she had pursued
Nancy Namme into Krinameh waters. They found a canoeman
who agreed to take them over the rocky waters to Krinameh.

As soon as they rowed past the rocks, Jagua saw – not the Krinameh she knew, desolate and impoverished, but a new Krinameh
with good wide roads and so many new buildings that for a moment
she thought of Port Harcourt waterfront. They arrived there at
closing time for the schools. The streets were filled with children
chattering, kicking rubber balls, and laughing. Their presence
seemed to fill Krinameh. She remembered Chief Ofubara's eternal
cry for education. She remembered too that with her altered circumstances she could answer some at least of his cry.

She took Rosa by the arm. 'Make we go back for Ogabu. I seen
all I wan' to see.'

Rosa gave her a glance of surprise, but Rosa did not yet know about Jagua's condition. In two months' time, everyone who looked at her would see the swollen belly. It was good like this, that Chief Ofubara should remain in her mind as her happiest romantic memory.

The child was turning over in her belly. Jagua leaned her back against the wall and watched the playful undulations of her own belly, swollen visibly now. She put a hand to catch the feet of the unborn child. Pain gnawed at her and she gritted her teeth. Sometimes she thought of a name for it. *Uzo* would be a fitting one, meaning *Road*. She had searched at home in vain for a child, but now the child had come to her from the road, from the shed of the seamstresses, a product of a casual affair with a vanished father. She would see to it that the child grew up straight and strong – and true. That night, out of sheer gratitude, she cried herself to sleep. Even if she went back to the Coast to live, to Lagos or to Port Harcourt, things would be on a new footing. She would never again be so reckless with the ingredients of the fast life and faster oblivion.

Jagua's mother was due to get out of mourning in a matter of weeks. Rosa stayed with them, waiting for the great day. One of the first things that Jagua did when she was able to, was to go across the river to the Postal Agency and to send to Chief Ofubara twelve bundles of £50 notes as a little help towards his education programme. Rosa saw the money and whistled.

'Jagua your hand too free! You goin' to dash all de money away finish!'

'Never min',' said Jagua. 'De Chief is a very kin' man. Very kin'. Is de only way I kin repay de love he have for me.' She looked at her belly. 'You see now, I done go get pickin from anodder man, so I no fit to marry am again.'

She took the receipts from the postal clerk, but as they walked home, Rosa kept telling her that she was too free-handed. Jagua merely laughed her fears away.

Sometimes Jagua took Rosa visiting. They went to the nearby village where the parents of Rosa's fiancé lived. He had since gone back to the college. By now Rosa and Jagua's mother joked freely about Jagua's condition and Jagua was pleased. She could see that her mother moved about the house with a new expectant freedom.

The time drew nearer for Jagua's mother to change her mourning clothes, and on the night before, Jagua had felt a violent searing pain inside her. She kept pacing the room like someone on the brink of insanity. Rosa hailed Jagua's mother who ran up, rubbing her eyes. Together they took Jagua into the inner room and sat her down, trying to calm her. Jagua heard her mother send someone to fetch the doctor.

Then the splitting pain came again, and they put her back against the wall and spread her legs apart. Rosa held her by one hand and her mother by the other, looking down on her bloated naked body.

'Give a grunt!' the mother cried.

Jagua grunted, to no effect.

'All your might!'

Jagua grunted, and fainted. Outside, the moon shone and the small boy who had been sent to fetch the doctor came running in and he was the first to hear the piercing note of the child: a boy.

Jagua's mother named the baby *Nnochi* which means *Replacement*. One old and dead, the other new and young and full of promise. And when at dusk the drums beat under the banana leaves, Jagua turned and listened to the rhythms that to hear meant happiness.

For two days, the child lived. Jagua, handling Nnochi in all his wetness and elastic gambols drew the maternal satisfaction she had long craved. On the third day, Jagua put Nnochi to the breast. It was early evening and her mother and Rosa had not come in from the farm. Jagua felt a sudden slackening of the lips on her nipple. She looked at the face of her newborn infant. It was turning an ashen colour. She gazed, not understanding. The life was draining out of Nnochi. Dumbfounded Jagua watched Nnochi stiffen, and then all movement ceased.

Jagua opened her mouth to scream, but could not.

Rosa and her mother came in from the forest and found her silent and stiff as an effigy before the oracle. She pressed the dead baby to herself and blubbering, would not part with it.

*

'When you are strong again, Jagua, what you goin' to do?' Jagua's mother came and sat beside her on the bench in the courtyard. It was a week after the burial of Nnochi and slowly Jagua was beginning to see the sun, to feel a thirst for water and a hunger for a little food.

She could read the fear in her mother's eyes, that she would forsake her; that Ogabu was not the place for her.

'Mama, I don't know yet. But I wan' some place – not too far to Ogabu. Dere I kin trade. I kin come here when I like for look you. Ah wan' try Onitsha whedder I kin become Merchant Princess. I already got experience of de business. I goin' to beg Brodder Fonso for advise me what I goin' to do. You see, Mama, now I got some money. Is going to be different. I kin buy me own lorry and me own shop by de river. I goin' to join de society of de women an' make frien' with dem. I sure to succeed.'

As she spoke, she saw the relief mount into her mother's eyes. 'Is good,' she said. 'I fear before whedder you wantin' for go back Lagos. Now is good I got me daughter on dis side of de Niger.'

Rosa came in from the forest while they talked. She looked fresh and sweet and completely one with the Ogabu forests. She was carrying a drumful of water which she had fetched. Her smile was bright.

'What you an' Mama plannin', Jagua? You already lookin' like you fine ol' self. You never kin grow ol', my dear!'

'Is God work, Rosa,' Jagua smiled. 'But I don' wan' to be me ol' self who suffer too much.' She looked from Rosa's face to her mother's and the expression of belief and goodwill she saw filled her with new hopes. 'I jus' told Mama dat I goin' to Onitsha. I wan' to become proper merchant princess. I goin' to buy me own shop, and lorry, and employ me own driver. I goin' to face dis business serious. I sure dat God above goin' to bless me.'

Evening had come once again to Ogabu and with its coming there stirred a gentle breeze that soothed. Jagua sat beside her mother on the log and dreamt. She thought how good it was to be dreaming while Rosa and her mother listened.

He just wanted a decent book to read ...

Not too much to ask, is it? It was in 1935 when Allen Lane, Managing Director of Bodley Head Publishers, stood on a platform at Exeter railway station looking for something good to read on his journey back to London. His choice was limited to popular magazines and poor-quality paperbacks – the same choice faced every day by the vast majority of readers, few of whom could afford hardbacks. Lane's disappointment and subsequent anger at the range of books generally available led him to found a company – and change the world.

'We believed in the existence in this country of a vast reading public for intelligent books at a low price, and staked everything on it'
Sir Allen Lane, 1902–1970, founder of Penguin Books

The quality paperback had arrived – and not just in bookshops. Lane was adamant that his Penguins should appear in chain stores and tobacconists, and should cost no more than a packet of cigarettes.

Reading habits (and cigarette prices) have changed since 1935, but Penguin still believes in publishing the best books for everybody to enjoy. We still believe that good design costs no more than bad design, and we still believe that quality books published passionately and responsibly make the world a better place.

So wherever you see the little bird – whether it's on a piece of prize-winning literary fiction or a celebrity autobiography, political tour de force or historical masterpiece, a serial-killer thriller, reference book, world classic or a piece of pure escapism – you can bet that it represents the very best that the genre has to offer.

Whatever you like to read – trust Penguin.